DEAD MAN'S ROAD

RANDY DENMON

PINNACLE BOOKS
Kensington Publishing Corp.
www.kensingtonbooks.com

PINNACLE BOOKS are published by

Kensington Publishing Corp.
119 West 40th Street
New York, NY 10018

All Kensington titles, imprints, and distributed lines are available at
special quantity discounts for bulk purchases for sales promotions,
premiums, fund-raising, educational, or institutional use. Special book
excerpts or customized printings can also be created to fit specific
needs. For details, write or phone the office of the Kensington sales
manager: Kensington Publishing Corp., 119 West 40th Street, New York,
NY 10018, attn: Sales Department; phone 1-800-221-2647.

ISBN-13: 978-0-7860-3538-0
ISBN-10: 0-7860-3538-2

First printing: October 2015

10 9 8 7 6 5 4 3 2 1

Printed in the United States of America

First electronic edition: October 2015

ISBN-13: 978-0-7860-3539-7
ISBN-10: 0-7860-3539-0

What do we want with this vast, worthless area? This region of savages and wild beasts, of deserts, of shifting sands, and whirlwinds of dust, of cactus and prairie dogs? To what use could we ever hope to put these great deserts, or those endless mountain ranges, impenetrable and covered to their very base with eternal snow? What can we ever hope to do with the western coast, a coast of three thousand miles, rock-bound, cheerless, uninviting, and not a harbor on it? What use have we for this country?

—DANIEL WEBSTER on the Senate floor in 1824, speaking in opposition to the development of the American West

1

Wyoming Territory
March 1868

Marshall Brewster looked out across the wide creek and magnificent new bridge under construction. In the gorge below, the deep, slithering, slicing canyon hid the river behind its rock walls and shadows. Fifty men worked at the end-of-track, where the new railroad pushed on into the unknown via their blood and sweat. Across the chasm, the masons finished the foundations for the bridge's abutment. Reaching out over the three-hundred-foot span, almost like a bird taking flight, the huge wood trestle, girders, and support piers crept to the other bank through the sound of hammers banging away.

The day had warmed under the noon sun. Behind him, men labored, touching up the shiny, new track with additional spikes and filling a large hole on the bridge's approach, the final obstacle to connect the track to the span. The rail descended a fifty-foot ridge to reach the bridge, and a series of small hills and draws had been flattened and graded on the bridge's approach to accommodate the rail's uniform grade.

Marshall inspected the stash of material on-site. Two kegs of black powder, beams and girders, bricks and mortar, and an assortment of fasteners. He correlated the material with the quantities required. To the south, over the horizon, the surveyors plotted the course over one of the most foreboding landmasses in the world—southern Wyoming.

"Whatchuh think, chief?" the bridge foreman, a short, stocky Irishman with weather-beaten skin, a big red beard, and a heavy accent, said.

"Looks good, Patty."

"I need twenty more crates of bolts and another car of those twenty-foot beams, else we'z be twiddling our thumbs by dark. We'll also need that last deck-span tomorrow so we can start rigging it."

Marshall nodded up the hill. "A new shipment of black powder arrived today. It's staged at the top of the hill. As soon as we finish the bridge, I want it moved forward to that next escarpment so we can start blasting. Looks like the work's going well."

"Aye, aye, they'll be through here in three days, no problem, then just a little cleanup work."

Marshall cocked his head and yelled to a young engineer under a tent, "John! Do you have that report for me on the two men injured in the blasting accident last week?"

One of the young engineers brought the report to Marshall before promptly returning to his work.

"The two men will be all right," Patty said, crossing himself. "Just an accident. The boys get careless with the frenzy of the work, the urge to hurry."

"It's inevitable." Marshall tried to keep an emotionless face. "This is dangerous work. The men know that. What's important is that we convey to the men we're doing all we can to minimize the hazards." Marshall paused to make sure he got the point.

"Aye, aye."

Marshall pointed to the bridge. "Tell all the men on the bridge there'll be a three-dollar bonus if the bridge is completed in three days. Do whatever we have to. Everything will come to a stop if we don't finish this bridge by week's end. Let me know if you need more men, anything."

"We'll make it." Patty laughed.

Marshall walked over to his horse, grabbed the reins, and put a foot in the stirrup. "I've got to get back to headquarters. Make sure you get what you need. Mail and pay train also runs today."

A scream ripped through the crisp, clean air. Four men ran from the bridge site. Back up the railway, a single flatcar rolled down the track to the bridge, picking up speed, its deck loaded with twenty wooden barrels of black powder.

Marshall shoved his horse to the side. "Run!" he yelled.

On the bridge the dozen men grading all dashed away from the track. One stumbled to his knees as he fled.

Up the hill, the railcar, now only two hundred paces from the bridge, gained speed. Marshall ran to a rock outcropping. Two workers sprinted across the bridge deck in his direction.

"Jump off!" Marshall yelled as he dove for cover. Landing face-first, he tasted the dirt as he rolled on his side. The steady squeaking of the car's wheels filled his ears. A loud skid. A thud. Metal screeched.

On the bridge, the two men, terror on their faces, leaped from the deck.

Marshall balled up, squeezing his eyes shut. The ground shook. The air flickered red. An earsplitting boom erupted.

A cool gust of air rushed over him. His ears ringing, he cringed as earth rained from the sky.

His breath heavy, his mind confused and racing, Marshall looked to the bridge site. The mangled remains of the flatcar lay among the flames, wedged into a large hole that was seconds earlier the bridge's abutment, now only fractured rock and masonry. A hundred-foot section of the bridge, a web of symmetrical timbers, careened over and slowly tumbled out of sight.

His vision blurred, Marshall struggled to his feet. In the smoke and embers, he saw a blood-covered man try to stand before falling back to his knees. He looked back up the hill. What happened?

2

Snow flurries drifted over Michigan Avenue, dancing and colliding with the large warehouses abutting Lake Michigan. Ambrose Graham tightened the collar on his coat. Beside the city-block-sized storage houses, activity abounded on the loading docks. Railcars moved along a myriad of tracks, and four ships were tethered to the man-made harbor, an array of wood piers protruding into the unfriendly, turbulent, and icy waters. All sorts of goods moved on and off the various forms of transport.

The day was gloomy, cold, damp, and windy.

"Uhh," Ambrose grumbled, walking another block to the office of the Illinois and Iowa Railroad Company, a modern, three-story brick building. He breathed a sigh as he stepped into the warmth of the building and looked over at the familiar face of the secretary, a lovely Irish girl in her twenties and dressed very professionally.

"Mr. Matson is waiting on you," the secretary said with a friendly tone and a smile. "You can go on up."

Upstairs, Ambrose strolled down a long hall trimmed with the finest mahogany. He paused to look at a large map that depicted the routes of commerce in the Midwest.

Chicago sat in the middle of the map, the transportation hub of the West. Shipping lanes from the Great Lakes and almost thirty railways converged here. Beef, corn, and all the raw materials of the Midwest moved to the hungry factories of the East through these facilities. And almost all the finished goods from the manufacturing hubs required to tame the West moved through Chicago—farming and construction equipment, dry goods, guns, and powder, almost everything needed for daily life on the frontier. In the last two decades, the tiny lakefront city had grown tenfold. The gateway to the West, founded less than forty years earlier, now had almost three hundred thousand residents.

Ambrose continued down the hall, where he knocked on an open door. Inside, his current employer, Benedict Matson, the president of the Illinois and Iowa, sat at a grand desk. Graying, dignified, and in his midsixties, Benedict wore an expensive black suit. Maps, sitting on easels, filled the room. Most were topographic or rail maps that depicted the company's dominion or future plans.

"Come in, Colonel," Benedict said.

Ambrose ambled into the office. He had no idea why he'd been summoned here. He wasn't a colonel anymore. After the Civil War, he'd surrendered his commission and command of the now disbanded 4th Illinois Calvary. But damn, Benedict only called him colonel when he wanted to pump up his ego or coax him into a difficult task. Ambrose stole a peek outside the large window to the lake and loading docks, a placid view from the cozy confines.

Benedict stood and extended a hand. He walked over to a large table covered with even more maps. He pointed to one and nodded for Ambrose's attention. "The Pacific Railroad, the greatest engineering achievement of the century. The Union Pacific building from the east, the

Central Pacific from the west in a great race. The prize: The West. I'm just upset I'm not in the race." Benedict paused and put his well-manicured finger on the map. "The Union Pacific will be over the Rockies by the fall. Most people think it's being built to connect the country, east and west, to California, but it also has a second purpose. That's to subjugate and settle the West."

Benedict flashed his pale blue eyes at Ambrose. "Colonel Graham, a half a million people have immigrated to America in the last fifteen years. Those numbers will quadruple by the end of the century, and the number of people living west of the Mississippi has increased fortyfold in the last decade and a half. We have opportunity here. And where will these people live? The West. Not to mention, the resources of the frontier are only now being realized. It will be the greatest treasure chest in the world. Great cities will spring up out of the wilderness along this railway, just like Chicago."

Ambrose stared at the map. Being in the railroad business, he was obviously familiar with the Pacific Railroad, currently under construction by the Union and Central Pacific Railroad companies with considerable support from the federal government. The epic rail enamored the Republic's citizens, regardless of social standing, and reports of its progress filled the American papers almost daily. In fact, it had lately dominated the news, especially with the reduction of national press since the end of the Civil War. He'd read that even the Europeans had begun covering the story. He had little contemplated, nor had any knowledge of Benedict's statements about the future of the West, but they seemed to make sense. Ambrose rarely doubted the logic of his boss and his keen eye for business. The man had attained a fortune analyzing potential markets.

"The Pacific Railroad," Benedict continued, "will

reduce the time to travel between the East and West coasts from six months to a week. It currently takes a month just to mail a letter across the continent. There's only three options now: Overland by wagon, around Cape Horn, or a ship to Panama, across its isthmus and then another ship to the West Coast. These options provide the traveler with ample hazards—yellow fever, malaria, hurricanes, Indians and banditry, starvation, succumbing to the elements, or even predators. Moving freight is time consuming and expensive. The new rail will bind the country, East and West, like the war has bound North and South."

Benedict paused, scratched his cheek, and looked up at Ambrose before continuing, "If we're going to stay profitable, we're going to have to move west, else our competitors will lock us out, not only of the new markets, but also our existing network. They'll reroute around us using their lines. That's why I've been in Washington the last month. I've secured a land grant for a new spur west of Cheyenne, south into Colorado. I've chartered the Colorado Northern Railroad Company. The new Railroad Act will also issue us government bonds, fifteen thousand dollars a mile." He shuffled a few maps around and moved one in front of him, then slid his finger over the map. "A one-hundred-mile line to Jeremiah, a small mining town in the Front Range. Silver's been discovered in the area. This may be bigger than the gold rush of the fifties."

Ambrose studied the map carefully. The line ran directly south from the Transcontinental over the plains, then worked its way up into the mountains, drawn on the map by one-hundred-foot contour lines. The map documented almost nothing around the line other than a few small towns and military forts he'd never heard of, three rivers, and several wagon trails.

Construction would be costly, he thought, but most

likely profitable, especially with a land grant. Ambrose was familiar with the grants, a scheme concocted by Congress to help finance rail construction through public lands, especially in the West where the government owned almost all the land. In addition to the revenue of rail traffic, the railroad was given approximately half the property adjacent to the rail line. If the area held silver or other mineral deposits, the grants themselves could be worth millions. The grants could be used in a number of ways to finance the rails. Companies could borrow against them or sell them during construction. The most money was often made by selling the land after construction when the grants would be choice rail-front parcels but only if the grantee had the financial strength to weather the expensive construction. The bonds would also help. They were only low-interest, long-term loans to subsidize the work. Of course, the rail had to be finished to complete the land transfer and bonds.

Rails were some of the most risky and profitable enterprises in America, requiring great capital investment, but also reaping mammoth profits. Sometimes the money was made in the construction and grants, other times through operation. Many times both. Each rail was unique, and a study of history usually gave no hint to where the profits lay, the grandest form of speculation. He felt Benedict's gaze bearing down on him and turned back to his boss.

Benedict said, "You've done well managing several of our rail projects. Quite well, I'd say. And you've been rewarded amply for it. That's why I've chosen you for this. But this will be much more difficult than anything you've done. Silas Jones and the Southwest Pacific also have a grant to build into this area from the south, but their line won't be to Denver for at least another year. We've got maybe two years. The grant covers three counties, two in Colorado and one in Wyoming."

Ambrose turned again to the map, then back to Benedict. A few awkward seconds passed.

"I want this line," Benedict said, his voice turning solemn. "And I want you to build it."

"I've never failed you. Or at anything."

Benedict stiffened, raising a hand. "I'm aware of your record, Colonel. I don't care what you've done in the past. I made you, and I can break you. Don't forget that. This is a race. And I mean to *win* it."

He had no idea if the construction would be complicated. The site was certainly isolated and distant. The contour lines made the mountains appear big and inhospitable. Were there problems with the Indians similar to those so often publicized by the press? He wasn't an engineer, but more of a manager, an organizer, a problem solver. He had acquired and mastered these skills on a large scale in the war.

Building a railroad was complicated. There were landowners, local governments, and labor and supply problems to deal with. In addition to managing the exactness of science and engineering, the inexactness of men and their egos had to be tamed. Just in the last few years working for the Illinois and Iowa, he'd undertaken numerous tasks, everything from working out the vast, complex logistical and organizational problems of construction down to arming and leading men to protect the company's claims.

"Denver," Benedict said, "is the second biggest city in the West outside California and growing. This line will span more than half the distance to Denver, and be part of the network that eventually connects it with the Pacific Railroad. A sure moneymaker. I'm putting all the resources of the Illinois and Iowa behind this. But the grants and bonds are only for the *first* rail built, to be delivered in twenty-five-mile segments. I have enough money to pay for the construction of the first twenty-five miles, then we'll have to borrow against the bonds and grants. As you may assume, time will be of the essence."

"Who do you have in mind for an engineer?" Ambrose inquired.

"I've already hired Marshall Brewster. He's the best available, especially in the mountains. He and a crew of about fifty men are already working. Our grant requires we get started this month. Their work to date is really only symbolic, but they've laid about a mile of track."

Ambrose rubbed his chin. "I thought he was going back to work for the UP after their winter break?"

"He was, but I got to him first. We have another problem. We've already had an accident, two men killed. Brewster thinks it was sabotage."

"Silas Jones?"

"Don't know." Benedict grabbed a bottle of bourbon off his desk and filled a tumbler. He turned it up. "My sources say the UP has already made Brewster another offer. I need you to get out there and convince him we mean business. Convince him to stay." Benedict handed Ambrose a large envelope. "He's somewhere along our route, south of Cheyenne. There's nobody else available, at least not anybody the UP will part with. His terms of compensation are in these papers. You leave this week."

"And what if he doesn't agree?"

Benedict's eyes narrowed. His voice grew loud and stern. "That's *your* problem. Make him agree. You two are friends. You fought together in the war. You speak the same language. As you'll see when you go through the details, I'm giving you and him a combined fifteen-percent stake in the new company if you beat the Southwest Pacific . . .

take your daughter with you if you have to. He's got a fancy for her, if I recall."

Ambrose cringed. His throat got thick as he mumbled, "But she's supposed to be graduating from finishing school this spring."

"Your concern for your daughter's education and well-being is moving, touching, Colonel Graham, but I only give a damn about getting this railroad built. Send me a report the end of the next week when you find Brewster."

Benedict filled two glasses, handing one to Ambrose. "The weather, the location, and the Indians will make this more difficult than anything you've ever done, but don't be distracted by that. Your real obstacle will be Silas Jones. He'll use all his considerable resources to stop us. And I want to beat that crooked son of a bitch to northern Colorado. I'm not going to lose to him again. Is that *clear*? You'll have to deal with that if you want what you deserve—a stake in the new fortune of the West." The Dutch immigrant's eyes focused on the maps.

A self-made man, Benedict had worked his way up from the slums of New York's Lower East Side to become one of the nation's leading industrialists. A stern, driven businessman, he'd learned the game and mastered it.

Ambrose swallowed. Men like Benedict and his arch-enemy, Silas Jones, got what they wanted, no matter the cost. They stepped on everything, pushing, shoving, and ruthlessly tearing their way to the ends they sought. *Nothing* got in their way. Despite their cruel exploitation and devious maneuvering, society draped praise on these men, the net benefits of their actions greatly outweighing their dirty deeds, at least to the general public.

Ambrose, whether he liked it or not, was now a tool in these men's battle. He turned up the bourbon, downing it.

3

A loud knock on the door interrupted Ambrose's thoughts. "Cheyenne, fifteen minutes!" the steward yelled, walking down the railcar's hall.

The train scooted over the tracks, the only sound the monotonous clicking and clacking of its iron wheels. The rhythmic noise and gentle rocking put even the most well-rested traveler in a lazy mood, and Ambrose rubbed his eyes. For hours, he had been dozing on and off. Out the window of his private car, the bland, brown country of Wyoming rushed by.

Beside him, his daughter stirred. He prided himself in few things more than her. Slim and healthy, almost five foot, six inches tall, she had long blond hair, blue eyes, and an impeccable fair complexion. To go with her good looks, she was as spunky and intelligent as any woman in Chicago. At twenty-two, she had bloomed into one of the most sought-after young ladies in town, catching the eye and attention of many of the city's well-to-do young men.

"Bridget," Ambrose said in a soft voice. "You should get up. We're almost there."

Bridget shook her head and yawned. She stretched out her broad petticoat, straightened her blouse, then stood and smiled as she looked out the window with an animated face at the immense nothingness. "I'm almost beside myself. I can't wait. How long have we been on this train?"

"Almost forty hours. Eighteen to Omaha via rail. Then six hours there waiting to change trains and ferry across the Missouri River. I hope they have that rail bridge completed before we go back." Ambrose looked at his watch. "And another eighteen hours from Omaha."

Bridget exhaled a long breath. "More flat, boring land."

"I thought the Platte River area was scenic, the gentle rolling sand hills and unbroken sea of grass. All the antelope and prairie dog cities were nice. It's starting to look a lot drier. But don't tell me you didn't like the hour stop to let the buffalo herd cross the tracks. That was an alien and magical sight, like being transplanted into one of the sketches of the West so frequently filling the eastern newspapers."

"Probably gets boring fast. I noticed most of the passengers didn't even bother to look."

"I guess the good news is we haven't seen any Indians."

"Not much of anything."

The sights had been minimal all day. The vast plain, almost treeless, stretched as far as the eye could reach, colliding with the distant, big, blue sky. The lack of trees worried Ambrose. Rails, even short ones, required ties, hundreds of thousands of them that could literally consume a forest.

He stood up, looking out the window beside Bridget. "I've read about the enormous size of the Great Plains, but one has to see it to truly grasp its dimensions. Its verdant fields of grass span forever, unbroken and unscarred by man. I bet it's something in spring or summer, a kaleidoscope of wildflowers and innumerable shades of green and yellow grass. We're ahead of the march of civilization. If nothing else, this ride should give you some appreciation of railroads. The Union Pacific has now subjugated the great desert. We're moving effortlessly and efficiently through untamed and hostile territory."

Ambrose pointed ahead to the towering peaks of the Rockies, their apexes covered in white snow. Since they had passed Ogallala five hours hence, the road had moved away from the Platte and began to gain elevation. Ambrose's ears had popped twice in the last hour. He had heard that water was a rare commodity here, and since the rail had diverged from the Platte, he had not seen a drop. His nose craved the clean, fresh air surely outside.

Little record existed of what lay beyond Cheyenne in the almost impenetrable wall of mountains. The only detailed scientific mapping had been done by the Union Pacific, typically only a few months ahead of construction, and then only of the proposed route. Out there somewhere, the construction crews of the Union Pacific toiled on, but exactly where depended on which paper you read.

Bridget sat, producing a big frown.

Ambrose grabbed her hand. "I like your black dress."

"I'm in all black today, a symbol of my depression at being here."

"You're going to like this. You've got an adventurous spirit."

Bridget poked out her red lower lip. "Oh, I do, but pulling me out of school—and in the middle of winter. There was the society ball next week. You had just bought me that new dress for it. And why am I here again?"

"Mr. Matson thought you might be of some help on a

new project of ours. You should feel proud he thinks so highly of you. The trip will be fun. You'll be the talk of the town when you get back after such an epic journey. Everybody will want to come see you. The paper might even do a story." Ambrose paused as he watched his daughter take in his words. "I know how you like attention. All those men will be doting over you. Your friends will be jealous."

Bridget's blue eyes grew big, her cheeks turning rosy. She bit her lip, then produced a big mischievous smirk. "But what can I do to help your new project?"

"As I told you earlier, we'll be seeing Mr. Brewster. I know you pretend you're not fond of him, but I know better."

"How old is Mr. Brewster?"

"Early thirties." Ambrose grinned. "I want you to use all your social charms on him, everything I've taught you. I've spent a tremendous amount of time and resources to have you educated to be a perfect lady, and you radiate it with every movement. You've learned well, but now I need to teach you about the real world. How it works. How to get things done. And getting Mr. Brewster to work on this project will mean a lot to us financially. I could send you to Europe, or buy a big house like you want on Prairie Avenue, or give you a big dowry so you will have every eligible man in the city at your doorstep."

Bridget brushed her blond hair and smiled. "Well, Father, now that you've explained it to me properly, I think you are right. Mr. Brewster is handsome, rugged, and smart, a real gentleman and man on his way up. Maybe this project will make Mr. Brewster so rich he might end up an apt suitor for me."

"That's more like it, like you've got more of my blood than your mother's. A woman on the way up." The car slightly jerked to the side. A few buildings rushed by the window. "Now, get your things together. We're getting off here."

Ambrose grabbed Bridget's hand as he stepped off the train. "There," he said, nodding, as he read his name written on a sign raised above the commotion at Cheyenne's small rail depot.

Pushing his way through the throng, he led Bridget to the man holding the sign, a short, stout, middle-aged gentleman with a big red beard.

"Mr. Graham, I presume?" the man said.

Ambrose extended a hand. "Yes."

"Patty O'Brien. Mr. Brewster sends his apologies. The UP line west of here is closed for some maintenance. I'll have a lad come get your bags. In addition to preventing Mr. Brewster's personal welcome, it has resulted in some complications for your trip, but I've made arrangements. We'll go by horse and wagon this afternoon to Fort Collins. It's about a four-hour ride, but with lovely scenery." Patty paused to look over Ambrose's shoulder. "Am I to presume this lovely peach will also be joining us for the trip?"

Ambrose stepped to the side. "Yes, this is my daughter, Bridget."

"Aye," Patty extended a hand to Bridget and laughed, "it's always a pleasure to meet a refined woman. Especially in these parts."

Ambrose studied the strange setting. The wind blew cold and raw, the air clean and fresh. In complete contrast to the idyllic setting of the plains, scores of rough, tough-looking men of every distinction roamed the planks.

"A sight for sure," Patty said, "but no place for a lady. Let us go down to the café at the hotel for some coffee. The crowd will clear shortly, and I will pull the wagon up here to get your bags. Then we'll be on our way. Mr. Graham, I've got a spare pistol belt for you. No need to worry, but you can't be too careful."

"Careful of what?" Bridget said.

Patty smiled. "You never know out here."

4

Around the end-of-track, the Colorado Northern's men worked to remove the debris from the destroyed bridge. At a table under a tent, its sides rolled up, Marshall looked over a stack of material shipping tickets.

A foreman entered the tent and handed Marshall three envelopes.

Marshall thumbed through the correspondence. "How many days until the foundations are shored up?"

"Two," the foreman said. "We've got every spare man on it."

Marshall opened a telegram from Ambrose Graham, noticing that it had been sent from Cheyenne.

MARSHALL
BRIDGET AND I SHOULD BE IN FORT
COLLINS BY FRIDAY 3/21 THE CITY HOTEL.
PLEASE COME WITH ALL HASTE.
                         AG

Marshall folded the paper, checking his calendar. Today was Thursday, March 20.

He took a deep breath as he spied the rugged landscape. Almost no one lived here other than Indians, and this land consumed white men. Hot in the summer, cold in the winter, something always seemed to be falling from the sky—rain, snow, ice, hail, and lightning that produced troublesome grass fires.

In his days on the Union Pacific, the rail moved forward through it all. But an exciting undertaking it all was. He loved it, building out in front of civilization and with only a vague idea of what lay ahead.

He had fallen in love with rails from the first time he'd ridden one twenty-five years earlier as a boy. He'd seen the benefits of them. Everywhere they went, civility and prosperity followed. What a challenge, every day something different, sculpting a path over God's green earth, all for the betterment of mankind.

He had studied rail engineering in his hometown of Troy, New York, and in the war built and repaired rails for the Union army under General Grenville Dodge. In the last decade, he had built rails all over the south and Midwest, but all that paled in comparison to building here. But he had never encountered anything like the bridge explosion a week earlier. His head still spun, his nights almost sleepless as he replayed the events in his mind. He was still trying to sort it all out. What had happened?

A man walked up.

"Who are you?" Marshall asked.

"Emory Chapman. You sent for me."

"Yes." Marshall dug through some papers on his desk and gazed up at Emory. The Colorado farmer had a classic frontier look, square face and strong, stocky frame. Contrary to local custom, his black hair was cut short and trimmed, and his face was clean shaven. The man had steely gray eyes and was very short, probably not even five feet tall without his boots. "Says here you served under Colonel Jacob Miller."

"Yes, sir, discharged in sixty-three. Then came out here for a new life. Was tired of the war, the death. Wanted a fresh start."

Marshall lifted a piece of paper, reading notes he had made of Emory's mortgage and records he had viewed at the courthouse.

"What went wrong?"

"Weather's worse than I figured, Indians, nobody to sell the crops to, no way to get them to market, or get anything else here. Wasn't as profitable as I thought it might be."

"Says here you've borrowed seven thousand dollars against your place, and owe almost all of it. You're three months behind on your note."

"I've put a lot into the place."

"I looked at it. Big, well-built house, two barns. A corral and a bunch of fences. I'd say you have thirty of the two hundred acres fenced."

"Yes sir, I built most of it myself."

"I'm going to make you a fair deal. I've done some checking on you. Sent a few telegraphs. I hear you're an honest man. The rail company will need an office and staging area. Your place will be perfect. It sits halfway between the start of our line and where it turns into the mountains. We'll give you the seven thousand dollars you owe on the place. And I'll put it in the conveyance documents that you can buy it back from the Colorado Northern for the same price once the rail's complete. Property will be worth something then. My only condition is you come to work for us. I've been told you were a deputy sheriff, too. We need someone with local knowledge. I have a feeling some of our recent problems are not simply accidents."

Emory narrowed his eyes, crinkling his nose. "What do you want me to do? I don't know anything about railroad building."

"Well, I need someone who knows the land, the people, the way around. And we'll also need someone to guard the rail and supplies, the payroll. We'll need more men for this. You can help recruit them. Colonel Miller says you were a fine sergeant for him." Marshall put down the paper. "A deal?"

"How do I know you're not going to cheat me?"

"You don't. You'll just have to trust me. You could have a lawyer look over the documents, but I don't know where you'll find one, maybe Cheyenne or Denver. But I don't see where you have any choice. This is the best deal you're going to get. Mr. Chapman, I can assure you, we have no interest in your claim other than for the railroad. When this rail is finished, I'm going back to Chicago. We have no desire to face any more Colorado winters or Indians than we have to. Your pay will be four dollars a day."

Emory swallowed, then stood and extended a hand. "Guess you're right. The bank will take it in a few months anyway. Deal."

Marshall felt the firm handshake. "Good." He stood. "I've got to go to Fort Collins to meet the vice president of the railroad. I'll be back in a few days."

"I've got to go that way too," Emory said. "To take care of a few things before I sign on. That's Indian country. It'll be safer to follow the stage road, at least until we get close. Best to leave at first light. We can make it by late afternoon."

* * *

From the saddle of Marshall's tall roan colt, the brown grass spanned to the horizon. To the west lay the impressive Front Range with its tall peaks slicing into the sky. He loved the big sky and wide views where the wind blew free. The great space exaggerated everything and made man seem insignificant.

The sun, almost directly overhead, shone down on the stage road, only a worn dirt path that weaved through the patchwork of rolling sand hills. "How much farther to Fort Collins?"

Emory whipped his reins. "About three more hours. We should make it by late afternoon. There is a stage depot about ten minutes ahead. We can stop there and stretch our legs a spell."

Shortly, they topped the next ridge and reined up. Against the wide panorama stood the smoldering ruins of a wood cabin.

"What the hell?" Marshall said.

Emory pulled up and raised his spyglass. "Seems quiet. But let's be careful." He pulled a carbine from his scabbard. "Let's ride up there, slow and alert."

Marshall removed the revolver from his hip and held it high. As he neared the stage depot, he saw the bloody bodies of two men, pierced with arrows and scalped. His skin got tight and warm. The smoldering wood frame of the two-room building popped and cracked, the smell of soot fresh, the heat still radiating from the dwindling fire.

Emory turned to the rough road behind them. A small dust tendril rose above a few horses in the distance.

Fear filled Marshall. "What is it?" he said, his voice hollow.

"Looks like an army patrol. In one hell of a hurry, too."

A few minutes passed as the four-horse patrol approached, reining up at the depot. Marshall tipped his hat to a sergeant, then to the three privates. Dust covered the men's uniforms and faces, and salt lines stretched along their horses' wet coats.

The sergeant leaned back in his saddle, tipping his hat.

"We just rode in," Emory said.

"Just down from Fort Russell." The sergeant paused to let his breath catch up. "Got word some of Roman Nose's braves are raiding in this area. They hit a stage station fifteen miles east of here this morning. Looks like we're late. We haven't had any trouble with the hostiles for months. Maybe it's this little splash of sunshine we've had lately." The sergeant dismounted, inspecting the ground. "I'd say a group of about eight Cheyenne warriors, but these tracks and this fire are fresh. Just a few hours old. I'd say they're still in the area."

Marshall took three gulps of air in an attempt to tame his queasy stomach.

The sergeant leaned his carbine on a hitching post and continued to study the tracks, kneeling and putting a hand on the ground. He pointed to one of the dead men and then a pair of long drag marks. "He had a wife. Her fate was worse than theirs. They likely took her . . . we're going on to Fort Collins, find somebody to come out and get these two, have them buried proper. You two can tag along with us."

Marshall rode, his mind uneasy, his hand gripping his pommel as they weaved along the road bisecting the grass. For thirty agonizing minutes since they'd left the depot, he had passed the time constantly scanning the horizon or ridgelines when they descended into a gully. The troopers had been silent, also scrutinizing the land.

One of the troopers darted left. Two shots rang out. High-pitched squeals filled the air.

"Left," the sergeant yelled, "over that hill."

Marshall spurred his horse. He saw nothing, but two more bullets zinged by. As he and Emory topped the hill, the four troopers leaped from their mounts, twisting their horses' necks to bring them to the ground. Marshall quickly dismounted, grabbing the Winchester from his saddle. He fell beside Emory.

"There," the sergeant said.

The four cavalrymen opened up.

Six horses raced across a knoll three hundred yards away.

"Put some lead up," the sergeant urged. "Make them think it will be costly. We don't want them to encircle us."

Through his sights, Marshall saw nothing. The sun hanging half down from its apex restricted his vision. He twisted around. To their rear, they were exposed, defenseless. There was only the big sky, the open plains—nothing else. His palms got wet. He shivered.

"Just shoot!" the sergeant yelled. "At the little hill at ten o'clock.

Marshall pulled the trigger, quickly cocking his lever and firing two more rounds.

More wicked screams came from afar.

The soldiers amped up their firing, the earsplitting barrage reaching a crescendo.

"Should we make a run for it?" Emory said.

"No." The sergeant grunted. "This is our only chance."

Movement came from their left, a group of horses riding away, a quarter-mile into the setting sun.

"I think they're hightailing," Emory said, getting to his knees.

The seconds passed slowly. The shots waned. The sergeant stood and lifted his field glasses. "Everybody reload.

They may be circling around." He turned and scanned the area to their rear. "No way to know but wait."

His breath heavy, his hands jittery, Marshall shoved six more shells into his rifle.

Emory stood, putting a hand over his eyes. "They probably used the sun to cover their departure."

The sergeant continued to study their rear, everything illuminated with the sun at his back. "I think you're right. Let's just sit tight five more minutes before we're off. Just our lucky day. They likely wouldn't attack into the sun."

5

Still dazed from the near deadly run-in, Marshall looked ahead to Fort Collins, a onetime military base, now a small town and staging area for settlers moving East and silver miners headed for the mountains. He pulled up on his reins and rubbed the mane of the tall colt beneath him. Why did Ambrose have his daughter with him?

Marshall had courted several other women in the last decade, but none stuck in his brain like Bridget. Two years earlier, he'd almost passed on the offer to work on the Pacific in hopes of further pursuing their brief courtship.

Why had she made the arduous trip? What was Ambrose up to? The last month had been long and turbulent. And the day's events had reminded him that he was ready to put his brief stint with the Colorado Northern Railroad behind him and get back to building the country's great new road.

He wheeled his mount around and spurred the colt toward town, only a quarter-mile distant. Marshall's first sight of Fort Collins disappointed him. The town had maybe forty buildings and only the absolute minimum in support facilities—one general store, a small hotel, a blacksmith's shop, a single café and bar, and the stage station as commercial establishments. In front of the hotel, he dismounted, tying his reins to a hitching post. His watch read four thirty.

Marshall sauntered into the hotel, where he turned to a clerk sitting at a desk. "Excuse me, but I was supposed to meet Ambrose Graham here at four. Do you know if he's here?"

The clerk nodded to a door at the back of the hotel's foyer. "He's in that private office there."

At the door, Marshall knocked twice and then opened it. He removed his hat and stepped inside. Ambrose sat behind a desk. "Benedict Matson must want this railroad awful bad to send the hero of Shiloh out here."

"You're late," Ambrose said, his lips forming a slight smile as he stood.

"Time ain't real precise out here, if you haven't noticed." Marshall took a second to inspect his old friend he hadn't seen in four years. Nearing fifty, Ambrose had a flat, serious face covered with a full beard. His black hair was receding and starting to gray, though the colonel's long, thin body still held its youthful veneer. But Ambrose's eyes and body had lost some of their zest and alertness since their time together in the war. His skin had gotten pale and softer. Unlike him, Ambrose looked like someone who had given up the rigors of a life in the field for an office.

Marshall stepped forward and accepted Ambrose's hand.

"Good to see you," Ambrose said.

"You too."

"I'll get down to business." Ambrose looked down at the papers and maps on the desk. "I know Matson has hired you to do some initial work on our rail, but I'm not sure our plans have been fully presented to you. We want you to come on board for the duration of this project. I know the UP has made you a new offer to return to work on their behalf."

Ambrose sat and gestured for Marshall to do the same.

Marshall looked at a map Ambrose had pushed across the table. "It's true that I had planned to go back to work for the UP when they get moving in earnest again this spring, but I cannot ignore an inquiry from a powerful rail interest like Benedict Matson."

"We've got a land grant to build a rail a hundred miles south of the mainline, here to Jeremiah and the silver mines. Got financing and capital, too."

Marshall nodded. "Makes sense. The Southwest is working its way up here from the south. You could connect in the future. Would be profitable, and the grants will pay— ore, iron, timber, and silver."

Ambrose leaned back in his chair, leveling his steely gaze on Marshall. "Mr. Matson is prepared to give you a five-percent stake in the rail, that's stock and grants, plus pay commensurate with your current salary."

Marshall looked back at the map as the words sank in. They surprised him. He'd never been made an offer like this, potentially this lucrative. How much money did the railroads make after construction? He usually moved on, but knew how much they cost to build. They had to be very profitable just to pay off the large cost of construction. Men didn't risk that kind of capital for meager returns. He had heard and read of the great estates the rails produced for their owners. The toll roads were revenue streams that went on and on and grew perpetually. He glanced up. "What's the catch?"

"The same problems the UP has."

Marshall didn't know the terrain, but knew how to read the contours and rivers on a map as they pertained to rail construction. "Why did I build this first mile here then? It would have made more sense to go south from Cheyenne, and you could avoid these hills. You'd just have to build it over the flatlands."

"I'd like to, but the grant doesn't include Albany County. Our first twenty miles will be easy, then we just cut through these hills, then we're back on the prairie until the last twenty or so miles where we turn back west and climb up to Jeremiah. These last miles will be difficult, but they'll be the last rail we lay."

Marshall studied the map trying to discover any major problems.

"What do you think?" Ambrose asked.

"Any other problems?"

"Let's see, the grants are only for first rail laid in the counties, so we've probably only got two years before the Southwest gets here. But our biggest problem will likely be Silas Jones. For obvious reasons, he doesn't want us to succeed."

"It can be done, but we'd have to start grading the hills and mountains first."

Ambrose nodded. "We can do that, but the first twenty-five miles are crucial. We get the grants and bonds on completed twenty-five-mile sections, similar to the Pacific. We'll probably need the money by then."

Marshall was familiar with these practicalities and problems in financing and building railroads. Engineers rarely built where and when they wanted, and he hated it. Politics, contracts, or legal details usually forced them to build in a location prescribed by somebody far away who had never seen a single spike driven. These demands increased the time and cost of construction. Building from an existing line made the most sense, since men and material could be brought to the construction site by rail, but he had at times lugged everything to construction sites by wagon only to build the rail back to the existing rail network. "What else?"

"How about the Indians?"

Marshall exhaled a long breath, his voice growing coarse. "They're here. Hell, we got into a fight with them on our way over here. Nearly my undoing. This is the heart of Cheyenne country."

"What kind of problems has the UP had with them?"

"Killed forty or fifty workers last year. Mostly surveyors or supply trains. They attack the small parties."

Ambrose scratched his stubbly chin. "Will the Indians be a problem?"

Marshall flashed his eyes at Ambrose. "You're the soldier. I'm just an engineer."

"What about the army?"

"We didn't have much luck on the Pacific. General Sheridan only has five thousand troops west of Omaha, spread pretty thin. How about the governor?"

"Doubtful," Ambrose answered, his bushy eyebrows rising and falling. "He's in bed with the Southwest. What do you think it will cost?"

"Pacific's about sixteen thousand dollars a mile over open terrain, three times as much in the hills, but with your reduced size, probably cost thirty to fifty percent more. The biggest problem is marshaling men and material out here, and you'll have to bid against the UP for all of it." Marshall wrung his hands. "I'd say you'll need five hundred men, minimum—a thousand would be better, if you can find them. In these parts, they run for the riches of the mines any chance they can get."

Ambrose removed his spectacles and stared unblinkingly at Marshall. "Well, what do you think? Are you in? This will be very rewarding financially. Mr. Matson would not be in it if it's not very profitable. He's never been wrong before, at least not since I've been associated with him."

Marshall's pulse quickened. A jolt rammed into his gut as he remembered the horrific accident at the bridge two weeks earlier. "It's a good offer. I'd like a chance to work with you again, but I don't really fancy fighting Indians or Silas Jones. I've only been on this job a month, and was damn near blown to smithereens by that runaway flatcar. I've heard about some of Mr. Jones's methods. I don't want to be planted out here."

"What about the rail accident?"

"Somebody caused it. I'm not sure who, but I checked the brakes on that railcar full of black powder myself an hour before it came crashing down on us."

"I'm here for the duration. And we could use you."

Marshall stood and put on his hat. "Building rails out here is much more difficult than back East. Give me a day or so to think about it. Indians, bandits, winters from hell, logistics nightmares, not to mention these other problems you have."

"Sure, but remember, I've got six hundred thousand dollars, in the I and I's money, plus another one and a half million dollars in guarantees, not even including the grants. This is big, and real, and I'm offering you a stake in it."

Sensing someone behind him, Marshall pivoted.

Bridget stood in the doorway. She was splendid perfection.

Marshall's heart beat faster. He removed his hat, instantly finding bliss in her wide smile.

"Well, Mr. Brewster," Bridget said, "I'm glad you could join us. Especially after I rode that train for two days and a horse for half of another to see you."

"We are trying to do something about that," Ambrose interjected. "With Marshall's help."

"Hello, Ms. Graham," Marshall said, grabbing Bridget's extended hand and bestowing a light kiss on it. "You look utterly captivating."

"Please, call me Bridget, and you look as robust and handsome as ever." Bridget waved her delicate hand in front of her face and blinked to her father. "I do believe I'm blushing. The descriptions in your letters don't do the plains justice."

"How was your trip?" Marshall said.

"Interesting," Bridget said, "I just don't know what a city girl will do around here. Mr. Brewster, will you take me for a ride tomorrow and show me the country? I don't know if I can take another day in this God-forbidden town."

Ambrose stepped out from behind the desk. "I was hoping Marshall and I might ride out and scout the line tomorrow. We'll be four or five days before we go to Denver. I'm sure you'll find your accommodations there more to your liking. Maybe Mr. Brewster will take you for a ride before we go. It's probably not safe for you to join us tomorrow."

"Excellent." Bridget turned her captivating blue eyes to Ambrose. "Father, I'm not a doll. I can take care of myself, especially with Mr. Brewster around. If you say so. I'd prefer a recreational trip anyway."

"I'm sure it's safe," Marshall said. "But we should look it over first. Then we'll go for a ride."

Bridget produced a big smile. "Let's hope so, Father. I'll certainly need to find something exciting to do if you want me to stay for a couple of weeks. I'm bored to death." She turned on her heels. "Now, I'll let you two get back to work.

And Mr. Brewster, please find me a pretty horse for our ride in a few days."

She'd be here for weeks! Marshall filled his mind with things they might do. He didn't know if he would take this job. It would provide him financial independence, something he craved, and possibly the woman of his dreams, but the Colorado Northern clearly had real enemies and obstacles. Was it worth dying for?

6

Wesley Loomis studied his cards without enthusiasm. A stinking pair of eights. He then squinted from the late-day sun filtering through the saloon's only window at the pile of money on the table. How much was there? Probably more than a hundred dollars.

"What'll it be, Sheriff?" one of the men across the table said.

Wesley no longer held the office of Arapahoe County Sheriff, but still answered to the title. He looked at his watch and then down at the bottle of whiskey beside his stash of coins. He wanted to turn it up and finish it, but had been summoned to see Silas Jones, the president of the Southwest Pacific Railroad, in twenty minutes. He already had a light buzz and thought better of it. Mr. Jones only made the trip here from Kansas City if he had urgent business. Wesley needed to sober up.

The little bar had twenty customers this afternoon, two tables of gamblers and four or five at the bar or entertaining the establishment's three young waitresses. He looked over his shoulder to Peggy, the prettiest of the three. "Goddamn it, next time I come in here, I want some real whiskey, from Tennessee or Kentucky, the stuff you keep under the bar, not this rotgut shit." He picked up his money, turned back to the table, and tossed his cards in. "I'm done."

Peggy said, "You come back and see me later, I'll get'cha the good whiskey."

Wesley pinched the girl hard on her ample rear and strode outside. Just a few blocks down Wazee Street, Denver's most prominent thoroughfare, stood the shiny new office of the Southwest Pacific, and as Wesley made the five-minute walk, he tried to shake loose of the alcohol's effect. Whatever his temperament, the whiskey amplified it, and today he wasn't in the best of moods. Nothing in particular stirred his gut, just the general state of things, and he tried to dissipate his feelings before he met with the county's most powerful man.

When Wesley entered the Southwest's office, he found no one in the reception room but heard voices down a hall. Walking in that direction, he stopped at a large mirror to inspect his appearance. Of average height and with a strong frame, he wore all black, including his Stetson. He brushed some dust off his arm and straightened his hair. Though he was only forty-four years old, his hair had already turned completely gray. He noticed his departing youth. His skin had gotten rough and flaky, and his blue eyes always appeared aged and bloodshot. Still, he looked good, the perfect image for a man in his business. Someone that other men looked at and thought: That's not someone you fuck with.

Walking on toward the conversation, he entered a large conference room. To his surprise, he found the mood in the room informal. Mr. Jones and two other men sat at a large conference table sipping wine and smoking cigars. Wesley recognized one of the men, Boss Smith, the railroad's hard-drinking, hard-talking manager in Colorado.

The other man was only in his early twenties, probably some type of aide.

"Good evening," Silas said. "Would you like a drink? Have a seat."

"No thanks, sir." Wesley sat.

Silas, a huge man in both width and height, had a bald head and a loud, authoritative voice, and usually didn't mince words—the no-nonsense type who typically got right to the point and wasn't afraid to say what needed to be said, or do what needed to be done. . . .

Silas rested his elbows on the table and leaned forward. "I've got a problem and I need someone to solve it."

Wesley set his hat on the floor. "What is it? I may be your man."

Silas lifted up some papers. "That damn crooked scoundrel, Benedict Matson, has gotten a land grant and government financing to build a railroad in northern Colorado in the new Railroad Act, the Colorado Northern Railroad Company. It's parallel to our planned route to Cheyenne. He probably had to pay dearly for this. No telling who he had to bribe. How he slipped this in on us I don't know." Silas paused and turned to the younger man beside him. "I want that son of a bitch that's looking out for our interests in Washington fired, today."

The thin young man replied, "It does look like the rail route is awkward, will be difficult to build."

"Probably all he could get." Silas chuckled and turned back to Wesley. "Now I can't have this. That's my railroad, and I don't plan on letting anybody else have it. They've already stolen the Pacific Rail from me, moved it from its best route through New Mexico and Arizona."

"I thought it was pretty common knowledge," Wesley said, "that the rail was started up there to stay away from the war, and the passes up there are much easier to cross."

"That was their *excuse*," Silas snapped. "Anyway, I need somebody to help me impede the building of Matson's rail until we build through there in a couple of years. Our line will have a better route, better for Colorado and Denver. We have a land grant too, and I want our grant protected. We'll lose it if he's successful."

"Sir," Wesley said, "with all due respect, I'm a lawman, not a bounty hunter or paid thug."

Silas leaned back in his chair. "Then why didn't you run for reelection?"

"I thought my talents might be of better use elsewhere. I plan to become a businessman. There's opportunity in Denver, the West. The papers are always raving about all this opportunity. I'm sure you read them."

Boss Smith butted in with a sardonic tone. "And has that panned out?"

"Been in a few things," Wesley said. "Nothing's panned out yet, but something will."

"I know you fancy yourself an honest man," Boss continued, "but you're just a polished-up outlaw in new clothes. Being elected sheriff in this county doesn't change that."

Wesley's blood got thick. He squirmed in his chair and flashed a stern glare on Boss, staring him down.

"Calm down, Boss," Silas said in an unruffled voice, turning to Wesley. "What Boss is trying to say is we know you're a man that can get things done. A man that's not afraid to step on a few toes that need stepping on. Things for the betterment of us all, Colorado. We have the support of the governor. I'll cut through the bullshit. We only need someone to slow down the progress of Matson's railroad. If he can't build it timely, he'll run out of money before he gets the grants and aid. Slowing down the work should not require much. Then I can come in and finish it."

"Hell," Wesley said, "why not just leave him to the Injuns?"

"I know Matson," Silas said. "That won't work. He's more resourceful than that, and troubles with the natives might allow for a government extension, or help from the army. I never trust an Injun to do my bidding anyway."

Silas paused, shaking his head and rolling his eyes. "There's another thing. Nobody needs to find out the railroad is behind any of this. What I'm trying to say is accidents happen. Men and materials perish in accidents, especially in the railroad business. Bandits and outlaws raid railroads all the time. It's the nature of the business, but I don't want anything that can be traced back to the Southwest. Is that understood?"

Wesley leaned forward. "I've read in the papers that they've already had some problems."

"We won't comment on that," Silas said, "other than to say we've already employed some people in our interest, but those parties were a little . . . how do I say this, too bold and ungovernable for our liking. Their employment has been terminated. We need somebody who obeys instructions and keeps a low profile."

"I know how these things work," Wesley replied, taking a long look at Boss and Silas. Opportunity lay here. He only needed to exploit it. "I'm tired of doing the rich man's bidding for scraps, and I'm tired of chasing two-bit outlaws for a workingman's wages. I've cleaned up every dusty town this side of the Republican River. If I was still sheriff, you'd have to deal with me on equal terms. You never know, I may run again. I'll do this job, but it won't be cheap. Fifteen thousand dollars, a third in advance, plus there'll be expenses, and I'll need some men, four or five good hands. I'm sure you can find somebody cheaper, but not anybody with my brains and grit. I've always gotten my man. I'm a safe bet. I've got a pretty young wife now and a family to think about."

The room got quiet. Silas and Boss exchanged a silent stare before Silas spoke up. "Let us discuss it, and come by tomorrow morning, say around ten."

Wesley stood and put on his hat, pulling the brim firmly down on his forehead. "Don't discuss it too long. That's nothing to the Southwest, probably less than building a mile of track. I'd hate it for you if I were to get an offer from someone else, maybe one of your competitors. And I want to be paid in gold. A small price to be the only railroad in northern Colorado." Wesley tipped his hat and turned for the door. "Been a pleasure. I hope we can do business."

He quickly stepped out of the room. Walking back down the hallway, he had a hard time concealing his smirk. He wanted this job. Working for the railroad would give him legitimacy. He had done some outlawing in his younger days and hated how that shadow still followed him. He considered himself as honest and hardworking as the next man. His indiscretions had resulted from his circumstances. He hadn't done anything anyone else wouldn't have done given the situation. Even being elected sheriff hadn't cleaned his record. The citizens had voted him in because they thought he was the only man around with the stomach to clean up the county. He'd succeeded, but with somewhat ruthless tactics.

Even in his outlaw days, he'd always considered himself a notch or two above his fellow thieves. He had more education and brains than most, and men followed him. He dressed and spoke well and had a glossy shine that most outlaws lacked. For years now, he'd looked back on his life in disappointment. What could he have accomplished if he'd taken another course? With this money, he'd be able to buy a large ranch, be a major landowner that everybody looked up to.

He smiled again. Silas would take his offer. Maybe he'd try to whittle him down some. He'd surely ask around, but all the answers he'd get would lead back to the reliable Sheriff Loomis. In the end, Silas would pony up. Wesley had read the desperation on his face and almost regretted not asking for more.

7

"You see it?" Marshall said to Bridget, looking ahead to a lovely meadow in Jeremiah Canyon where a moose grazed a few hundred yards ahead.

"Yes, it's wonderful. Are they dangerous?"

"Sometimes, if you spook them, especially the mamas if they have calves."

Bridget handed the binoculars back to Marshall. "The weather is perfect. I'm so fortunate you've spent the morning showing me around."

The midday sun had warmed the day. Marshall looked back down the main barrier of the proposed Colorado Northern Railroad, where the wonderful Jeremiah River Canyon parted the Front Range, slicing a westerly path through its granite walls. In stark contrast to the calm of the plains, the roar of the little river, raging from the snow-melt, filled the air as it rushed down the boulder-strewn stream, tumbling over cascading rock falls. He and Ambrose had scouted the canyon the day before on a well-traveled wagon trail from Fort Collins that led here and up to Jeremiah and the silver mines.

A few cloud blankets still hovered in a side valley. Overhead in the distance, the snow-covered peaks silhouetted themselves against the sky like a portrait. The temperature stood in the sixties, but still with a morning nip.

Marshall pointed to the yellow plain below. "You see, right there, the rail will turn, go between those two foothills, and then start its climb up the canyon."

With his hand chisel, he knocked loose some rock from a small outcropping. He picked up the material, feeling and inspecting it for hardness.

"What's so important about the rock?" Bridget asked.

"The quality of rock matters. It can be used for grading material in soft spots. You need to determine how easy it can be graded, and more importantly, how difficult it will be to blast away. The hardest rock only breaks free at about a foot a day, the softer maybe four feet a day. The difference seems small, but on a tunnel or cut of several hundred feet this can mean a difference of months in construction time."

Marshall pointed to the upturning layers of stone strata and eroded edges. "Look at all the different rock types— granite, limestone, sandstone, shale, quartz. Some of those I don't recognize." He lifted his little pad and made some notes.

"A splendid day," Bridget said, "haven't seen any Indians either."

"You won't see them," Marshall laughed and looked up the valley, "until the arrows or musket balls are headed your way. . . . Sheriff in Fort Collins says this road up the canyon is safe. The hostiles are on the prairie." Marshall looked back down the stream. "The canyon has a good slope, pretty gradual." He pointed up to a ridgeline that could be used to gradually ramp up the mountains, allowing the iron horse to chug its way up the canyon. "There's several places we'll have to blow. That new nitro-glycerin works wonders, but you have to be very careful with it."

"How do we build over those?" Bridget pointed to a large side draw, a huge hole in the gradual grade up the canyon.

"Not a problem. A temporary Howe truss can be built over them. Once the track is laid, we can bring in embankment to fill them. That will allow us to use a steam excavator. We've also been using some steam pile drivers that have worked out well . . . we'll need to do a good survey through here on the front end of construction."

"We? Does that mean you want to build the rail?"

Marshall grabbed his writing pad. He loved challenges. He was so busy planning out the construction in his mind, he had forgotten everything else. The weather here was highly variable—deep snow, high winds, and sudden blizzards in the winter. Opportunity had a way of passing men up. He didn't want to be passed over. He wanted to do something, make a name for himself. He'd worked and served but never left his mark on the land.

But could he leave the Pacific Railroad with all of America watching? One of the current problems on the Pacific Railroad was accommodating the droves of reporters that the UP brought out to the construction site every week. The last few weeks had been tough, more than he wanted or anticipated. This was an untamed and dangerous land. The bridge explosion had traumatized him.

The encounter with the hostile Indians two days earlier had spooked him, rekindling fears he hadn't experienced since the war. He wanted to put that behind him—the days of uncertainty, anxiety, and never-ending fright. It made him tremble. And Ambrose was a pain in the ass. A driven man and harsh taskmaster.

"What a challenge of mind and men," Bridget said. "If I were a man, I think I'd be a railroad engineer."

Marshall chuckled. He loved Bridget's feisty nature. Today she looked magnificent in a red dress, and he pondered fond thoughts of the two of them together. He always sensed Bridget liked the chase instead of the catch, at least when it came to men. But she was attainable.

Bridget frowned. "The most incomprehensible thing in the world to a man is a woman who is his equal." She looked away. "Well, I've decided I'm going to stay, at least for the summer. I won't get back in time to complete school this year anyway. This will be a journey I could never know otherwise, how exciting. A chance to do something, help civilize this land. What freedom. I will get a break from all those burdensome rules back home."

"Have you discussed this with Ambrose?"

"I will. My charms are rather effective on Father."

Marshall's blood pumped. To see such an amazing woman every day. . . . He'd seen nothing but dusty towns, hard work, and tough men for more than two years. He yearned for the soft touch of a woman, but could he pass on the Pacific Railroad, an engineer's dream? Had Ambrose put her up to this?

Marshall pushed up the brim of his hat and put his hands on Bridget's hips, pulling her closer. "You've got a lot of your father in you. All those times I called on you in Chicago. . . ." His stomach flipped as he took in Bridget's fresh scent. He put his hand gently on the back of her head, turned her face to his, and forced his lips onto hers.

"Mr. Brewster!" Bridget said with a deep breath, recoiling.

Marshall heard the words of resistance, but felt Bridget's

welcome as she consented, returning her lips to his, and putting her hand on his shoulder. The warm, wet kiss and soft skin consumed him as he closed his eyes and placed his other hand on her cheek.

Bridget stepped back, exhaling a long breath. "Maybe it's the fresh air, but I don't remember you as such a strong, confident gentleman."

Marshall openly inspected her. "This country's not for everyone. A rose like you can wither here."

"I'll be fine." Bridget smiled and grabbed the brim on Marshall's hat. "I'll certainly need to get some clothes more fit for my Western adventure. And one of these big-brimmed hats. . . . Have you decided if you're going back to work for the UP, or will you help us build this rail?"

Marshall removed his hat and ran his hands through his hair. "I don't know." He glanced at Bridget from the corner of his eye.

"We can take morning rides every day."

"I could see the benefits of morning rides with such a lovely and spirited lady, but railroad engineers are often too busy for such things."

"Let's hope you find some time for recreation no matter where you are." Bridget smiled and grabbed Marshall's hat. She fanned herself with it. "This morning has been a pleasant surprise. Certainly, a man who can build a railroad through this canyon could brighten my coming days with more surprises."

Marshall glanced at his watch. "We better get moving. Your father will be waiting on us. If I remember correctly, he guards you like a hawk." Marshall laughed. "Are you worth me having to butt heads with him?"

"More than worth it. And why would that matter?"

Bridget fanned herself as her eyes got big. "I make my own decisions on all such matters."

"We better get going." Marshall cleared his throat. "How many men back in Chicago are going to be upset that you've taken up with these rough cowboys and railroad workers?"

"There's a few."

8

Ambrose pulled out his briefcase and opened it on the table. He'd spent days studying the requirements of the land grants and bonds. The small details were important. The document had dozens of his check marks scratched on it—the maximum grade and the width and pound per foot of the rail required. The grants allowed the I&I to excavate minerals and cut timber on grants for railroad construction even before conveyance. For the rail to be considered completed, it had to be connected to the Pacific Railroad. Additionally, twenty percent of the bonds remained in escrow until the completion of the entire rail, and telegraph lines had to be stretched along all of it.

Bridget and Marshall walked in.

"I'm exhausted," Bridget said, "what grandeur."

Ambrose nodded to Marshall. "So what will it be? Do I need to make other plans? You know as well as I do, the railroad goes on."

Marshall put his hands on his hips. He turned to Bridget, who produced a big grin.

The room got quiet. Ambrose looked at his daughter, her

face tinted from the fresh sun, and then studied Marshall. Had his daughter worked her charms? The ex-army captain's physical attributes were average at best. He was of medium height and build; his brown hair fell down to his square shoulders sitting atop a lean, fit body. Marshall's skin was parched beyond his age from years under the sun, but his alert green eyes exuded confidence. Up close, he had an uneven, coarse appearance, but at a distance, he looked young, fit, and polished, and his mannerisms signaled someone educated and refined, the type of man people typically expected to excel.

"Okay, I guess I'm in." Marshall winked to Bridget. "I'll telegraph General Dodge and tell him I'm employed."

"Send my regards," Ambrose added. "What now?"

"We need men, all the men and equipment the Illinois and Iowa has, everything, sent here immediately. We're wasting working weather now."

"I've already telegraphed the main office. We have three hundred men on their way with grading equipment. I've got the turnouts and the rails on the way also. First fifty men will be in Cheyenne next week."

"You'll need everything that's required on a typical rail job, but you'll also need telegraph people, cooks, everything to house, feed, and supply the men. I'd go to Cheyenne and talk to the Smith brothers about cutting ties on our grants. Then go to Omaha and see Buck Johnson and Company. Have ten of those sleeper cars made, two dinner and office cars also, just like the UP cars. Buck'll know. Put twenty-five percent down on all of it and pay for everything on time. You pay all your bills on time, you'll usually get what you want. The UP is often very late with payment. The only reason they get material is everybody knows they'll eventually get paid by the government.

Everybody working for the UP is cash-strapped. Overorder everything, because everything will be late."

As fast as Marshall talked, Ambrose jotted it all down on his little pad.

"And start working on the nitroglycerin," Marshall continued. "You'll need to find somebody to mix it on-site. Find somebody that knows what they're doing. That shit can kill men a dozen at a time. We'll need it by summer. We can start the grading next week. Most of the first twenty-five miles will be easy. We can probably get that completed by the middle of June. As soon as we begin laying track, I'll start surveying the line, finding trouble spots."

Ambrose set down his pencil and reached up to offer his hand to Marshall. "I'm glad you're staying. You won't regret it. Make me a list of everything you'll need, and make a schedule. The boss likes schedules." He turned to Bridget. "Instead of Denver, I guess we should go to Omaha and Cheyenne to start buying supplies. You can catch the train back home from there in a week or so."

Bridget stepped forward, flattening the front of her dress. She stumbled with her words before spitting them out. "Father, I've decided I want to stay here with you and help with the rail. How exciting. I would never be allowed to do something like this back home—actually conduct business."

"Out of the question," Ambrose said impassively, putting his pencil to his mouth. "I promise you can come visit Mr. Brewster and inspect the rail work often, but a rail camp is no place for a woman, not to mention what else might lie out there."

"Father," Bridget grabbed Ambrose's hand, lifting it, "I'm as capable as any man. You know it, and you'll need an orderly, someone who can read and write well. You'll be so busy. I can help you write your reports. Oh, think how committed and convinced Mr. Matson will be with me here at your side. And you need someone to take care of you. I want to stay. I mean it. Just let me stay a few more weeks. If then you think I should go, I will. I promise. I won't resist. You know I'm not a problematic creature."

Ambrose raised a brow at Marshall. Both remained silent. Had Bridget promised this to Marshall? He cast his gaze back on his mischievous daughter. Did she really want to stay or was she only doing everything in her power to help him? This and his daughter's powers of persuasion made him proud. "We'll talk about it on the train. Stage to Cheyenne will be through here this afternoon. We'll follow it on horseback to Cheyenne. Marshall, I hope to be back here within a week, but I'll be in touch through the Cheyenne telegraph office."

Bridget bounced up onto her toes. "Thank you, Father. I won't let you down."

"Don't go celebrating. I haven't decided anything yet."

"But you will. After I look after your every need and help you with the paperwork this week in Cheyenne and Omaha, you'll see how useful I can be. Not to mention, I know how you enjoy my company and conversation." Bridget turned to Marshall and smiled, nodding back to her father. "I'll see you next week. Oh, how exciting, building a railroad."

9

Wesley sat at the kitchen table in the new house he had just purchased in Boulder, looking over the map Silas had given him. The rudimentary map covered the three counties of the Colorado Northern's railroad grant, but only identified a few small towns, some stage trails, river fords, and details of several mountain ranges. In the week since his meeting with Silas, he had sent a half-dozen telegrams to men he had worked with over the years about employment, but mostly he thought how he'd spend the five thousand dollars of his advance. Almost smitten, he conjured up dozens of ideas for the money. His thoughts only led to grander schemes and desires that required more money.

Wesley generally knew the area of the proposed rail, almost unpopulated, and mostly grassland except for the mountains that thrust in from the west. By basic common sense, he figured the rail would be built somewhere on the flat country. He had no idea how to slow down or halt the construction of a railroad. Boss Smith had given him a few suggestions, but mostly implied that he should delay the work any way he could.

Turning up his cup of coffee, Wesley studied the four men in the kitchen. Two of them he had deputized on several occasions for dirty jobs when he was sheriff. The other two had gotten wind that he needed some men for a special job. All four looked similar—toughs, with unshaven faces, steely eyes, and shiny, oiled pistols hanging loosely from their belts—and all dressed in attire for riding and weathering the elements. He needed to give these men a pep talk, some instructions, but didn't want them to know who employed him.

The two new men were surely ex-Confederates. The country was full of them. After the war, they'd come West by the droves looking for a fresh start or running from their pasts. Likely, many had nothing to return home to.

Wesley lifted a little leather pouch and then poured the gold coins on the table. He turned to the two men he'd employed in the past. "Pay is seventy dollars a month, gold. Tex, I want you and Johnny to go up to Fort Collins and sign on with the Colorado Northern." He raised a copy of the Denver newspaper and pointed to an advertisement. "Says here they're paying four dollars a day and need as many men as they can hire. If you can get on as guards, that would be best. With your pay plus the seventy dollars I'm paying you, you'll be well paid."

"What do you want us to do?" Tex asked with a deadpan face.

"Nothing for now, just keep me posted on what's going on. I want weekly reports. There'll be more pay if we need anything else." Wesley counted out half the money and placed it in two stacks, enjoying the smiles on Tex and Johnny's faces. "Here's half in advance. Don't spend it all in one place."

Both men scooped up the money and put it in their pockets.

"Don't just stand there. You're on the job. Get on up to Fort Collins *today*," Wesley snapped. He then patiently waited a few minutes for the men to depart before looking at the other two. He turned around and opened a drawer with six more sacks of gold, taking special care to make sure the two other men saw all the loot. He removed two pouches and set them on the table.

"Amos, you two will be paid six dollars a day, plus bonuses for commendable work." Wesley eyed both men. He knew how to read men, and both of these satisfied his inspection. They looked hollow inside, without conscience or regrets, and capable. "This is dangerous work, but I want that railroad work stopped or slowed down considerably. I'm wondering if you two are cut out for this work. I'm not a man to slight."

"Hell, me and Dog rode with Bill Quantrill," Amos said, his shit-eating grin exposing two gold teeth. "We love a sporting life. Blood don't scare us."

"No need for blood. This job probably won't require it. Don't want a bunch of law and newspapermen on us. But that's not to say we can't shove a few people around. Most men aren't like us. They *are* scared of blood."

"What'd you have in mind?" Amos said.

Wesley nodded to the corner of the room. "They're likely to have several hundred men working on that rail. Three of us ain't enough to do this with bullets. It'll take brains. That bag over there is full of black powder sticks. I'm thinking the easiest way to shut the work down is to blow up the new rail or water tanks. That way their supplies won't get to the end-of-track where they're working. We need to wait until they've laid enough rail to be a few miles away from the Pacific Railroad. They will then spend most of their time and money fixing the rail instead of building it."

Amos turned to his partner. "Pretty smart, Dog."

"The further back from the work that you blow the rail, the better. Just takes a little thinking, but don't do anything to the Pacific Railroad. That would probably get the army sent after us." Wesley grabbed both bags of gold and threw them to the men. "Half a month's pay. There's plenty more where that came from. Money is not a problem but not a word of this to anybody and don't go sparingly with the powder. I've got a warehouse full of it we can use. Now you two just hang around until I give you the word to do something. Shouldn't be more than a day or two."

10

"What about those two wagons of black-powder kegs?" Marshall asked Ambrose as he led him through the construction site on the first of two sets of foothills that protruded out from the Rockies. The rail would have to cross these hills to get from the Pacific Railroad to the flat plains. They poked up over the land only a few hundred feet, but they were the first major impediment to the rail's progress.

"Be here this afternoon!" Ambrose yelled over the sound of mauls banging away.

"And the nitroglycerin? It sure would speed things up."

"I've got some coming. It has to come all the way from Europe. It, and a mixing man, will be here by midsummer. Let's hope so, anyway. What are your problems?"

"Let me show you around." Marshall led Ambrose to a rock face where fifty men drilled holes in the hard rock. The labor-intensive work consisted of two-man teams. One held a drill and a long piece of iron, while a second man drove it into the stone face with a large sledgehammer. With each blow, the drill advanced a fraction of an inch, and the man holding the drill turned the iron instrument to reset the head in a different location. The work required guts and tremendous concentration. A flinch at the wrong time often resulted in broken bones, if not worse.

Marshall put a hand on the rock and studied a few fracture lines. Picking the location of the drill holes took a trained eye.

Upon completion of a dozen or so holes, black powder was packed into the crevices and detonated with a fuse. The powerful blasts produced thundering sounds, sent shock waves over the land that rattled men to the bone, and sent deadly debris flying in all directions. The excitement of the blasts was tempered by the small quantity of rock broken free that was then removed and the process initiated anew. For a railroad to triumph over time and space, it sometimes had to move mountains.

"Rock is harder than I expected," Marshall said. "It may present a problem in tunneling because of the lack of access, but now we need to utilize more men to attack this face in every possible location. We've been back to work three weeks. We've now laid eight miles of track. Not a stunning pace, but the work crews are now grading and laying almost a half-mile a day. Nothing like the Pacific Railroad or other rails back East, but we're moving along."

"More men and material will be here tomorrow," Ambrose said. "Including a second engine and twenty more flatcars to move the men and materials to the end-of-track."

Marshall frowned and raised a finger. "The end of rail is now only eight miles from these hills. Our progress is about to come to a screeching halt. What about moving more men and materials here? You should have let me move more men here a week ago. This is now the critical-path activity. Balancing how far in advance to grade is more than art. Well done, it keeps the rail moving along at a uniform pace."

Ambrose grunted. "I don't give a shit about that. Grading and working far in advance of the line requires too many men and too much material to be hauled here with horses and wagons. We needed to get some track laid first. Getting going, showing progress does the most for the morale of the men, the bosses, and bankers. By tomorrow we'll have almost four hundred men on the payroll. You can have fifty more men."

Marshall moaned. "You're going to get us in trouble thinking like that."

"Where are Emory and Patty?" Ambrose's posture stiffened and he stomped a foot. "I want to get to the bottom of these rail accidents we keep having."

"They're here. Up this trail." Marshall stepped to an overlook to catch a breath of the fresh, clean air. Below, green grass flickered as far as the horizon, like waves in the sea.

"Hell," Ambrose said, "all I ever heard or read was that everything west of Omaha was a desert. Just a little sunshine and warm weather and this land turns as rich as anything in Illinois. It's plenty adequate for farming. I can almost see the miles of crops that will follow the rail."

Hearing steps coming up behind him, Marshall turned to see Patty and Emory descending the trail. He pointed. "Let's walk on up a piece. Get away from this racket, and there may be an ignition in a few minutes." As he strode on, he reached over to pet a gray German shepherd following Emory. "What's with the dog?"

"He can smell Indians."

"We've seen a few," Patty said, "but only at a distance. They don't seem threatening."

"Indians ain't our problem," Ambrose said. "The rail was blown up again last night. This is the third time in two weeks. Worse, the perpetrators are crafting their skills. This one caused a derailment. About four miles back of end-of-track. The engineer didn't see the mangled track at night, but it did give us time to start getting the engine back on track and make the repairs before daylight. We only lost half a morning. I went down there this morning. Tracks are leather boots. Whoever it was took off in the direction of Fort Collins. I don't have to tell you how bad this is for morale or progress. Fortunately, the engine was not damaged, but if these outlaws' skills continued to evolve, serious problems lay ahead."

Emory said, "I got three men guarding the track now."

"That's not *enough*," Ambrose snapped, clenching his teeth. "Pull twelve more men from the ranks as you see fit and outfit them. There's two boxes of Henrys and ammo at headquarters. Pull the horses off the carts to mount them. I want a three-man outpost every two miles. Twenty-four-hour surveillance. Patrol a mile each way constantly. Only one man sleeps at a time. Shoot to kill. This will only get worse as the rail stretches out. We've probably only got to catch one of the bandits to end it." He narrowed his eyes. "I bet Silas Jones is behind this."

"Will do, Boss," Emory said.

Ambrose cocked his head to Patty. "What about the men?"

Patty rubbed his red whiskers. "A few grumblings, but nothing we Irish don't do, even in good times."

Ambrose removed his hat. "You assure the men that I will not rest until I solve this problem."

Marshall studied Patty's alert, shifting eyes. No amount of formal education, wealth, or power helped gauge the men's mood, and keeping their willing consent was as big a hurdle for rail construction as any outlaw band or deep canyon. Patty knew the men. Marshall thought about Ambrose's off-the-cuff remark. Would killing or scaring off one outlaw do the trick? He doubted it. And Patty probably did too. His gut tumbled. This wasn't his first railroad war, but out here, in the middle of nowhere with no prying eyes and little press, things could get bloody in a hurry.

11

Wesley sat on the porch of his new house, looking off to the west at the great mountains towering over the land. In the distance, a thunderhead loomed, its cool wind whipping the ten-foot-high grass in all directions. The onrushing dark clouds blocked out the sun, turning the mountains to shades of purple behind the thousand-acre plot he planned to buy.

Out of the corner of his eye, he saw two horses approaching. Boss Smith sat atop one of them.

Boss, his face flushed red, pulled out his pocket watch, checked the time, then closed the watch with a neat click. "Let's talk business."

"Name's Parson Simpson," the second man said.

Wesley knew the name, a hired gunslinger, known in the Southwest as a paid taskmaster for ranching interests with his own personal posse on the payroll. His methods were extreme, but effective. Parson had long, straight black hair, hard, flat, emotionless eyes, and a rangy, slender body and big shoulders. Two polished Navy Colts hung from his waist. Wesley knew the type—someone who made a living with a gun.

"Okay," Wesley answered.

The two men dismounted and tied off their reins. "Mind if we come in?"

Wesley slowly stood and opened the door, following the two men inside.

In the kitchen, Boss picked up a piece of new china. "The Colorado Northern has built fifteen miles of track in six weeks." Boss paused, casting a stern gaze on Wesley. "We're paying you to hold up the rail. Looks to me like you ain't doing anything but spending that money we gave you."

Wesley stole a glance at Parson, noticing the gunslinger's patronizing smirk. "I've got two men hired on with the railroad. Two more sabotaging it daily. We've derailed the locomotive twice, cut the track three more times, destroyed a water tank, and cut their telegraph lines at least a dozen times."

"I don't give a *shit* about the details," Boss snapped. "At the rate they're building, they'll finish the rail in advance of the time allotted in their government grant. You're not doing enough." Boss dropped the cup, and it broke into pieces as it collided with the floor.

"What Boss is saying," Parson said, "is the railroad may need someone competent, not a two-bit, washed-up sheriff. This job may be beyond you."

Wesley's blood rushed. He stiffened up, squaring himself to Parson and fighting off an urge to slap the shit-eating grin off the gunhand's face.

Boss cleared his throat. "What I'm saying is that for the money this job pays, there are obviously other parties interested in the work. From the railroad's position, we don't care who we hire. We're prepared to pay anyone who will look out for our interests. That's just business." Boss stepped toward Wesley, stepping on some of the broken china with his stride. "I can break you and will if I don't see some more results. I want that rail stopped. I don't care what you have to do. I would suggest you quit sunning on your new porch and get your ass up there, put some fire in your men, or do it yourself before Parson collects the rest of your pay. Is that clear?"

"Yes sir," Wesley said, "I'll get up there tomorrow."

Boss reached over, feeling the starched collar of Wesley's new cotton shirt. "They've got more than five hundred men on that rail. Derailing a few trains and cutting telegraph lines won't work. I don't care what *does* work. I just want the rail stopped or slowed. Get your hands messy if you have to." Boss nodded to Parson and stepped to the door. "I'll be up there myself in a week. By then I want to see some progress, else Parson will be back here to collect the gold we've paid you."

Veins pulsed on Wesley's forehead. He cocked his head and yelled, "The next time you see me, it will be to congratulate me for bringing the Colorado Northern to a dead stop! You can bank on it."

"How far away are we?" Wesley said, turning to Amos and Dog, both lying beside him and looking at the acre-sized staging area beside the Colorado Northern's new railroad. Behind him, the top of the sun crept above the horizon, sprinkling a few rays of light over the prairie.

"Five hundred paces," Amos said. "We stepped it off last night."

Wesley lifted his long rifle and flipped up its sights, adjusting them for a five-hundred-yard shot. He studied the grass, barely rustling. "It's calm. That's good."

"What kind of rifle is that?" Dog asked. "Ain't never seen one of those."

"It's British," Wesley whispered, "less than an inch pattern at five hundred steps." He picked up his spyglass and studied the scene, still just a patch of darkness draped in the shadow of the small hill the three men currently hid behind. "Where's that powder contraption I gave you?"

"Right there," Amos pointed, "this side of the powder storage. Placed it there four hours ago. Nobody seen us."

Wesley strained his eyes. In the shadows, he saw a black monolith of powder barrels, fifteen feet tall and more than a hundred paces wide. "How many kegs of powder down there?"

"A bunch," Amos answered. "Probably a couple hundred."

"And you did like I told you," Wesley continued. "You filled that iron bucket up with an inch of powder, then turned it on its side." He stared at Amos with serious eyes. "You laid down a six-inch-wide powder trail to one of the kegs that you burst open? Made sure it touched the hole in the bottom of the bucket?"

"Yeah, put two lines down."

"And you've got the hole in the bucket near the ground?"

"Uh, huh, we looked it over well. You designed it up real good. You hit that bucket, whole thing's going up. Just hope we're far enough away."

Wesley turned back to the staging area, straining his eyes even more.

"That bucket is right there." Amos pointed again. "Still too dark to see it, but you will in fifteen or twenty minutes."

Wesley checked his rifle. He'd packed the powder and ball in the muzzleloader carefully the night before. He turned to the west. He had been up for several hours and here for more than an hour to make sure his eyes acclimated to the twilight. The tops of the distant mountains already glowed from the rising sun. Below their apexes, the shadow line of the sun slowly crept down the slopes. He sucked in a deep breath.

In the last month, he'd been a headache for the Colorado Northern, his actions certainly slowing the work. Blowing the quarter-acre stash of the rail's powder stocks would do considerably more. He would essentially be declaring war on a five-hundred-man army of rail workers. He'd never envisioned anything like this when he'd signed on, but after several days of pondering his options, he had finally reconciled himself that something on this order had to be done to impede their progress. No wonder Silas had so hastily met his demands.

He had spent a few days checking around on Parson Simpson. Sorry-ass Boss Smith and Silas Jones had already hired him, but it would be later in the year before Parson's full crew of cutthroats were available. They were busy in southern Colorado on another job.

What lay ahead? This wasn't what he had in mind for a new career. Despite his thoughts, he couldn't retreat. He'd never taken on a job that he had not finished. His reputation and pride were on the line. This was a tough land where tough men like him thrived and excelled. That's the way it was. Either he or the Colorado Northern would succeed. No other options existed. He was now cornered. And he meant to win.

"You boys get your Spencers ready," Wesley said. "Ain't likely, but in case I miss, you two fire away at the bucket when I fire." Wesley lifted his rifle, placing the butt firmly against his shoulder. He then set the rifle's supersensitive double-set trigger. "Anybody down there?"

"Usually two men," Amos said with a soft voice, also putting his cheek against his rifle stock. "They change guards just around first seeing light. Probably about fifteen minutes. They usually meet over there on the south side when their relief arrives, on horseback."

"God have mercy on their souls," Wesley mumbled, "because I won't. Maybe they'll get lucky. This is just business, not personal. You boys are going to learn, I mean business, no matter what it takes. Next time I send you two to do a job, I want it done. If I have to come back again and do it, you're off the payroll. We're going to stop this railroad, one way or the other, no matter how nasty it gets. Now sit tight, and be still. There'll be enough light to shoot in about fifteen minutes."

12

Marshall sat on his horse examining the five rust-colored outcroppings of granite at the end-of-track that the rail had to slice through. Ranging from twenty to forty feet above the rail grade, each fifty to a hundred feet wide, they spanned more than two miles in both directions and had to be surmounted.

The work crews had completed two of the five cuts, narrow slits in the stone barely a foot wider than the train, their walls almost vertical. Beyond the cumbersome, time-consuming obstacle lay open plain where the grading crews marched forward. Past this barrier, only six more miles of track needed to be finished for the Colorado Northern to receive its first grants and bonds.

Just thirty minutes after daylight, Marshall watched the work site transition from a chaotic mass of confusion to an organized army of men and materials as the crews arrived and found their workstations. With the rail dead-ending into the natural obstacle, the track laying had ceased, and almost all the men had been put to work on the cut.

Around him, foremen checked the quantity of materials. Blacksmiths hammered away at a machine shop built on-site. Young boys carried water buckets to the thirsty men. A man hobbled along on a bandaged ankle, probably whacked with a hammer.

Patty approached. "Now that the critical construction is centered here, you don't hafta ride twenty miles a day up and down the rail solving problems. Will help on the ol' backside."

"Here," Marshall handed Patty several newspapers, "these came last night. Pass them out to the men tonight."

"Anything going on in the world?"

"Yeah, the Union Pacific has reached Laramie. The Central Pacific has completed construction to Donner Lake. The Republicans nominated Grant for president, and Andrew Johnson avoided impeachment by one vote. Reading the papers reminds me that we're in the middle of nowhere."

"Ah, General Grant will make a fine president. Why we all crossed an ocean to come to America."

"That's not the biggest news. Red Cloud and the Sioux have agreed to stop their war on the whites and the army in return for ownership of the Black Hills and the removal of all the army forts from the Powder River. It's all in there. Sitting Bull, Lone Horn, and Big Mouth all signed the treaty."

Patty opened one of the papers. "What about Roman Nose and the Cheyenne? Did they sign?"

"Nope." Marshall watched Bridget, attired in denim pants and a pullover sweater. Horseback, she rounded up some of the railroad's stray cattle.

"You twos is fond of each other. I see it."

"Probably too fond for her father's liking."

Patty chuckled loudly as Marshall spurred his horse and rode in her direction.

Bridget wheeled her horse and galloped toward him. She pulled up, gasping for air. "What a great adventure. I love the mornings here and this life in the open. Keeps me out of breath."

"It's the altitude," Marshall answered, the smell of manure fresh on his nose.

Bridget, her face flamed pink from several days of sunshine, her lips full and rich in complete contrast to the rugged setting, fanned herself.

"We're over five thousand feet here. You'll get used to it in a few more weeks. This may be fun for you, but your father and I have our careers on the line."

"We're going to finish the first segment in three weeks." Bridget smiled. "Any news of importance in those papers?"

"Yeah, Red Cloud has licked the army." Marshall smirked. "You're not going to love it so much if we run into Indians. They would love that yellow hair of yours."

Bridget grinned back at Marshall. "You'd never let that happen. Who would you flirt with then?"

A thundering blast rolled across the land. He turned to the north. A chill fell over him as a half-dozen subsequent explosions popped in the distance. Only one thing could produce a blast so large. All sounds ceased. He shifted his gaze to the work crews, the men all now looking to the north at the dark tendril of black smoke rising.

The scene was horrendous, a hell on earth. The little acre of prairie that only an hour earlier held a trove of the Colorado Northern's materials was now only a huge hole in the ground. Dozens of little fires flickered. Beside the crevice, two hundred feet of the new railroad lay uprooted. Covering the land for a hundred feet around the hole, shards of wood lay everywhere. A few railroad workers milled around the site, astonishment written on their faces.

Black soot covered everything, the charred scent falling on Marshall's nose. Cracking and simmering filled the air. He felt the heat of the smoldering cinders. In all directions, the buffalo grass bent away from the epicenter of the explosion. Two ties, forty yards from the crater, stabbed into the ground like spears. Around them, rails and dozens of hand tools lay spread out everywhere. The skeleton of a wagon still burned, turned upside down from the force of the blast. He'd seen accidents before, but nothing like this.

Hands on his hips, Marshall turned to Emory. "What about the dead?"

His face as cold as stone, Emory said, "Only one of the guards. The other is scratched up good. Lucky for us, they were the only ones here. The teamsters hadn't arrived yet."

"Where's he at?"

Emory twisted around to a wagon where a doctor currently wrapped a bandage around a man's arm.

Marshall stepped to the wagon. The injured man sat on its tailgate, his feet dangling to the ground. Several small lacerations blotted the man's smut-covered face. The doctor finished the bandage and wiped the man's face with a wet rag. "He going to be all right?"

"I'll be fine," the man said.

Marshall turned to the doctor. "Can I have a second?"

The doctor finished his cleaning and then reached into the wagon for a bag.

Marshall put his hand on the man's shoulder. "Any idea what happened?"

"It just blew up. Just about twenty minutes after first seeing light. I was over here waiting on the wagons. Don't know where Bo was."

"See anybody around here?"

The man shook his head, his bloodshot eyes wandering, his lips twisted in despair.

"You hear anything?"

The man picked up his canteen, took two big swigs, and then wiped his eyes on his sleeve. "I'm just now getting my senses back. But now that you've mentioned it, I do think I remember a couple of thuds, and maybe something like the rattle of a hammer on iron just before it all went up."

"Well, we're going to get you fixed up," Marshall said. He walked over to the rail and stood on what remained of its embankment.

Emory stepped to the track. "What you think?"

Marshall studied the land silently. "I'm guessing this is sabotage. Those sounds he heard. What you reckon they were?"

"Couldn't have been anybody around here. That would have been suicide."

"Maybe some gunshots at some type of rigged powder keg." Marshall nodded to the east to a little hill. "The sun came up right over that hill. Would have perfectly hid the shooter." He took off toward the rise.

A few minutes later, Marshall looked down at an area just behind the ridgeline where the grass lay bent over. With his foot, he pushed aside the thick turf to see a set of boot prints in the disturbed soil.

"How many you think?" Emory said, bending over and picking up a spent cartridge. He handed the gold casing to Marshall. "A Spencer repeater."

Marshall nodded to the south, to a horse approaching. "Here comes Ambrose."

Emory stepped around the scene, pushing aside the grass with his boots. "Looks like three. They took off that way." He pointed to the rolling hills of grass stretching to the horizon.

Ambrose arrived and reined up his buckskin mare, his

face red and lungs heaving. He removed his hat as he stared down the hill at the devastation without speaking.

Marshall held up one of the spent cartridges, his throat dry and thick. Below, Emory's dog snooped around the worn turf. "Somebody blew our powder stock. One man dead. Looks like three men. Took off that away about an hour ago."

"Emory," Ambrose said, still sizing up the scene. "You and your best man pick up this trail. See where it goes."

"Don't follow too close," Marshall said. "Ride slow and careful. Wouldn't want to rush up on a man who can hit a powder keg from five hundred paces." Marshall threw the Spencer cartridge on the ground.

"Not a word of this to anybody," Ambrose said as Emory stepped off. "I don't want a bunch of rumors going around. This might cause us serious problems with the men, especially if it's seen as more than an accident. I don't want a strike or a work stoppage. Emory, find out who's behind this. Go to Denver if you have to. All I can figure is the Southwest Pacific is behind this. This is more than I thought they'd ever resort to. Find out what you can."

"We've got bigger problems than this," Marshall said, turning a grave face to Ambrose. "I've got about two days of powder left. Don't know where you're going to get anymore, quickly. We've still got three more cuts to blast before we finish our first segment for payment. Any meaningful work will come to an end tomorrow night."

"We'll keep grading," Ambrose said. "I'll find some more powder, somewhere, and I'll talk to all the men tonight. We'll keep them on the payroll until we get back to work. It'll be expensive, but we don't have any choice."

13

"Mr. Graham," Patty said, "it will go a long way if you will let me say a few words first, ah? I will provide you an introduction."

"Okay," Ambrose answered. "How are the men?"

"They're a little spooked, but with good reason. They just need reassuring. Most of these men are veterans of the war. They've experienced men like you leading them through much worse."

Marshall's insides tingled as he studied Ambrose's alert eyes, a big knot moving in his throat. Patty's words reminded him of the war. There, he had seen Ambrose often do the unfathomable, almost willing things done with the sheer nature of his character.

An hour before dusk, a strange crimson hue hovered over the rock-strewn work site of the Colorado Northern. The setting sun's rays merged with the treeless plains to produce a rainbow of colors, fluttering against the horizon.

The Colorado Northern's work camp stood out as the only man-made thing for miles. The square silhouettes of the housing and dining cars and the dancing shadows of the workers were in complete contrast to the setting. The war had developed the organization and structure for an undertaking on this scale.

The operation had discipline and a military structure; the construction crews were the new front line with the entire country lending men and materials. This factory under the sun put down more than two thousand ties and ten thousand spikes per mile, all at a rail a minute.

"Let's get on with it," Ambrose said, and he and Patty climbed up on the flatcar.

The men gathered around them, an ocean of hats, mustaches, beards, and glowing cigars. They got quiet as a late-day breeze sliced over the land, dropping the temperature by the minute.

Patty stepped forward, raising a hand. "Just a few words before we have a fine dinner. And yours truly will say grace tonight to bless the food and the dice in hopes I may get back some of my hard-earned money with the nightly recreation."

A few men laughed.

Patty continued, "Mr. Graham has asked that everyone gather here for a few minutes before dinner so he might share a few words with you about the accident today. Myself and several other foremen visited the accident this afternoon, and to the best of my knowledge, Mr. Graham will be providing you all the information he has."

"Thank you, Patty." Ambrose stepped forward. "First, I'd like to put an end to the rumors. Our powder stock blew up this morning. Unfortunately, one man died. I don't know what caused the accident, but we are investigating it, and every reasonable effort is being undertaken to safeguard the work area. A second problem has arisen in the fact we only have about two days of powder remaining, and it may take five or six days to get some additional powder. But I want to assure everyone that the railroad is strong enough, financially, to weather this, and the rail will be finished. If for some reason there is a work stoppage, you men will be paid, fed, and housed until work recommences."

The land had turned purple in the fading light. A half-dozen torches threw their light into the work site, illuminating a few faces. Marshall studied the men for a reaction, their gazes all locked on the boss. Other than the general labor, men of all make worked on the line—water boys, game hunters, cooks, gaugers to guide and space the rails, tunnelers, cattlemen, explosive experts, carpenters, masons, woodcutters, blacksmiths, telegraph operators, and guards to protect it all.

Ambrose's speech seemed to be accepted positively. In reality, it would likely buy the railroad a week to find some supplies before the men would start wandering off to the mines, saloons, or the Union Pacific. More important, he thought about the desperate crime, what the saboteurs had done. He'd been involved in railroad wars before, but had never seen anything like the destruction from the powder supply's explosion. They were lucky dozens of men hadn't been killed. This was serious. The hair rose on his neck. Someone wanted the railroad stopped. And they were prepared to kill to do it.

Sitting at his desk, Ambrose removed his hat and scratched his beard, his head spinning. A single gas lantern lit the office, its yellow flame casting fluid shadows on the office's walls in an eerie dance that mimicked the grim atmosphere. Outside, the night was deathly quiet. At a desk, Marshall studied some profile maps.

Ambrose's problems were almost immeasurable in size

and scope. Unlike the war when solving problems typically only required grit and determination, albeit at the cost of life and limb, he was usually in total control. Now, he was not the master of his domain, and this was becoming abundantly clear. His forehead grew hot, and he ran both hands through his hair.

"We'll be all right," Marshall said. "I thought you handled the men well."

Ambrose cocked his head back. "We've got bigger problems. The Colorado Northern, and the Illinois and Iowa, are stretched to the breaking point. I know we're only six miles from completing the first section of the rail, but the cost has been almost twice our initial estimate."

"We started a little slow," Marshall said, "but the pace is picking up."

"I figured that much, but the bidding for materials against the UP has run up our cost considerably." Ambrose lifted a stack of papers off his desk. "The price of rails, spikes, almost everything was double what we typically pay back East, plus the cost of shipping has been astronomical and beyond my wildest imagination. The railroad has all but depleted its initial capital. All construction is now operating on credit. With this delay, we may hit a crisis point. Secondly, the entire operation's morale is frayed to a breaking point. Without pay, the men will quickly turn nasty and irritable. I'm worried if just some of the men start drawing their wages, this will increase the money crunch before I have time to solve it."

Ambrose looked at the papers scattered on his desk, his vision turning blurry. "For weeks, I've been studying the finances and the details of the government support. I've calculated the value of the land grants, what we could sell them for on the current market. I know the value of the bonds. I've checked over all other prospects, anything the railroad can milk money from on the front end. I'm convinced this railroad is a profitable endeavor if we can build it. With two-thirds of it complete, investors will pour in."

Ambrose flashed his eyes to Marshall. "Instead of just sitting there with that dumb-ass stare on your face, say something."

Marshall picked up some engineering drawings. "You should have let me finish that cut weeks ago like I wanted to. We wouldn't be in this mess. We'd be a week from our first milestone, celebrating with the government inspector. You *never* let the work bunch up on a single task. This is what can happen."

Ambrose gritted his teeth. Anger washed over him and he grunted. "You were right and I was wrong. I don't want to argue about it anymore, goddamn it. There's nothing we can do about it now."

Marshall pointed to a map. "If we can only finish this first section, then the initial bonds and grants will be conveyed, and we should be on a better footing. The next two segments cross open range, without a cut or fill more than twenty feet. They can easily be laid in two months, thus reaping more viable capital."

"*If.*" Ambrose moaned.

Bridget handed Ambrose a glass. "Here, I made you some tea. The men trust you. If a woman can read anything, it's men."

Ambrose took a big gulp. His daughter's words eased his tension some. "I think that Emory is a good man. He'll find something out, and we'll get to the bottom of this. At the rate we're going, we're going to have to employ a coffin maker full time. I want to make sure we have a nice funeral tomorrow for the man killed."

Bridget's face grew pale. "Why can't we get any help from the army?"

"Matson is trying," Ambrose said. "Go into the money vault. Have Bill bring me all the gold we have. Go on, now." He then turned to Marshall. "How many kegs do you need to finish the cut?"

"Five hundred should do it."

"I'll get them. I'll probably have to pay twenty dollars a keg for them, but I'll find them somewhere."

The accountant entered the room, the iron box of coins jingling as it hit Ambrose's desk.

"How much is in there?" Ambrose asked.

The accountant said, "About four thousand in gold, another two in scrip."

Ambrose wrung his hands. "I'm going to Omaha tonight. I'll pay gold to siphon off some of the UP's powder. You should have some in a few days. Then I'm going to Chicago, see if I can find some more money." He turned to his daughter. "Bridget, you'll stay here. Keep the books. Don't pay any bills that aren't essential. We've got eight days before payroll is due. Sell the excess ties we've cut, but only for cash, no credit. The Smith brothers will probably give us seventy cents on the dollar for them."

Marshall stood. "You know that's a breach of our contract. We cut those off government land."

Ambrose's temper rose, his cheeks growing warm. "Not building the fucking rail is a breach of our contract. These are obviously extraordinary circumstances." He paused and continued to think. "You have enough rail to finish this last few miles?"

Marshall picked up a piece of paper, briefly scanning it. "Just about, we've got enough ordered to finish. Should be here by the end of the week."

"Put your pencil to it." Ambrose grunted. "Determine exactly what you need. Have the order cut back to that. Come up with a good excuse for our reduction so our suppliers won't think we're squeezed. Tell them we're moving our staging area or something like that. What else is there for the men to do?"

Marshall lifted his sketches. "We've still got two miles of track to lay, and some chores back up the line that need to be finished."

"I will find the money for the payroll, somewhere." Ambrose dropped his feet to the floor with a loud clunk. "We're going to finish those cuts and finish this first section of line if I have to get out there and drive the spikes myself. And when I find out who blew up that powder stock, I'm going to shovel the dirt over his grave."

14

"Beautiful country," Marshall said, looking into the small valley on the plains, "I bet it's easy to get lost in."

"Easy enough," Emory said, standing in the saddle as they topped a small hill. "I think that river crossing is around here somewhere. Unless we get a big rain, you should be able to get your wagons across it and onto the rail corridor."

Marshall checked his watch. They'd been out scouting most of the morning. "We're supposed to meet with Patty at one. In the five days since Ambrose left, he's managed to send us enough material to keep working, but I want to make sure I can move men and grading equipment ahead to prevent a work stoppage just in case." He put a hand over his eyes. A small dust tendril rose above a few horses in the distance.

Emory raised his spyglass, studying the scene for a few seconds. "Might be Indians."

A nervous shiver raced up Marshall's spine. He raised his field glasses. Five more horses topped the ridge, maybe five hundred paces away.

"Probably Cheyenne," Emory whispered.

"Hostile?"

"Doubtful." Emory chuckled. "You'll never be so lucky to see hostile Cheyenne coming. Most of the Cheyenne have gone south of the Arkansas River. The ones left usually try to stay away from the white man except for a few bunches fighting with Tall Bull and Roman Nose. But they're almost all to the east. Probably a hunting party out with this break in the weather. Been a long winter. Likely they're more concerned with refilling their beef stocks than mischief." Emory reached to his saddle and grabbed a piece of a white sheet. He tossed it to Marshall. "Do us a favor. Put this on the end of your rifle. Raise it high."

Marshall's face grew warm. His stomach tumbled as he scanned the lonely hills and the hazy silhouettes on the far ridge.

Emory squinted into the spyglass. "Looks like about twenty. They're just checking us out. Let's not do anything that looks threatening and they'll likely move on."

Thirty tense seconds passed.

"Looks like we're going to find out." Emory lowered the spyglass. "Two of them are breaking out and heading this way. Just be calm. All we can do. We'd have no chance in a fight or by fleeing. I don't see any war bonnets."

Bland images of surly, ugly, and warlike savages filled Marshall's mind. He'd seen a few Indians at a distance over the recent years, but he had never had a close encounter. He thought of all the newspaper stories and books he'd read. Some painted the Indians as polite and helpful, aiding the earlier settlers, but volumes of print documented the gory details of the Cheyenne's bloody raids and depicted them as ruthless, born fighters, the greatest in the world. Visons of the two disfigured white men at the stage depot rammed into his head as he leaned back in his saddle, exhaling a long breath.

The two horses raced forward, growing more visible by the second.

Emory raised his spyglass. "Looks like one of the riders is a half-breed, maybe even a white man. The Cheyenne have quite a few of each in their band. Lower your rifle and put it away."

The riders approached, reining up ten paces in front of Marshall. Both riders wore buckskin pants and shirts, decorated with beads, and both wielded Spencer repeaters that sat in their laps. On the far ridgeline, the other Indians stood in a line, their horses facing them.

One of the riders raised a hand. "Name's Foster."

Foster's perfect, unaccented English surprised Marshall.

The other man stared at him with a kind face and honest, sincere eyes. The Indian had a big nose and an expansive, broad forehead. His cheekbones were ample and sturdy, and his lips narrow and straight. The mosaic image of the young brave gave no hint of gentleness, only the perfect portrait of a warrior. Marshall hoped he'd never have to fight this man one-on-one, a struggle he was sure he would lose.

"Emory Chapman, we're only out for a morning ride."

Foster nodded to the Cheyenne beside him. "This is Yellow Horse, a cousin of mine." He mumbled a few words that Marshall didn't understand, and Yellow Horse patted his chest.

Foster said, "We were just trying to pick up the trail of a small buffalo herd one of our scouts found this morning. Just looking for a safe place to cross the river and making sure you weren't an army patrol or buffalo hunters."

Emory waved his right hand across his waist. "We ain't seen anybody all morning."

"Much obliged." Foster turned to Yellow Horse, again spitting out a few words of Cheyenne.

Yellow Horse spurred his horse and galloped back toward the other Indians. Halfway to the line of the Cheyenne, he yelled something, swung his horse around, and the line of Indians raced ahead.

Foster lunged forward in his saddle and spurred his horse.

Marshall flinched. He felt weak, alone, his fate to be determined by things out of his control. His heart pattered. He wiped his forehead on his sleeve as Foster disappeared into the ravine. In less than thirty seconds, the twenty Cheyenne raced into the cover of the river. Smoothly, with hardly a sound, they quickly disappeared like deer running off.

Marshall broke the minute of silence. "How often does something like that happen here?"

"About once a year I'll run into a bunch of Cheyenne. But that's the first time it's ever happened in such an isolated place. . . . I've heard of that Foster. He's the son of a trader and Cheyenne squaw. There's a few people around here on good terms with him, and I've never heard of his band doing any raiding."

"Let's hope so." Marshall whipped his reins. "We've got enough problems without the Indians. Let's get back to headquarters."

Marshall sat at his desk in the new Colorado Northern's headquarters reading a telegram. An endless stack of papers covered almost every inch of the desk. The papers constituted dozens of material tickets, payroll receipts, bills to be paid, labor contracts, and the daily correspondence from Ambrose telling him to do this, do that, speed up the work, et cetera. Just feeding and watering the rail's horses, oxen, and donkeys, numbering more than a hundred, required several men's complete attention.

Now late May, the days growing longer and the weather better, the railroad needed to be utilizing the prime working season to the fullest instead of surviving.

His days had become a dizzying maze of paperwork. He sent and received no less than thirty telegrams a day, sometimes almost communicating with Ambrose or material suppliers in real time. Even under the existing conditions, the work crews had to be fed material on a gargantuan scale. Building a railroad was like moving pieces on a large chessboard.

"Bridget," Marshall said, studying a shipping ticket, "you need to have these tickets checked against the actual stock of every car. The logistics of building a rail requires impeccable organization, especially now. The material has to be staged so that the exact number of ties, rails, spikes, splice bars, and spike plates, et cetera, arrive at the end-of-track simultaneously on the same car so they can be laid in place."

Marshall stood and held up a piece of paper. "If a flatcar arrives with a shortage of one item, or the items aren't stacked correctly, lengthy delays ensue. More ties than rails means the car cannot move to the end-of-track and the one-hundred-and-fifty-pound ties have to be lugged ahead by hand. Anything that means carrying the five-hundred-pound rails is problematic. Adding to the problem, a flatcar has to be moved back almost a mile to a side track to get another car to the end-of-track. That's why we have several men stretched along the rail between Omaha and Cheyenne to update us on supplies heading to the work site."

"I know, Mr. Rail Engineer. We have ten orderlies and foremen handling the material staging, constantly inventorying and calculating, but there will always be problems."

Marshall hated the tedious, nerve-racking details. He never quit worrying about them. What he loved was progress on the ground, which gave him his only satisfaction. As he looked over a few bills, the door to his office opened and Patty entered.

"We'll need to add two more small curves," Marshall said as he sat at a desk. "One degree only, but they'll make the best crossing of that creek we scouted this morning. I'm having the timbers for the bridge hauled up there today. Patty, will you check on this right now?"

Patty nodded and walked out of the office.

Marshall said, "Bridget, can you bring me the shipping schedule for the rest of the week? A bigger problem than the material staging is our general supply of material. It looks like we'll have enough black powder to get through the first cut this week, then we'll need more of everything. Success requires that when the work crews get moving, they stay working. Men are stretched up and down the line for miles accomplishing different tasks. Once this operation gets up and going, any breaks in the supply chain force the process to stop. Then, precious hours, if not days, are required to get it back up to speed."

Marshall thumbed through some papers, scratching his ear. "I think we might make it."

"Of course, we're going to make it." Bridget leaned over him to pick up a ledger, brushing her shoulder against Marshall's chest.

Marshall eased forward in his chair. He grabbed Bridget's hand and she twisted to face him. "When we do, I think I'm going to celebrate by taking you for another ride into the canyon."

Bridget sat on Marshall's desk, lifting her feet off the floor. She leaned back, turning her blue eyes to him. "Mr. Brewster, Father did leave me with strict orders to honor your every wish while he was away. Possibly, you will finish this first section of railroad and come up with some more entertaining and recreational tasks for me before he returns." She then jumped to her feet.

Marshall skipped a breath. He leaned back, putting his boots on the desk. "We're not there yet. You likely wouldn't be so optimistic and in such high spirits if you'd been with me yesterday when we stumbled onto that big group of Cheyenne. A tad unnerving. . . . Tomorrow I'm going to join the surveyors for a few days, finalize the route ahead in case we have to move the men there and start grading. I was supposed to be up there four days ago, but your father's absence has forced me to stay here. If there's a problem, send for me. And if it looks like material will run short for anything, you need to let me know promptly. I can move men to grading, but this needs to be predicted several days in advance to ensure the men stay busy. Idle men often quit or make for the mines."

"Yes, sir."

15

From his pony, Yellow Horse looked down at the strange figure. Several hundred paces away, few details of the white man were discernible, even in the midday sun. Out for a day of hunting and general scouting, he had topped a small hill and found himself staring down at the man. Silently, he turned to Little Bear and Crow Eater behind him, raising a hand to stop. His instinct told him to ride off before he was spotted, but as the seconds rushed by he noticed that the man had spotted their horses silhouetted on the little ridge and slowly turned to face them.

He squinted and saw no rifle in the man's hands. He and his two companions lingered, the four shocked men staring at each other in deathly silence.

Yellow Horse *hated* these people. Four years earlier, at the still young age of twenty, he had survived the massacre at Sand Creek where almost a hundred and fifty Cheyenne and Arapahoe, mostly women and children, had been slaughtered by the army while camped peacefully under the bluecoat flag and promise of protection. Through the years, he never shook the images of the women and children cut to pieces and lying dead along the placid stream, many of them scalped, their private parts cut off and used as decoration on the soldiers' horses. The image of the soldiers' evil green and blue eyes enjoying the murderous rampage remained as vivid as that day when he cowered in the bushes, his knees shaking. He still heard the babies crying and saw the noses and ears severed with the shining sabers.

A strange shot of energy rushed over him. He'd been a member of war parties raiding the new rail lines and frontier towns in retaliation for the injustices. At the village the white men called Julesburg, he'd helped burn the town, even killing women and children.

But in the seasons since, his elders and the chiefs had taught all the Cheyenne to avoid the white faces. He stayed away from the white man's roads cutting through his people's land, and his villages had always fled from just the rumor of the oncoming invaders. He kept his gaze locked on the white man.

He needed to end the illicit endeavor. Yellow Horse gently clicked his heels and wheeled his horse around broadside to the man. He raised his lance high, wielding it. His heart exuded confidence and bliss as he rode off.

Then he heard a sharp splatter, the snort and grunt of his horse below him. What seemed like seconds later, he heard the rumble of the shots and a few yells echo over the land. The mare buckled to her knees and then over on her side to the ground. Yellow Horse's head collided with the ground. The weight of his horse fell painfully onto his thigh. Around him, he saw only a maze of green grass. His mind rushing with fear, he scrambled to gather his senses as he struggled to free himself. Pulling his leg loose from under his horse, he grabbed his knife from his belt and slit the mare's throat to end her hawing.

Breathing heavily, he briefly stood. Beside him, Crow

Eater's horse had also been shot, and he now lay behind it, his Henry rifle aimed in the direction of the shots. Little Bear had dismounted, grabbed his musket, and shooed away their only remaining pony. He then fell to a prone position and also pointed his sights in the direction of the hostile firing.

Yellow Horse hunched over and hurried to Crow Eater concealed in the three-foot-high grass. He strained his ears, but heard nothing. In the quiet setting, his mind worked hard. Just seconds earlier, he had been simply riding along peacefully, minding his own affairs. Now he lay hidden beside his two dead horses, wondering what had just happened.

"There must be more," Crow Eater said.

In the thick grass, Yellow Horse still saw nothing but the green haze around him. Now buried low in the lush vegetation, even his two friends beside him were out of sight. Yellow Horse cautiously rose to a knee, but still saw nothing. "Why are they shooting at us? We showed no hostile intentions."

"You see anything?" Crow Eater whispered from the grass. "The shots came from the river."

"I see nothing," Yellow Horse said, looking at a knoll a few hundred yards away, the highest point around and fifty feet above them. He then fell back into the thick grass. "Crow Eater, follow me. We're going to crawl up to that little hill we rode over where we can see something. Little Bear, when I raise my rifle toward the sun, get up and ride behind this hill and meet us."

Through a white man's spyglass, Yellow Horse stared out at the two white men. The day was now late, and the setting sun at his back illuminated the scene and ensured his concealment. The two white men worked alone, one looking through a long glass sitting atop a three-legged stand while the other sat beside him writing. The early stars glittered in the sky. A coyote howled in the distance. This country where the wind blew free and the waters roared unchecked seemed bland and peaceful. It was all he'd ever known, and the two whites looked like a hideous scar on the land.

The three Cheyenne had spent the afternoon tracking the two men on foot, being careful to conceal their every movement. Yellow Horse had spent the hours trying to piece together what had happened earlier in the day. As his nerves settled and his mind cleared, he wondered if he had done something to provoke the strangers. He replayed the events over and over, his anger growing by each breath. Apparently, one of the two men had simply fired at his party for no reason, maybe with the intent to kill, or possibly in an attempt to scare them off. The shots were too well placed to be only warning shots, and worse, he had lost two valuable ponies.

Yellow Horse spied the whites' two healthy horses, both with rifle scabbards affixed to their saddles. He turned to Crow Eater, who wore amused contempt on his strong, confident face. Crow Eater was a burly giant with a hearty laugh, but now he lay flat in the grass as still and quiet as a mountain lion. All three had removed the silver ornaments from their buckskin attire and left them with Little Bear's horse, then they hobbled over a hill behind them.

Yellow Horse handed the spyglass to Crow Eater. He moved a piece of grass and continued to stare. These two whites had hearts set on mischief and competed against him for the verdant, rich soil. Yellow Horse checked his bow. All three men also carried rifles. It was much easier to kill the men with their rifles, but their ammunition was sparse and needed to hunt game. The white man had scattered, killed, and spooked the abundant animals to such a degree that hunting them now required the white man's weapons, where once a little stalking and the sharp aim of an arrow was more than ample. Killing the two white men required less skill than killing the buffalo, even in years gone by.

"They are packing up, getting ready to leave," Yellow Horse said and pointed to an area behind the men about a hundred yards away. "We'll move there. When they ride by us, we'll kill them. Don't use the guns unless you have to."

Yellow Horse crawled in the knee-high grass. As he moved through the green wall on his hands and knees, his mind raced with anxiety. He crawled faster and faster. Seeing the grass get deeper and greener he stopped, knowing he now lay in a small draw. Behind him, Little Bear and Crow Eater lay on their bellies.

He rolled over on his back. His companions did likewise. He grabbed his bow and carefully set the arrow before laying the weapon on his chest at the ready. Staring into the darkening sky, he strained his ears, waiting to hear the riders approach.

In the distance came the low murmur of voices, slowly growing louder. Thrill, worry, disgust, an endless array of emotions raced through his body, and sweat built on his chest. The voices got louder, along with the horses' footsteps. His entire body stiffened in a frightful pose. Yellow Horse closed his eyes, letting only his ears guide him. Finally, the voices growing so loud they were chilling, he sprung to his feet.

He pulled back on the bow. The land stood quiet. His actions were quick and effortless. The two white men never saw the three Cheyenne. He heard his bow uncurl, the quick zip of the arrow plunging through the air. All three arrows dove into the soft flesh before either man knew their time on this earth had expired, each riding and talking as they grunted. With lightning-quick efficiency, three more arrows found their mark.

Then the timeless sound of the rustling grass retook the land.

16

Marshall's skin got tight. He covered his nose, removed the revolver from his hip, and held it high. Below his horse, sprawled in the thick grass, lay the bloody bodies of two men and a mule. More than fifteen arrows pierced the two men, both scalped. The hindquarters of the mule had been removed.

Emory's jaw hung open as he dismounted, inspecting the ground. "I'd say three or four Cheyenne warriors, late yesterday."

Marshall took three gulps of air in an attempt to tame his queasy stomach. "I've read about the maiming of the bodies, but why the mule?"

"That's just food," Emory said.

Marshall's vision got blurry, his breath heavy. "Had it not been for Ambrose's departure, I'd be lying here without hair." He rubbed his face. "What's this mean?"

"Can't rightly say," Emory replied. "Most of the Cheyenne and Arapahoe signed the treaty last year at Medicine Lodge and went south with Black Kettle. Almost all of the ones that stayed are only hunters like the group we ran into a few days ago. But there's a few bands of warriors left, mostly young bucks. Some are just stealing, others are more idealistic. General Hancock stirred them up last summer, burnt a bunch of their villages. He's since been replaced by General Sheridan, who's moved most of the army up to protect the Pacific Rail corridor. I've heard some of the ones that went south have already returned. Everybody's hoping that last summer's bloody raids don't reoccur. None of them are much of a threat to the railroad unless they unite. Likely they'll only attack isolated workers and settlers like this. It's difficult to catch them. No white man can ride with them. They're too skilled on horseback."

"Looks like their horses, guns, and ammo were taken."

"May not mean anything." Emory put a hand to his chin. "Horses and guns are their favorite loot."

Marshall sighed. Someone, white men he believed, daily tried to sabotage his work, and now they had Indian problems. "Any suggestions?"

"The good news is . . ." Emory rubbed his chin. "They only attacked a two-man survey team. They're not likely strong enough to do more. I would send more guards with the surveyors. Have everybody else keep a good eye and make sure nobody antagonizes the natives."

Marshall groaned. "I guess it's good news if you're not the one or two they get." He stepped down from his horse, inspecting the survey equipment. "Let's keep this as quiet as possible. Have these two taken to Fort Collins and buried instead of back to the railroad. I don't want the men to get alarmed, especially not now. Last thing we need is an Indian scare. We've only got three surveyors left. I'll see if I can find a few more. Probably have to get them back East." He cocked his head up to Emory. "Do you know someone we can send to talk to the local natives, possibly appease them?"

"I'll ask around. See if I can find somebody who knows that Foster we ran into the other day. But you're right. We need to keep this as quiet as possible. If word leaks out, the local press will be all over the story. They love this. They embellish these Indian raids to their worst, all the gory details. The fear of Indians, instead of the Indians themselves, can cause serious problems."

From the crest of a little knoll, the infinite horizons of buffalo grass constantly fluttered under the big, turquoise sky. To the north, a small storm moved across the land, the thunder rumbling freely over and over. In the distance, a dust storm hovered between the foothills.

For a week Marshall's skin had been clammy, his nights sleepless, the images of the dead surveyors branded into his brain. He was only here now working on the railroad by chance. The thoughts of the arrows piercing his chest, of the sharp, dreadful pain of his scalping, caused him to cringe. More discouraging, the reality of building the Colorado Northern's rail was setting in. This was a life-and-death struggle fraught with deadly perils almost daily.

Below, the track-laying crew marched on. The foremen's voice blared as the men lifted the five-hundred-pound rails with the iron tongs. He loved the foremen's authoritative and repetitive calls of "down rail."

The healthy, sweat-laden, and rough-handed men drove the spikes, three strokes at a time in an effortless rhythm as more men operated the cantilever that lifted the rails off the cars. The sledges rang. The crews worked deliberately, only spiking down each rail with ten spikes, enough for the supply carts to move forward. Forty more spikes per rail would be added after the end-of-track moved forward a quarter-mile.

Around the work crews, men laid out ties, spikes, splice plates, and graded rock ballasts as a foreman walked along, gauging the rail. The end-of-track raged with life like no other spot along the line. Everything—men, materials, and money—supported it.

Bridget rode up beside him.

"The space never gets old, does it?" Marshall said.

Bridget removed her hat, shaking loose her long blond hair. "I never cease to be in awe of the space. The clean air is intoxicating, and you can see forever." Bridget pointed to a large, isolated rock cylinder poking five hundred feet above the lush fields. It sat like a citadel, commanding and looming over the land.

"For weeks we've been approaching that. I never thought we'd get there. Now it looks small and insignificant to our rear."

Marshall rolled a smoke. Gratification soothed his soul.

Bridget said, "Why do you look so worried? We're back to turning wilderness into civilization. In only two weeks, you and your men blasted and moved that rock out of the way. We only lost two days of work due to a lack of powder, and much of that time was spent moving supplies forward, repairing wagons and carts, patching up a few trouble spots in the rail, and grading ahead."

"I'm still a little flustered by my near undoing at the hands of the Cheyenne. . . . And don't go rejoicing just yet. Whoever it is that wants to stop the rail is dead set on doing it. Anyone prepared to perpetrate something on the scale of blowing our supply yard will certainly strike again. Not only do we have to build the rail, we will likely have to fight and kill to finish it. I'm realizing that's probably inevitable."

"Father sent you another telegraph."

"What's it say?"

"One word: Congratulations!"

"Well, I've got my fingers crossed, but it does look like we're going to finish this first section by tomorrow night." Marshall took a long puff. "I never thought he'd pull it off but he did."

"*We* pulled it off," Bridget said.

"When's your father coming back?"

"Says a week or two, maybe more. He wants to make certain he's shored everything up first."

"Since it looks like I'll have some spare time, I think I will now instruct you to spend some time alone with me."

Bridget walked her horse up directly beside Marshall's, the two horses almost touching each other. She casually reached across his lap and grabbed his canteen, taking a big sip. She smiled enough to show off her perfect, white teeth. "If I'm not too busy."

"This is a business trip of the greatest importance. But I may try to squeeze in some recreation."

Bridget laughed and reached back across Marshall to return his canteen. "The federal rail inspector will be here day after tomorrow to certify the first twenty-five miles."

"Right over there!" Marshal turned and yelled to two men in a wagon. "Where those stakes are planted. I want the machine-shop door facing east."

"What are you doing the rest of the day?" Bridget asked, brushing back one of her bangs.

"Figure I'll ride back a few miles, inspect the rail. Make sure we don't have any problems before that rail inspector gets here."

"Mind if I go?"

"Not at all, but aren't you supposed to be working. Who's taking care of the railroad's paperwork?"

A mischievous smile sprang across Bridget's full lips.

"Can't I have a little fun before Father gets back? It's stuffy in the office all day, and there's all this fresh air out here."

Marshall nodded to a horse approaching. "Just a minute. Let me take care of some business first."

Emory rode up, tipping his hat to Bridget.

Marshall wiggled his finger. "Tell me about this Wesley Loomis you telegraphed me about."

"I know 'em," Emory said. "Use to be the sheriff of Arapahoe County. Word around Denver is he's come into some money. Been seen at the Southwest Pacific's office a couple of times, too, and in Fort Collins lately. He's tough, with more brains than the typical bushwhacker. A gunslinger with a restless, driving personality, but not the outlaw type, only hires on or kills for money, not sport, a professional."

"The worst type." Marshall moaned as he discarded his smoke. "We'll have to deal with him, before he deals with us. When Mr. Loomis and Ambrose run into each other, it'll be like two trains headed for a deadly collision."

Marshall rode down Fort Collins' dusty, pothole-strewn main street. A few blocks ahead, he saw the sign for the telegraph office. Beside him rode Bridget, Emory, and Mr. Terrance Coleman, the federal government's rail inspector, an elderly man with a hard face but a gentle and understanding voice.

The Colorado Northern's contract stated that once Mr. Coleman had inspected the twenty-five-mile stretch of new rail and it met government standards, he was required to send a telegram to Washington from somewhere other than the rail's telegraph office.

The four had spent the morning in the company's finest railcar, rolling up and down the line, stopping on a few occasions to get out and inspect the new track. Familiar with the process and how most of the federal inspectors tired of hearing the railroad's problems, Marshall had given Emory and Bridget strict orders not to complain to the government inspector about all their problems. For the most part, both had held their tongues when it came to the railroad's trials and tribulations, allowing Marshall to do most of the talking.

"I do believe," Bridget said in an exasperated voice, "that if I were back in Chicago, I would have measured for a new dress for such a momentous day."

Pulling up on his reins, Marshall dismounted, tying his horse off to a hitching post. He reached over and did the same to Mr. Coleman's horse.

Bridget hopped off her horse, handed her reins to Marshall, and straightened her long, white dress. She stepped on the porch of the telegraph office and opened the door. "After you, Mr. Coleman. And you will have to come visit us again. I make a terrific dinner."

Marshall slowly strode inside. Mr. Coleman handed a handwritten and signed note to the telegrapher as Bridget set a dollar on the little desk. The telegrapher lowered his glasses, reading the destination. He then tapped out a few seconds of code on the telegraph key before raising the paper to his eye.

Bridget tried to hide a smile beneath her glowing pink cheeks.

The telegrapher finished tapping, and then spent a few seconds listening to the broken hiss from the telegraph sounder. "Confirmed. It went through."

Marshall stepped forward. "I'd like that confirmation, with the telegraph company's seal on it. I'm going to file it and one of the copies of Mr. Coleman's certification in the courthouse. But first, we're going to have a drink." He waited for the telegrapher to stamp the confirmation, then picked it up, folded it, and put it in his shirt pocket. Turning to Mr. Coleman, he asked, "Care to join us? The saloon is just a few doors down."

"Wish I could," Mr. Coleman replied, "but I've got some other things to tend to. You will get me back to Cheyenne by tomorrow?"

"Mr. Coleman," Bridget said, her frown producing two large dimples. "I had hoped I might spend the afternoon enjoying more of your delightful company."

"Meet us back here in two hours," Marshall said, opening the door. "How's that sound?"

"Excellent," Mr. Coleman said, tipping his hat to Bridget. "And to you, Miss Graham, I do look forward to a return trip to inspect the rail's progress."

Bridget extended a hand that Mr. Coleman raised and kissed. "As do I," she said, "but I will expect you to allow me to cook you a fine dinner then."

Mr. Coleman produced a wide smile.

Marshall studied Bridget. Through the morning, she had completely charmed Mr. Coleman. Almost eerily, like a machine, she had turned on her outgoing personality and refined manners. She enjoyed men's attention, and like her father, she liked to get what she wanted. Her constant flirting with him had amplified his desire for her, keeping his knees weak and his insides about to burst. Was all her attention just a game, something she only engaged in to get something else?

They walked down the wood sidewalk fifty steps to the door of the local saloon. The blaring sound of a piano came from within. He grinned at Bridget. "Are you old enough to have a drink of whiskey?"

"Let's find out," Bridget answered, pushing open the swinging doors and stepping inside.

Emory let out a loud chuckle.

Marshall also laughed as they went inside. To his surprise, the little bar was lively in the midafternoon. Through the cigar smoke, the clinking of glasses, and the piano banging away, six people sat at two tables and two burly, unclean, and unshaven men danced with two women, probably employees of the establishment.

Marshall approached the bar. "What's the cause of all this celebration?"

Emory removed his hat and set it on the bar. "Probably a couple of miners that hit pay dirt. Or railroad workers squandering their pay. Hope they don't work for us."

"Hello, thar," the barmaid said. "What ye be?"

"We'll take three whiskeys." Marshall turned to the barkeep, a plump, greasy woman with a wrinkled, aged face. "Your best bottle."

Only seconds later, he grabbed one of the shot glasses, raised it high, and bumped it against Emory and Bridget's, also held high. All three turned up the whiskey and finished it.

"You see," Bridget said, "I'm as tough as you railroad boys."

Marshall grabbed the bottle and poured three more shots. "Not a word of this to your father. And don't throw up on my new boots." He felt Emory's elbow against his ribs, then a hand cup his ear.

"You see that man over there sitting at that table," Emory whispered. "The one in the white hat and blue shirt? That's Wesley Loomis. Wonder what he's doing up here?"

Marshall pivoted. The man sat with two companions who looked like drifters. Wesley had a flat, wide, unshaven face with small, cold, calculating eyes. An insatiable anger washed over Marshall. He felt an urge to walk over and whack the man likely responsible for putting their entire project in jeopardy. But that would accomplish little. Instead, he studied the man, locking his image into his memory.

"Who's that?" Bridget inquired.

"Wesley Loomis," Marshall answered softly.

"Is it so?" Bridget picked up one of the shot glasses, downed the whiskey, and stepped toward the man.

Marshall grabbed Bridget by the arm, spinning her back to face him. "What the hell you doing?"

Bridget jerked free, turning her back to the bar and yelling, "Mr. Wesley Loomis, will you come have a drink with us?" She grabbed the bottle with one hand and gestured to Wesley. "A drink on me."

Wesley stood and took two steps to the bar.

Marshall again grabbed Bridget's arm, pulling her behind him.

"Something on your mind?" Wesley said in a flat voice, stopping a few feet in front of Marshall.

Marshall's chest got tight. Emory had squared his back to the bar. "In fact there is."

Wesley grabbed the bottle from Bridget, poured himself a shot, and turned it up. "I'm listening. Go ahead."

Sweat built on Marshall's forehead. "Actually, we've changed our minds about the drink."

Wesley glanced at Emory then to Bridget. "Well, get out of my face then."

Bridget stepped forward, her face growing red, her cheeks crinkled. "You washed-up outlaw. You don't know who you're messing with."

"What's she's saying," Marshall said, jerking Bridget behind him, "is your company is no longer wanted."

Wesley's face contorted. He poked out his chest. He grabbed Marshall by the jaw. "You little smart-ass."

Emory jumped forward, pulling his pistol, its barrel aimed at Wesley.

Marshall felt his temples pumping. He jerked his head back from Wesley. The bar got completely silent. A half-dozen seconds passed, the only sound was his heavy breath.

Wesley took a step back, narrowing his eyes at Emory. "You ever pull that gun on me again, you better be ready to use it." He then strode for the door.

Bridget stepped forward, poking her head around Marshall. "You mess with the Colorado Northern Railroad and you'll wish you'd never met us."

Wesley stopped, turning to the three again with a cold stare before walking out of the bar.

The bar still deathly silent, Marshall felt his heart settle, his mind quit spinning. He grabbed the bottle and took a big swig before turning to Bridget. "You're turning into a little fireball, a better-looking version of Ambrose. No more whiskey for you."

17

"I know the local politicians are in bed with Silas Jones," Bridget said, "but you would think the murder of a few of our workers would be enough to have Mr. Loomis arrested."

"We can't prove that he's done anything," Marshall answered, helping Bridget off her horse. "We'll see how long Mr. Loomis stays around after he butts heads with Ambrose a few times."

Bridget took off her hat. "I hope so. We can't let these heathens stop progress. It's inevitable that this land will be civilized, and we're the ones Providence has deemed fit to do it."

"It's not that simple. There are other interests involved, powerful interests."

"I *know* that." Bridget rolled her eyes. "Have you forgotten I'm more than just your hired assistant? We're not going to allow ourselves to fail. I'm beginning to have the same distaste for Silas as Father has."

Marshall dipped his hand in the little mountain stream and splashed some of the cool, clear water on his face. He looked up at the titanic walls of Jeremiah Canyon. The midmorning sunlight broke across his face, and he felt the slight burn of the high-altitude rays on his neck. The hills, the granite chimneys, and the rock spires took every shape imaginable in a montage of otherworldly, staggering beauty. He loved the cool breezes in the high country, the variety of smells and colors—the yellow, green, and orange of the fauna and the red, gray, and brown of the rocks.

It was the day after the rail's certification, and for the first time in weeks Marshall's mind didn't race with things to do.

Bridget, as bright and pure as the mountain stream, was dressed nicely in a red shirt and long black skirt. She had unbuttoned five or six buttons down one side of her skirt that occasionally exposed her long, supple legs.

"Why are we going up to Jeremiah?" she asked, unfolding a blanket and flopping down.

"I'm going to talk to the mining boss, a nice German fellow, give him an update on the railroad. I'm also going to ask him for some men, some help against whoever is sabotaging our work, and more importantly, the Indians if we have trouble with them. Another fellow will be there, a colonel with the Colorado Volunteer Infantry, Rufus Bates. Just going to ask them to have some men at our disposal if we need them. It's in their interest." He gently pinched Bridget on the cheek. "That's where you come in. I've noticed your powers of persuasion over men are quite remarkable. I want you to use those for the benefit of the railroad."

"How much farther is it?" Bridget turned up her canteen and took a drink.

"About two more hours' ride."

"Next week for the 4th of July, I'm going to have a big barbeque for the men, real fancy. I've ordered everything. Since we're engaged in the most American of enterprises,

I was wondering if the men might get off a few hours early for it?"

"Yes, it will be good for morale." Marshall looked back at the towering canyon. "I'm going to start surveying this canyon in earnest next week. I just had a small cabin built up here for the surveyors to stay in. We've got to find a way to push our avenue of glory through this canyon. I figure we'll complete another fifty miles of rail by winter, be almost to this canyon. During the winter, we can do some blasting and grading in here. By next spring, all we'll have to do is build this last twenty miles of track. We'll have six months to build it."

Marshall scratched out the topography in the dirt with a stick.

Bridget paid close attention to his primitive drawing. She constantly prodded him to tell her of his plans or stories of his experiences building railroads, always listening alertly to his responses. He loved how curious she was about all things. She reached over Marshall, grabbed a twig, and quickly delineated the rail in the dirt sketch. Her neck brushed against his cheek.

Marshall grabbed Bridget by the shoulders, pulling her close.

Bridget rolled over on her side, her movement brushing her skirt to the side, her bare leg touching his.

Marshall skipped a breath and looked down at Bridget's thigh. "You like flaunting your beauty in front of me, don't you?"

Bridget chuckled. "You have a high opinion of yourself, Mr. Brewster. Freeing my dress a little aids in riding."

Marshall pulled Bridget closer, pressing his lips to hers.

Bridget reciprocated, putting a hand behind Marshall's head.

Voices sounded in the distance.

Bridget lightly kissed Marshall's neck, then gently pushed him away, keeping her eyes locked on his.

Marshall turned to look down at the wagon trail leading up to Jeremiah. Two men sat atop a wagon, cursing, prodding, and whipping their reins as they urged the four horses pulling the wagon over a hill and up the steep road.

Bridget wiped her hand across her red face. "Let's go see the mining boss and take care of the railroad's business."

Bridget said, "Mr. Kramer seemed like a nice man, and Colonel Bates seemed like he'd be willing to help."

"Maybe," Marshall answered as he wheeled his horse around, "especially since we're over Table Rock Pass and back on flat ground. Kramer's not worried about the Indians. They don't care about white men in the mountains. They never bother the miners, but they hate white men on the buffalo-grazing grounds. We'll go back and see him again. We just need to remind him that our interests are the same as his and if we can't build a rail on the prairie, he won't get a rail. I don't know what to make of Colonel Bates. Not sure who pulls his strings, but he could be of great aid to us. He's got almost three hundred volunteers under his command. Maybe the mines are paying him off."

For an hour, he'd been watching the sky darken. The distant rumbling of thunder grew louder and louder until the storm now appeared to engulf Jeremiah Canyon. The tempest was huge, powerful, spanning as far as he could see. He was familiar with the terrible storms of the plains, sprouting out of nowhere and lasting for hours, pounding the earth with unchecked rain, wind, and hail.

The dark clouds overhead dodged and swirled in every direction. The gray curtain of rain readied to crash into the mountains. A cold gust howled through the canyon and knocked off Marshall's hat, only restrained by his chin string. A bee-sized drop of rain stung his arm. The wind bent the trees in every direction. A quick flash of white filled the sky. A bolt of lightning ripped across the clouds, followed only an instant later by the roar of thunder that shook the ground.

Marshall's horse threw back his head, blowing and snorting. Marshall reached over and untied Bridget's rain slicker, handing it to her. He then quickly untied his poncho and pulled it over his head. "Put this on. This might be a real gusher. Let's go, follow me. That cabin we built is just over here, maybe a five-minute ride."

Marshall galloped off. Five minutes later, soaked, he jumped off at the one-room cabin built of shiny new planks. He opened the door, then grabbed Bridget and pulled her off her horse. "There's a stove in there, see if you can start a fire. I'll tend to the horses."

Marshall led the horses to the cabin's small corral and removed the saddles and bridles. He grabbed all the tack and walked into the cabin. Dripping wet, he set the saddles on the wood floor. The cabin smelled of pungent new timber. It contained only three old mattresses, a woodstove, a table, and a wooden chest.

Bridget started a fire in the stove and let her thick, blond hair fall to her shoulders.

As the rain beat on the roof, Marshall unbuttoned his shirt. "Might be here awhile. That chest probably has some blankets and towels. We should dry our clothes over the stove so we don't get sick." He walked over to the chest and pulled out four blankets.

Bridget turned to Marshall, her wet clothes snug against her body and accentuating her burgeoning womanhood.

Marshall grabbed a blanket. He walked to Bridget,

dropped the blanket on the floor, and put both hands on her hips, pulling her to him and forcing his lips onto hers.

Bridget's breathing increased rapidly.

Marshall reveled in her rising and falling chest. He raised a hand to unbutton her shirt.

"No," Bridget said, taking a half a step back.

Marshall moved closer.

Bridget retreated two paces until her back found the wall.

Marshall's heart rate soared as he felt her firmness. He kissed her neck.

Bridget cocked her back, pushing her chest forward. She raised her hands and shoved on Marshall's chest. "It's not time yet. We shouldn't."

Marshall resisted Bridget's limp attempt to restrain him. His eyes turned downward to the long, smooth curves of her cleavage pressing against her blouse. "I think you like all this, your charades. But you also want to play rough. We're a thousand miles from anything. The rules are different here. Let's see if you're the woman you pretend to be." He unbuttoned two more of Bridget's buttons and kissed her upper chest.

Bridget's chin quivered. Her chest heaved.

Marshall moved his mouth lower down Bridget's chest, securing her waist firmly. "You're ready for the next step, a real man instead of those city boys."

Marshall stood in the cabin's open doorway. In all directions, moonlight bathed the grass and trees in white light below the now clear sky. A cool wind scooted through the rustling trees. His watch read two thirty. He shut the door and crawled back in the bed, snuggling up beside Bridget's naked body under the blankets. Amazingly, he'd been asleep for seven hours.

Months had passed since he'd slept so well. Usually he spent his nights worrying, lying in bed for hours watching the moon and its shadows move across his room. If he did sleep, it would only be for thirty minutes before waking for an hour or more. Maybe it was the two hours of passionate lovemaking with Bridget, or the soft, gentle rubs of her hands that had put him into such a deep, carefree sleep.

"What time is it?" Bridget mumbled, turning up the burner on the little gas lantern beside the mattress. She then turned on her side and put her hand on Marshall's bare chest.

"Two thirty."

"You think our clothes are dry yet?" Bridget laughed.

"Doesn't matter. We can't leave till daylight."

Bridget smirked. "When did you build this cabin? You *have* been doing something with your time. I thought you only rode up and down the line barking orders and complaining."

Marshall reached over her and grabbed the lamp. He placed it on the floor behind him so the torchlight shone on Bridget. He loved the light in her eyes and the sound of her voice. In the minimal light, her smooth, fair skin, and plentiful curves stood out.

"What are you doing?" Bridget said with a playful smile.

"I just wanted to see you. I've been waiting for years to see all of you." He half grinned. "This is two days in a row that you're not going to tell your father what I've had you doing."

"He can hardly say anything," Bridget said in a soft, sincere voice. "I haven't told you this, but he brought me here with explicit orders to charm you into working for him. What can he expect? Like you said, I'm good at that."

She rubbed Marshall's chest. "Did you enjoy giving me an education?"

Marshall loved the small tickle and long strokes. He couldn't remember the last time he'd felt a woman's feminine touch or gotten such devout attention, much less from the girl of his dreams. "I thought it might be like breaking a wild mare, but you broke rather easily."

Bridget laughed loudly. "Is that how you saw it? Talk about charades. It was more like a mother feeding milk to her hungry and misbehaving baby. Cowboy, in your wildest dreams you've never had any forbidden fruit like that."

A few awkward seconds passed.

Bridget said, "You think we'll finish the next fifty miles this summer and get all the government aid?"

"Maybe. I'm realizing we'll have to take this railroad as opposed to building it, from the Indians and Silas. Kind of like I took you tonight."

"Fortune awaits the bold." Bridget smiled. "What do you think about the Railroad Act, the land grants, and loans? Some people think it's a scam."

"It's not a scam. The roads wouldn't be built without the government's help. The government will actually make money off the grants because the remaining land that they don't give to the rail companies will increase in value, tenfold or more. Plus it promotes commerce, increases tax revenue to the government, and improves everybody's life. Even in Chicago, most of the food you eat wouldn't be available without a railroad, and all the new immigrants have to live somewhere. For the last fifty years, rails have been built between existing populated places. The new paradigm is to build the rails into the wilderness, let development and settlers follow them, to nation build. They're the tip of the sword in taming the West. Great cities will rise out of the wilderness."

"Sounds like a railroad engineer's point of view." Bridget rested the side of her head on Marshall's shoulder. "You slept like a baby. Father never sleeps good. He still has nightmares about the war. Mother can barely take it sometimes, but he never talks about it. Tell me about the war. How you met Father, what you did. Do you still have nightmares?"

"I used to have bunches of nightmares. I was just a captain, a railroad engineer. We repaired a lot of the railroads in the South that the Rebs destroyed. We never really got much done until your father was put in charge of us. We were shelled a lot. I've never seen a man like Ambrose. When the shelling or fire got so bad the men wouldn't work, he would take charge personally, storming into the falling lead. Several times I thought he was ordering us all, including himself, to our death. My worst fear wasn't dying, it was having my legs or arms blown off. I still have the bad dreams, but not as much now. The work helps take your mind off of it." Marshall sighed. "If your father finds out about this tryst, he may shoot my ass."

"He will certainly be enraged. But he'll have to live with it. You're the key to the Colorado Northern and all he wants. And like you said, you'll have to take it no matter what." Bridget crawled over on top of Marshall, straddling him and letting her hair dangle into this face. "We've already infuriated Father, we might as well enjoy it for now."

18

"What kind of mischief have you been in," Gray Man said to Yellow Horse with a laugh, "that you so urgently wanted to discuss it? I had planned to go scout some of the new buffalo range with the summer moons and get away from all of these squabbling women and kids."

Yellow Horse laughed and took a seat beside the two other young chiefs and Gray Man, the eldest of the four. Beside him sat Sun Walker and the Arapahoe warrior Medicine Bear. Around them, Gray Man's little village of fifty continued with their daily lives as the four held council. Five more young braves stood around them, all permitted to listen, but none allowed to participate in the conversation.

Gray Man, probably thirty-five winters in this world, had relaxed eyes as he always did, never wearing a look of concern. Honored and celebrated, the chief was known for his bravery, hunting skill, and wisdom. Yellow Horse had seen few men as calm under pressure. Once in a clash along the northern road of the iron horse, he'd seen Gray Man dismount to lead ten braves into a hail of the white soldiers' bullets. The flying steel bounced around Gray Man, his actions giving his braves confidence and demonstrating to his people that they should not fear the white invaders. And even today, the sound of Gray Man's easy voice filled Yellow Horse with warmth, making him feel optimistic about the future.

"The next time you ask for a council," Gray Man continued, "come earlier and bring some of your beautiful squaws for my young braves."

Medicine Bear lit a large pipe. "You mean bring some of our pretty girls for *you*."

Gray Man grabbed the pipe and turned to Yellow Horse. "Tell me about these white men you killed."

"They worked on the new road for the iron horse."

"This is no good." Gray Man scolded Yellow Horse with a disapproving glance. "Killing the rail workers might bring more of the hair-mouth soldiers to us with hostile intentions."

"But they shot at me first, killed two of our ponies. We were only there observing. We topped a hill, and they were there. What else was I to *do*?"

Medicine Bear took the pipe and puffed on it twice. Short and stocky, the Arapaho warrior had a long, serious face with healthy muscles covered in decorations. He handed the pipe to Yellow Horse and spoke. "The white man is greedy. We never harmed the whites but in defense. They've run off all our buffalo. We have been wronged by the whites, but I have hope. We must try to avoid the whites."

Gray Man said, "The whites' children are as many as the leaves on the trees. The silver and gold rock has been discovered in the hills. Why it's so important, I do not understand, but it drives the whites crazy. The iron horse moves with great speed, breathing smoke, and making loud noises. It drives away the game."

He held his hands wide apart. "No matter how many we kill, more come. Many new settlers will be coming with this new road, as numerous as the antelope. Black Kettle and Lean Bear have both been to the land of the rising sun to meet with the whites' Great Father. They say the whites are too many and too strong to defeat. We cannot defeat the whites. We must learn to live in peace with them. We don't want more war with the whites. I once fought, but now I realize it does no good."

Gray Man took the pipe from Yellow Horse as he continued, "I do not agree with the great warrior Roman Nose and his braves who always fight the whites. Some say Red Cloud has defeated the whites, but there are not many whites in the North and no iron roads. I also did not agree with Black Kettle when he left for the South. I did not sign the white man's treaty at the Medicine Lodge when the leaves last fell. The white men have lied to Black Kettle and not provided him with the provisions they promised. We should stay here where the Great Spirit has put us where we can provide for our people. We must find a way to do this."

Yellow Horse was the youngest at the council and usually only spoke when asked. He had attended dozens of these councils in the last few years. Most of the meetings were useless babbling. The chiefs, especially the older chiefs who had all now fled, went on and on discussing the problems and why the white men had come to desecrate their land. They always discussed and complained about it. Little talk revolved around the subject of what to *do*, only complaining about the changes forced on them.

"I only want to remain what I am," Sun Walker said. His deep voice carried more age and knowledge than his appearance. The heavy-set, dark-skinned warrior was usually quiet. "A hunter. But the new road will run off the buffalo." He turned to Medicine Bear. "And the white man will kill them for fun. I would like to be friends with whites, but they didn't want peace. I see through their schemes. They lie to us. What is there to live for? I would rather die fighting than starve. We will live like our fathers before us."

Gray Man leaned back against a stump. "I know some of the young Cheyenne do not like this. Many fight the whites now, raiding and killing out of anger and revenge. My word is true, none will be around in ten winters. These new roads will cause us much trouble. I know it is difficult, but we need to keep our young braves away from the whites. We must keep the white man from turning us against ourselves."

"The whites kill Cheyenne and Arapahoe whenever they *can*," Sun Walker said. "We are superior to the whites, even with their better weapons. I say we fight the whites. Many of our great warriors, Tall Bull, White Horse, and Gray Beard, are coming back north because as you say, the white men have lied to them."

Gray Man asked Yellow Horse, "What do you think?"

Yellow Horse nudged himself forward a few inches. He knew Sun Walker well as a hothead, who was jealous of Yellow Horse because of the esteem he had earned at a young age and because he had once been in love with Yellow Horse's beautiful wife, Bird Woman. Sun Walker's eyes, as they often did, looked condescendingly at him, probably unhappy Gray Man had asked for his opinion.

"I agree with Sun Walker," Yellow Horse answered. "I am not afraid of the white man. He cannot ride as fast as us. He suffers in the climate. He is not as strong and agile as us and is less observant and moves with less conceal-ment. It is true that in large, organized groups, the hair-mouth soldiers are much stronger than us, even when we outnumber them. But I also agree with Gray Man, learning to live with them is the only way."

"If it is to be," Medicine Bear added, sucking on the pipe. "We should parley with the whites building the rail and find a way. I do not want to go live on the reservation and depend on the white man's handouts. Cheyenne and Arapahoe must roam free. Cooped up we will die. We must live beside the whites. I will send for Singing Man. We will discuss it with him. Maybe we can arrange a council with the whites building the iron road."

Sun Walker stood, balling his fist and patting his chest. "The councils with the whites do no good. Everyone only complains. The whites only tell us the way it is, the way it has to be. They tell us we have to conform to the white man's ways and submit to their leaders. Why? I am growing restless of the white man's broken promises."

Gray Man stood. "We must survive as a people. We will only fight as a last resort. It will be tomorrow before Singing Man gets here from Medicine Bear's camp. We should eat and rest and continue our council tomorrow when he is here. Singing Man may be able to give us some advice. We have time to settle these matters. Now, during the season of green grass we need to hunt and let our ponies fatten up."

Wesley rode down the dusty street of the makeshift, ramshackle community adjacent to the Southwest Pacific's new rail line on the outskirts of Denver. A half-dozen shacks had recently popped up here to cater to the railroad's workers—several stores, and three bordellos, all only wooden porches attached to canvas tents.

Late in the day, he stepped into one of the seedy bars. Tough, unshaven men stood over the rough planks. The stench of sweat, cigar smoke, and fetid food filled the dark room. It reminded him of why he had taken the job from Boss Smith. He was above this. And he meant to stay there. He ordered a glass of whiskey.

As he downed it, he wondered about the two men and lovely young girl he had run into a few days earlier. Were they with the Colorado Northern? How did they know who he was? Where did they get their inclinations that he was behind some of the railroad's problems? To date, he hadn't put a face or thought to his opponents. Were they as ruthless and capable as Silas Jones and did they solve their problems like he did? He walked outside to the Pullman car parked on the railroad.

Stepping up on the car's rear porch, he knocked on the door.

A well-dressed young man opened it. "Yes."

"I'd like to see Boss. Name's Wesley Loomis. He'll know."

The man stepped away from the door, returning a minute later. "Come in and have a seat."

Two fine leather chairs adorned the plush car. Engraved crystal sat atop the office's little bar.

Boss entered and nodded to the doorman, who stepped outside, shutting the door upon exiting. Boss swelled his massive chest and turned up his chin. "I'd prefer if you wouldn't come see me here. I told you, I'll send for you if I need something."

"I just wanted to discuss a few things."

Boss fired a cigar. "I read in the papers that the Colorado Northern's having some more significant problems lately. Speaking from the railroad's position, it always pleases me when our competitors have problems. But I see where they completed their first segment for government support. Mr. Jones was in town last week, and we discussed their progress. The current situation is completely unsatisfactory, but he felt that if the Colorado Northern's recent problems continue, or get worse, there could be opportunity for the Southwest to grow its current market in the state."

Wesley leaned forward. "I thought I might let you know that I bumped into some people involved with the Colorado Northern, upper-class types that made a few statements you might be concerned with."

"And what would that be?"

"They suggested I was associated with the Southwest and that I might have had a hand in some of their unfortunate events."

Boss shook his head twice. "What's so strange about that? Of course they think that. They're not idiots. If the Southwest's competitors were easy to deal with, we wouldn't need the likes of tough men like you. What does it matter? What matters is what can be proved, and more importantly, what they get done. Nobody gives a shit why you fail. When they're bankrupt and run out of Colorado, they won't be a threat to anybody." Boss lifted his glasses and rolled his eyes. "My advice to you is don't rest on your past achievements. If the Colorado Northern completes a second section of rail, the Southwest may be required to reevaluate some of its ongoing operations, if you know what I mean."

Boss picked up some papers, scanning over them briefly.

Wesley's blood boiled. He raised a hand to continue the conversation.

"That's all, Mr. Loomis," Boss said, not looking up from the papers. "And don't come down here to see me again without a summon."

19

On the western horizon, the tall peaks loomed over the heat waves still dancing above the grass, a wonderful display of colors in the late afternoon. Overhead, the perfect late-July sky sat like a giant umbrella, dotted with a few cotton-ball-like white clouds.

From atop a small hill poking up above the plains, Marshall looked through the viewfinder of his surveyor's transit, focused on the apex of one of the distant peaks. He rechecked the angles and some of his figuring. By his calculation, the peak was 6,996 feet above sea level.

Marshall was just playing around. He loved to survey the peaks, his little part in mapping the West, most of which constituted a blank slate on most maps. He planned to mail his findings and data, the longitude, latitude, and elevation, to the General Land Office in Washington. His findings would be added to the current collection of surveys in the West. Hopefully, the Land Office would publish his maps. Maybe they'd even ask him to name some of the six peaks he'd surveyed.

He had just returned from Jeremiah Canyon, where he had been surveying for ten days. The progress pleased him.

The Colorado Northern had now completed about fifteen more miles of track, reaching the company's headquarters. The chorus of clanging and pinging filled the air as the men banged one of the rails into a curve with their hammers. A handcar moved down the line that was only weeks before bare earth.

From above, Marshall inspected a huge field of buffalo bones on the prairie, all several years old and bleached white. Hundreds of skeletons lay in the grass, so many the workers actually had cleared a path through the graveyard for the grading. The precious hides brought two to three dollars each. In an afternoon, a good shooter with a couple of wagons could secure several months' pay.

Bridget rode up the little hill. He hadn't seen her since their night in the cabin ten days earlier, and his heartbeat quickened. Her image surpassed his delightful memories.

"Good evening, Mr. Brewster," Bridget said, lounging in her saddle, a big grin below her rosy cheeks.

Marshall nodded toward the bones.

Bridget turned to look. "What a slaughter. Very sad in some ways, but Father says killing the buffalo is good. It will help get rid of the Indians."

"It's the unofficial policy of the government. The army gives the buff hunters free ammunition. I've even heard people say killing the buffalo is doing the Indians a favor. It will force them off the plains, and hence, keep us from having to kill them . . . a strange logic." Marshall put his hands on his hips. "How long's your father been back?"

"Two days. How's your survey of the canyon going?"

"Fine. Too bad about Ambrose being back. I was hoping I might take you for another ride in the canyon before he returned."

Bridget put a finger to her lip. "That's wishful thinking.

Who says you're going to get another dance? I *am* a proper lady."

"If the Cheyenne get me, you'll one day realize what a good teacher I am. We'll see how your false front holds up the next time we're alone together. Though I'll have to use my imagination since your father is back, if I can find some spare time."

"Mr. Brewster, certainly if you can build a rail through that canyon, you can find a way to spend some time alone with me, if only for a walk this time. Possibly my indiscretions have led you to believe I'm here for your entertainment instead of the other way around."

Marshall chuckled. "I actually came down from the canyon because your father sent for me. He wants to discuss the progress tonight. I miss anything else while I was gone?"

"Yeah, generals Grant, Sherman, and Sheridan are coming to Cheyenne next week to look at the Pacific Railroad. Everybody's talking about it. And we had a terrible grass fire the other day. Cinders from one of the engines started it. This grass is starting to turn dry. Lost an entire half-day, but luckily nobody was hurt. We just lost a few wheelbarrows and hand tools." Bridget pointed to the north. "There, you can see the burnt grass."

The grass, lush green a few months earlier, had begun to turn golden, and he saw the outline of the huge black void. Too bad about the generals in Cheyenne. The press would surely be there in droves for such an event. If he were still employed by the UP, he'd also likely be there, shaking hands and visiting with the brass. "See all the fun I'm missing out on to build this railroad. Probably would have had my picture taken with the next president." Marshall removed the transit from its tripod, placing it in its travel box. "Those fires will likely get much worse before winter."

Bridget rode abreast of Marshall. She leaned back in the saddle, arching her back and proudly displaying her maturity. "It's not all sacrifice. There are things here you would rather do than see General Grant."

"Like getting shot by Wesley Loomis or scalped by Roman Nose?"

In the twilight, Ambrose looked over the Colorado Northern's headquarters. With the passing months, the old ranch had taken on a new character. Two sets of fresh elk horns hung over the front door, and dozens of people stirred around the complex. On the front porch, a cook churned butter while another swept the planks. Beside the ranch, several more men stood around the rows of meat cooking on long rods over fires, and another man pulled a dead antelope off the back of a horse. A banjo played somewhere over the sound of two men chopping firewood.

Ambrose turned with satisfaction to see one of the Colorado Northern's engines pass the headquarters. The engineer extended a hand out of the cab and waved. The shiny rails glistened in the moonlight, decorating the land. The ground shook. The trembling earth always thrilled him. It reminded him of the great force he unleashed with his daily labor.

He was glad to be back. The last month had been tense as the rail teetered on financial ruin, but the completion of the first section of track had secured the railroad's books for the time being. With the federal certification of the first twenty-five miles, he had managed to secure a short-term loan of two hundred thousand dollars. In a few weeks, the Colorado Northern would receive its government bonds worth almost twice the value of the loan. Better yet, the work crews only needed a few more weeks to complete their second section. That would allow for the full repayment of the loan and leave the rail with ample operating capital through the winter and in good standing with its creditors. Finally, he could get back to what he loved—building and worrying about the railroad's construction instead of its solvency. For the first time in months, he felt somewhat relaxed, his mind able to drift away from his problems.

He looked down to the only recreation in his life, the letter he had written to his wife the night before. He reread it.

My Love:

I miss you dearly, and after your recent 'scolding' I intend to write often. I'm already homesick and think of you often. The work is moving along fine, and I feel I will now have ample time to write more often. I received the tea you sent, and Bridget brewed us a large pot last night. The weather here is Divine. The fresh air and spectacular views make me feel young again. I cannot wait for you to come out in the spring.

Much work and many long days lie ahead constructing our road. We have had a run-in with the Indians, and I worry more troubles with them await us. I fear the construction of our road through their country will lead to fighting, but let us hope not. As I have often conveyed, your daughter is taking to the plains and work like I never expected. Do not worry. I will send her back to you at some point, but her clerical skills have been of great aid to me. The oncoming winter is no place for a woman so inquiring and naive of the

*world. I hope the Providence of God will see us
through the completion of our righteous work.*

*Wishing to hear from you soon
and send my love to everybody,
your loving husband.*

"Father," Bridget said, peering into his office, "quit rereading it and go ahead and send it to Mother. It's not what it says that counts, but that you're sending it."

Stepping into the dining room, he found Marshall and Emory standing next to the dinner table. "Let's go ahead and eat."

Bridget, sitting quietly at the table, stood and removed the dish covers from the dinner—steak, roasted red potatoes, cornbread, peas, jam, and tea.

Ambrose sat down, portioned some of the steak and cornbread to his plate, and then passed one of the bowls to Emory. "How's your progress, Marshall?"

"Good, the canyon is halfway surveyed, and we should have our next segment complete in a few weeks if we don't have any unforeseen problems. The canyon may be a little more difficult than I planned, but nothing we can't handle."

"I'm not worried about the work," Ambrose answered after swallowing a mouthful. "The crews are doing fine. We're not going to have any trouble building the rail, it's our enemies I'm worried about."

Marshall scooped some stew out of the bowl. "We ran into some surveyors on the southern portion of the line . . . about two miles west of our line."

"That's the Southwest," Ambrose said. "I did some checking. They have a claim also, but only if we fail to fulfill our obligations. Silas still thinks this line is his. That confirms my initial thoughts. They're behind our troubles.

Have we found out any more about the fellow Wesley Loomis?"

"Saw him in Fort Collins one day," Emory said. "Nothing much else. I'm still guessing he's behind the incident with the black powder."

"Been pretty quiet for almost a month," Marshall said. "Except for a few sections of track getting blown every few days. We're trying to catch the perpetrators, but they always strike in isolated areas."

Ambrose's blue eyes flashed. "What about this Colonel Bates you met with? You know anything about him?"

Emory paused his eating. "Yeah, I wouldn't trust him. He has ties to Denver, probably the Southwest Pacific, but he could be helpful. I'm sure he doesn't give a damn about your railroad, but he'll give you a hand if it's a good excuse to kill Indians. He looks like a gentleman, but he's a fiery Episcopalian preacher. Thinks killing Indians is the lord's work, a real John Brown of the West."

"Could be useful," Ambrose said, flashing his gaze at Bridget. She sat prim and proper at the end of the table with her hands folded in her lap. "What's wrong with you? Typically, it's all you can do to keep from telling us railroad men how we should build our road."

"I'm just listening, Father," Bridget said with a light smile, briefly glancing at Marshall. "Learning how the world works and how to get things done as you instructed me."

Ambrose set down his fork. "Tell me about the two dead surveyors."

Marshall said, "We sent what was left of them to Fort Collins to be buried. I didn't want to bring the bodies back here for the men to see."

"There has been some good news," Emory said. "The local Indians want to meet with us. I met with that fellow named Foster, the half-breed we ran into that day on the stage road. He's arranged a meeting with the local Cheyenne and Arapahoe chiefs day after tomorrow. He's arranging a meeting place. The Cheyenne will never let whites they don't know into their villages, and I can't blame them for that. The army's ridden in a few times firing away. We will need to bring some gifts—butter, coffee, tobacco, sugar, and some powder and lead."

"Powder and lead?" Ambrose grunted, displeased. "We're arming the Injuns so they can kill us?"

"Just a little," Emory said, spooning his coffee, "that's what they want. I did some asking around. It's normal that some powder and lead be given at a meeting. It's supposedly for hunting. I guess if they're going to fight us, powder and lead, bows and arrows, what's the difference? Foster will be here at ten in the morning day after tomorrow to lead us to the meeting place. He said it's about a two-hour ride to the west."

"Is it safe?" Ambrose asked. "Should we bring an armed posse or try to the get the army or state militia to send some troops?"

"No." Emory leaned back in his chair. He raised his eyelids, crinkling his forehead. "I'd say no more than eight of us. It's best not to bring a big, armed party so you don't show any hostile intentions. Foster said there will only be four or five Indians present. I'm thinking if we see otherwise when we get close, we can cut out and hightail it back to the rail line."

Ambrose set his fork down. He had never met an Indian, never even seen one up close. Now, in less than forty-eight hours, he'd be face-to-face with the feared warriors of the plains. Just a week earlier, he'd been in the safe confines of urban Chicago. What a change in time and place. His breath rose a tad. The words reminded him again that although he sat in the middle of a modern work site with five hundred men around him, in reality, he was the exception in this vast, untamed country. His financial problems had been grand, but without the possible consequences of his problems with the railroad's enemies.

20

The sun shone bright and hot directly overhead. Butterflies rumbled in Marshall's gut as he sat horseback amid a patchwork of tight, rolling knolls of fluttering grass flowing in all directions. Overhead, the sky was wide with a few clouds, but the earth lay broken such that a buffalo, standing less than a hundred paces away, might be out of sight.

For two hours, he, Emory, Ambrose, and five more men had been led here by the half-Cheyenne called Foster. The ride had been pleasant over the unvarying monotony of hills and grass. They all waited anxiously in the saddle. Twenty minutes earlier, Foster had stopped the group and struck out on his own to find the chiefs, leaving word for the eight to stay put until he returned. Foster, who the Indians called Singing Man, had been agreeable. Adorned in buckskin, he looked the image of a half-Indian with long black hair and a tinted complexion.

The day seemed strange. Though it was hot, a few gusts of refreshing wind blew up sand that stung the skin.

Ambrose said in a calm voice, "There he comes."

Foster rode over the ridge of a little hill, reining up in

front of the eight men. "They're about a half-mile ahead."
He paused and said to Ambrose, "There's no danger at all.
The Cheyenne would never fight at a peace meeting. They
think the Great Spirit would curse them for that. Bring no
more than four. There's only four of them. Everybody
should be on equal terms."

Ambrose pointed to Marshall and Emory. "The rest of
you stay here." He turned back to Foster, opening the saddlebags of one of the packhorses to show off the ample
rations. "Should we bring our gifts now?"

Foster inspected the gifts.

Ambrose unlaced one of the sacks.

"That's not much powder and lead," Foster said with a
frown. "Is that it? Not hardly enough to kill a half-dozen
buffalo. . . . But yes, bring the two packhorses. Now remember, when we get there, they'll likely wield their
weapons, fire a few shots in the air, maybe show off their
riding skills. Don't let it spook you. They're just showing
off their prowess before the meeting."

The grass rustled off to Marshall's left. He jerked up on
his reins and put his hand on his pistol. His nerves on edge,
he turned to see the grouse, spooked from the grass. He
wiped his sweaty forehead on his sleeve.

"Settle down," Foster said in a relaxed voice. "I told you
there's no danger. When we get there, the Cheyenne will
likely spread some buffalo robes. When that happens, we'll
dismount and sit on the robes with them. I'll do the translating. Gray Man will be their leader. I'll point him out to
you. Let's go. It's about a ten-minute ride. If they complain
about the scant powder and lead, I'm going to tell them
your supply is low."

The ride took forever, weaving up and down and around
the little hills where visibility, even on the great prairie,
never surpassed a few hundred steps in the wasteland of

mounds. The horses stepped through the thick vegetation, so high the stirrups seemed to glide over the land as if they floated on the grass. The group topped a little hill where vision stretched almost a quarter-mile. On a far ridge, four riders sat on their horses, only dots on the sea of yellow.

Foster slowly led the men to the Indians, sitting four abreast on horses. He stopped a hundred paces short of the four chiefs.

Marshall held his breath as two of the Indians raised their spears and squealed short, loud screams. Two Indians then raced forward, circling behind the three white men before returning to their original formation. The action unsettled Marshall, but he did his best to contain his apprehension.

The four Indians dismounted, walked forward to three buffalo robes already placed on the ground where they slowly sat.

Marshall strained his eyes, taking in the details. How quickly and effortlessly the four men slid off their horses. He recognized one of the chiefs, the Indian he had met that day with Foster, Yellow Horse.

"Okay," Foster said, dismounting and walking forward. "Bring the gifts and sit across from Gray Man and the others." Foster dismounted and walked forward. He said a few words in Cheyenne before sitting on one of the robes.

The scene was quiet. Around them, little ridges curved and weaved against the sky in every direction. How many more unseen Indians watched the proceedings?

As Marshall sat, Foster pointed to each of the white men, conveying their names. He then pointed to the Indians, one at a time. "This is Gray Man, Sun Walker, Medicine Bear the Arapahoe, and Yellow Horse. Present your gifts."

Ambrose stood and untied the five packages from the horses, opening them and laying them on the blanket.

The chiefs looked similar. All sported buckskin, but the one named Sun Walker also wore a blue army coat with its gold buttons. All the Indians were decorated in ornaments or decorations—body piercings, beads in their ponytails, earrings, elk teeth or bird feet hanging around their necks. They all looked capable and magnificent in a way. He realized why the Cheyenne called themselves the beautiful people of the plains. In contrast to the view from a distance, off their horses and next to the white men, the Indians seemed smaller than Marshall had expected, on average, each a few inches shorter and considerably lighter than their white counterparts.

Gray Man spoke a few sentences directed at Ambrose, and Foster translated. "Singing Man says you come to us for a peace council. We come in peace. We have no desire to fight the whites. Singing Man tells us you were a brave warrior in the Great Father's war with your rebels. We respect this."

Marshall and the other three men listened carefully, looking back and forth between Foster and the chiefs. Gray Man appeared the most imposing of the four. He had a hawk nose and big eyes that told of intelligence, and his face was determined and chiseled, like a statue.

Gray Man spoke again, his deep voice getting everyone's attention.

Foster said to Ambrose, "Gray Man says the Great Spirit made the earth for everybody's use, and they want to use the land alongside the whites."

Ambrose looked directly at Gray Man. "Ask him why they killed our surveyors."

Foster conveyed the message, and Gray Man spoke for some time in response. Foster then spent a few seconds translating Gray Man's words. "He says that they are sorry for killing the surveyors. Your men fired on his warriors first, killed two of their ponies. They did not start the fight. He says it is hard for the Cheyenne and Arapahoe. You come and hunt us, kill us. We are not the Sioux, the Sioux do not want to live beside the white man."

Ambrose nodded. "Ask him why they have not gone south with the other Cheyenne as agreed in the Medicine Lodge Treaty."

Marshall studied all the warriors' expressions while Foster went through the lengthy translation and listened to the response. Tension filled the air, written on all the faces. The long process of translation added to the strain and allowed for considerable thinking between exchanges.

"Gray Man says they did not sign the treaty at Medicine Lodge. There are not many buffalo to the south. Gray Man says he only wants to ramble across the prairie until the Great Spirit takes him. White men roam free, but why don't the white men want the Cheyenne to roam free?"

Ambrose quickly replied, "Tell him we don't care if they hunt buffalo. I am no longer a big chief with the whites and cannot speak for all whites. We are only here to build the railroad, nothing more."

After listening to the words, Gray Man turned to his subordinates and the Indians discussed things. Then Gray Man responded with calm and assuring words that Foster translated. "We do not like the rail. It will run off the buffalo. White settlers will come."

Ambrose swallowed a few times before replying, "This is true, but the Great Father, who commands many whites, as many as the leaves on the trees, has ordered the rail be built. I cannot do anything about it. It is the way it is. It will be built. If we don't build it, somebody else will. Many whites are coming to settle. There is nothing I can do about that."

After Foster translated Ambrose's response, the Indians mumbled among themselves.

Ambrose continued, "Ask him if he speaks for all the Cheyenne and Arapahoe."

Gray Man quickly answered, and the other chiefs laughed at his finishing remarks. "No, I do not speak for all Cheyenne and Arapahoe. There are good and bad Cheyenne and good and bad whites. Many Cheyenne have tried to live in peace, but you kill us without provocation. Many warriors feel you do not want peace, but we have to hunt buffalo, or we will starve. Do you think I would starve before I fight?"

The Indians' laughs eased the tension in Marshall's stomach. He turned to Ambrose, currently silent with a hand on his chin.

The chief named Sun Walker, the largest of the four, with wide shoulders and a big chest, spoke up.

Foster listened attentively, before turning back to Ambrose. "Sun Walker says the Indians didn't start the killing. This war was brought on them. They tried to love the whites, but the whites hunt them for no reason. When one Indian does something bad, white men punish all Indians."

Sun Walker began to cry as he continued, speaking fast.

"He says he is a brave hunter, a leader of his people, but the white men look upon him as stupid. He says the white man must treat the Cheyenne and Arapahoe fairly and respect their land. This is their land, the land of their fathers. It is sacred to them. The buffalo are sacred to them. They have to have buffalo for their existence. All they do is avoid the whites and hunt. They are backed up to the mountains with nowhere else to retreat. For the last twenty seasons of green grass, they have disappeared, their camps are now small with only a few fires."

Marshall sat up, startled. He had never imagined an Indian, much less a chief, could cry. These impressive warriors had emotions, feelings, problems, and hopes just like he did. And much of what the Indians spoke of dealt with long-standing issues, past troubles, issues that did not concern the railroad. The Indians had grievances with many whites, and the army, and they were using this setting to communicate them.

Gray Man gave a lengthy sermon, punctuated with a few smiles. Marshall waited with anticipation for the translation.

"Gray Man says the Great Spirit has made Sun Walker very emotional. He feels he has been wronged many times by the whites." Foster pointed to Ambrose. "Gray Man also says he likes your straightforward attitude. He sees no trickery in your words or eyes. It is not his intention to fight the whites. You are more and stronger than his people. That is the way of the Great Spirit. He does not like it, but he can't change it. He says if your men will not attack the Cheyenne, they will not attack the railroad."

"I give my assurances," Ambrose said.

Gray Man waited for the translation, then nodded and spoke.

Foster communicated the words while still looking at Gray Man. "Gray Man says the Cheyenne do not break their word. If they do, other Cheyenne will fight them. He, himself would fight any Cheyenne who broke his word, even if he had to fight alongside white men. He also says he hopes for peace, and if he becomes friends with you, you will bring him more powder and lead so he can have a big hunt."

"Yes, if we become friends," Ambrose said, nodding with a grin.

The chief named Medicine Bear spoke up, and Foster turned to Ambrose to convey the brief words.

"Medicine Bear asked if you will use your talking wires to tell all the white men about this meeting."

Ambrose again nodded.

Each man appeared content, though the Indians also wore a look of confusion. Had they made peace? These Cheyenne seemed to be willing to make peace, but admitted they didn't speak for all the local Indians or like the railroad.

Gray Man reached behind him and lifted a pipe. He turned to Foster and spoke.

Foster struck a match and lit the pipe. "Gray Man says now we smoke a pipe."

Gray Man took two deep puffs from the pipe, then handed it to Sun Walker.

Instead of finding the cunning, bloodthirsty savages bent on ravaging the plains that he had prepared himself for, Marshall had found the Indians thoughtful, intelligent, and willing to work with the whites. Still, he had concerns. Both parties had different visions for the ground around them, and both had demonstrated their willingness to fight for these visions.

Could they build a railroad through these Indians' land without bloodshed? He hoped so. More than most, he knew well who would inevitably win the struggle, but for the first time, he hoped no harm would come to these men, seemingly caught between two colliding forces beyond their control. Here on this buffalo robe in the middle of nowhere, his heart sympathized with these proud men.

Medicine Bear handed the pipe to Ambrose, who took it and handed it to Marshall.

"Tell him no offense," Ambrose said. "But tobacco has never agreed with me."

As Foster translated Ambrose's words, Marshall grabbed the pipe. He took two long drags. Exhaling the smoke, he handed the pipe to the man across from him, Yellow Horse, who had not uttered a word in the meeting. Marshall tried to read Gray Man's face as Foster restated Ambrose's message.

Gray Man uttered a quick response with a cunning smile, and the other chiefs laughed.

"What'd he say?" Ambrose asked.

"He said you should smoke the pipe. Refusing a peace pipe from a Cheyenne is not a sign of disrespect, but one who refuses the Cheyenne pipe is cursed in this land by the Great Spirit."

21

Marshall relaxed on the little cushioned bench in the last car of the Colorado Northern's supply train making its daily return trip from Cheyenne to the company's headquarters. He looked out the window at dusk. An afternoon shower had perked up the grass, which was now standing erect. The sun had just dipped below the top of the mountains, leaving maybe thirty minutes of seeing light. Overhead, the stars, already visible, shone as the train jerked and bumped along to the incessant sound of *cha . . . cha . . . cha . . . cha. . . .*

For three days his head had been spinning with thoughts of the meeting with the Indians. What an alien event. As he sat in this modern machine, scooting over the land at twenty-five miles an hour, out there somewhere entire villages were making their fires and preparing for another night as they had done for centuries.

Bridget sat across from him. They had both gone to Cheyenne that day. He to check on some bridge trusses being fabricated and her to pay some bills and receive the railroad's payroll, now in the front car and guarded by three men.

Marshall had hoped they might find some time for another discreet meeting, but his day had been too busy. Their initial encounter seemed more of a dream than reality. It almost magically transported him to another time and place. He longed for another passionate night to remove him from the harsh environment he had gotten accustomed to over the last few months.

"Find anything interesting in there?" Marshall asked.

Bridget looked up from the newspaper and pushed a strand of blond hair back under her hat. "Mostly articles about Congress forming the new Wyoming Territory last week, but also the Fourteenth Amendment has been ratified, granting citizenship to everybody, even ex-slaves."

"What's it say about Indians? Did they get citizenship too?"

Bridget read the fine print. "Nope, Indians, unless they pay taxes are specifically excluded from the rights of citizenship." She stood and walked over and sat beside him, putting her hand on his thigh. "How much longer until we get to headquarters?"

"We're about halfway back, about an hour."

The train jerked hard. The caboose's brakes engaged, producing a loud, lengthy squeal, followed by similar sounds from the cars forward. The railcar decelerated quickly, its rapid slowdown threatening to pull them out of their seats.

Marshall put one arm around Bridget, holding her firmly, and grabbed the bench's armrest to restrain the two. In just a few seconds, the train came to a stop, silencing the loud scream of the brakes.

"What is it?" Bridget said.

Marshall stood and walked to the window. The loud, quick roar of an explosion boomed. The car rattled and shook. His thoughts uncertain, he reached over and blew out the car's gas lamp as he slid open the door facing the sunset. Poking his head outside, he looked to the train's engine. Men shouted near the front of the train. Past the six flatcars loaded with material, he saw men, maybe a half-dozen, some horses, and a wagon. Still not believing his ears and eyes, almost like a dream, horror and panic jolted through him. He pulled his Colt from his hip and handed it to Bridget. "I think the train's being robbed. Here, you know how to use this?"

Bridget nodded. "I think so."

Marshall grabbed a Henry rifle hanging on a rack. He quickly cocked its lever, then stepped to the door on the east side of the train and opened it. Outside, the land lay in the train's dark shadow. He grabbed Bridget's hand, tugged her forcefully to her feet, and then shoved her out the door.

In the darkness, he saw nothing, but felt his feet collide with the ground. He stumbled to a knee. Bridget fell to all fours, her dress mangled around her. Marshall clenched her hand, urgently yanking her to her feet and slinging her away from the train into the grass of the prairie. "Run out there in the grass and lay down, *now*. Don't use the gun unless you have to, but if you do, just point it and pull the trigger. I'll be right back. I'm just going to go see if I can identify the robbers."

"Don't be a hero," Bridget mumbled, hustling off.

Marshall waited until Bridget disappeared, her image fading as she ran. He then turned. The brakeman stood in the doorway of the caboose. Marshall ran forward and pointed to the open grass as he whispered, "The train's being robbed. Get off it and go hide in the grass."

Gripping the rifle, his senses alert and his ears tuned, he hugged close to the railcars as he crept forward to the sound of the voices. Reaching the flatcar two back of the engine, he fell to the ground. From there, under the train, he saw the vague images of the men's and horses' lower legs.

On his hands and knees, he crawled under the train and then to the front of the flatcar, near the coupling, where prone he pointed his rifle in the direction of the commotion. He placed a hand over his ear, cupping it and trying to hear the words.

"Make sure the safe is tied down good," one of the voices finally said, "and let's get out of here."

The smidgen of light that remained diminished by the second. Marshall squinted. He thought he saw the men's legs disappear and the wagon turn. Anxiously and quickly, he crawled to the space between the cars, banging his head painfully on some hard steel.

Between the cars, he stood and peeked around the corner of the railcar. The men had saddled up, five in all. Two horses and the wagon had already departed to the north-west, but two more men still sat horseback looking over the carnage of the paymaster's car, still intact, but its windows all blown out. Beside the train, the engineer and two of the train's guards sat on their knees, their hands bound behind their backs. Glass and splinters of wood covered the ground. To his dismay, all the bandits wore bags and masks that concealed their faces.

Marshall eased back into the darkness between the cars. Out of sight, he squeezed the rifle in his hands, resisting an urge to spring from the train, raise the weapon, and fire. Killing these two men wouldn't even be a chore. His heart pounded and his hands shivered as he stood as still as a rabbit, listening. Should he jump out of his hole and fire or just let the men ride off? He didn't care about the money. He wanted to find out who they were. As he struggled with his thoughts, his mind jumbled, he heard the men's voices, then the horses' footsteps. He crept forward and stole a quick glance. The two outlaws had ridden to the front of the train.

Marshall turned to the west. The wagon had all but disappeared into the night, more than a quarter-mile distant. He looked again to the engine, but the men had disappeared. Alarmed and confused, he moved through the space between the cars to the other side of the train. There, the two men had crossed the track and now trotted off to the east. Marshall took one more look back over his shoulder before raising the rifle. He put his sights on the faint image of one of the men. He paused his breathing and squeezed the trigger.

Almost surprising him, the rifle's ignition pierced the silence. He felt the recoil. One of the men plunged from the saddle. The second horse shuddered sideways. Marshall cocked the rifle and fired again with less precision. The second horse wheeled around to face him.

Two quick flashes of orange broke the night. More shots erupted. Lead clanged around him. Taking a knee, he cocked the rifle again. Another shot sounded. A sharp pain ripped into his left arm. He gritted his teeth trying not to scream as he tried to raise the rifle with his right hand. The movement again sent a shot of pain into his wounded arm. His target now raced all out to the rear of the train at an angle that put him broadside but made hitting a moving target difficult.

Thankfully, he didn't the see the wagon coming back. He looked again to his left arm, bleeding above the elbow. Grasping his predicament, his inability to shoot accurately, if at all, he fell to his stomach and tried to put the rifle to his shoulder.

Bridget stood up out of the grass, extending the pistol.

"Get back down!" Marshall yelled, crawling out from under the train.

Bridget ran ten paces toward the bandit, stopped, and raised the pistol. She fired, the shot echoing, its muzzle blast visible against the night.

Marshall struggled to his feet. Two more shots. He ran to Bridget.

She stood in the grass, her arm extended. The outlaw lay sprawled out on the ground.

His mind still churning, Marshall relaxed his tense muscles. Silence again fell over the earth. His arm throbbed, but with less intensity. "Bring that pistol, hurry!" he yelled as he hunkered low and rushed into the dark field looking for the first man he had shot.

Bridget ran forward, her face filled with grit and resilience.

He grabbed the Colt, thankful he had a weapon that only required the use of his good arm. The outlaw he'd shot was only a blank outline twenty paces away. Stretched out on the ground, the dark image moaned without movement. Marshall took a quick knee and fired three shots at the man, only a vague figure. The body twitched with several of the shots, but continued to mutter. Marshall rushed forward, focusing. Lying on his back, the bandit, still veiled by the mask, was covered with blood.

The grass shuffled behind him. His hands still shaking, he wheeled around, raising the pistol. Bridget approached. Darkness now totally enveloped the land. The derailed engine sat leaning slightly to one side, hissing. Debris had been piled on the tracks to force the train's quick stoppage. The outlaws had apparently assaulted the paymaster's car, breaking a window and throwing in a stick of black powder. The train had eight passengers. In addition to the three payroll guards, an engineer and two brakemen worked the train. Where were they? Were they alive?

"Your arm," Bridget said, putting her hand on Marshall's shoulder and looking at his bloody bicep.

"I think I just got grazed. Let's go see where everybody is. Hopefully they're all alive. Let's gather everybody up in case those other bandits show back up."

22

The first rays of the early-morning sun lit Ambrose's desk as he sipped from a cup of coffee, pondering the previous night's train robbery. He reread a telegram he had spent the last hour scratching out.

BENEDICT MATSON
ILLINOIS AND IOWA RAILROAD COMPANY
200 MICHIGAN AVE
CHICAGO ILLINOIS

REGRET TO INFORM YOU THAT THE
PAYROLL TRAIN FROM CHEYENNE WAS
ROBBED LAST NIGHT. MARSHALL
BREWSTER SLIGHTLY INJURED. NO DEATHS.
PAYROLL STOLEN. TWO PERPETRATORS
KILLED DURING ROBBERY. PAYROLL CAR
DESTROYED. INVESTIGATION ONGOING.
HOPE TO PROVIDE FURTHER DETAILS
WHEN WE KNOW MORE. NO STOPPAGE IN
WORK BUT PLEASE ADVISE TO THE DATE

OF THE REPLACEMENT PAYROLL AS I
NEED TO INFORM THE MEN.
AG

Ambrose sucked in a deep breath. He ran his hands
through his hair, then rested his elbows on the desk as he
loathed the thought of the two or three scathing telegrams
he would get from Benedict during the day. He had long
ago discovered that trying to explain problems to Benedict
was a useless endeavor. Mr. Matson didn't care about
problems. He only wanted results but constantly required
meticulous updates on progress.

He looked to Bridget's empty bedroom as he tried to
imagine the events of the previous night, his daughter in a
shoot-out with one of the outlaws. He had regretted her
being here for months, even more so in recent weeks as his
daughter's fondness for Marshall had grown. In her eyes,
Marshall now superseded him as a figure of authority, and
his stomach turned as he imagined how close they might
have gotten. But today, for the first time, he thought about
the harm that could have come to her, an almost unbear-
able thought.

Emory entered the office. "The doctor in Fort Collins
says Marshall should be back on his feet in a couple weeks
at the most. Your daughter is fine, just a few bruises."

"We know anything?"

"I will meet with the sheriff this afternoon, see what I
can find out."

Ambrose handed the telegram to an aide. "Send this."
He stood and walked out on the porch. In the faint glow of
the morning, several hundred men moved from a dining car
to a train to be dispersed along the line for the day's work.
Behind the headquarters building, some men bickered

with Patty and one of the grading foremen, a long, slender man named Aden.

Ambrose strode quickly toward Patty.

A few of the men saw Ambrose approach, and Patty turned in his direction.

"Can I see you two a second," Ambrose said politely, "in my office?"

A minute later, Ambrose turned to face the men. "Is there a problem? It's working light now. Why is the morning train twenty minutes late?"

Patty rubbed his hands together. "Some of the men have been talking. It's the robbery last night. They worry."

"We will not die for this railroad," Aden said, rolling his eyes to Emory.

"Say what you *mean*," Ambrose snarled as he studied Patty's face. The merry Irishmen wore a rare look of concern.

"I think the men will be fine," Patty said, "These continued accidents have them concerned and for good reason."

Ambrose scrutinized the two foremen, then Emory, thinking over his words carefully. Labor problems had the potential to be as big an obstacle for the railroad as anything, and managing the men required as much skill as any of Ambrose's daily tasks. The men were the one entity capable of shutting down work on the rail, and nothing would undermine his credibility with Benedict or the rail's financial bankers more than a work stoppage resulting from the men's discontent.

"Patty," Ambrose said, "tonight, after dinner, I want you to meet with all the foremen. I want the men to get together and tell me what they want to make them feel comfortable. If it's doubling the guards, we'll do that. But what I want is for you and the men to tell me what you want within reason. If the railroad consents to that, there should be no grumbling. If we have some additional problems, it then becomes our fault instead of mine. Is that clear? I want them vested in the railroad's safety as an equal partner."

"Aye, aye," Patty said.

Ambrose turned to Aden. "What more can I do?"

"Okay," Aden said. "That is fair. The men will understand that."

"Thank you," Ambrose said, "now let's get some work done so the men will get their bonuses. Patty, I will give you an update on the new payroll train tonight so you can tell the men."

As the two foreman walked out of the office, Emory poured himself a cup of coffee. "Spec' I'll be back mid-afternoon after I meet with the sheriff. Just let me know how the men want to handle this."

Ambrose sighed. "I want you to adhere to the men's wishes exactly. Believe me. I know what I'm talking about. I've been through this before. It's important that the men feel they are being treated fairly and respectfully. We have to make them a part of the solution." He lowered a firm stare at Emory. "Right now, we cannot afford a labor walkout. That will make our problems with Silas Jones seem minor."

23

Wesley balled his fist. "What in the *hell* are you doing robbing the train? I didn't give any orders for that."

"We got almost thirty thousand dollars, gold," Amos snapped, returning Wesley's icy stare. He stood and grabbed his gun belt hanging on a chair and put it around his waist, slowly fastening the buckle. "Derailed the train and partly blew up one of the cars, too."

Wesley took a long drag of his smoke. The little sod house nestled on the prairie about twenty miles east of Fort Collins had a rough inside. He had found Amos here after two days of searching and asking around. The abandoned, one-room building had a dirt floor, a table, and two cots. He'd been thinking about this conversation for two days. The train robbery had caused a stir all through northern Colorado and southern Wyoming. Only a few weeks earlier, he'd thought he had finally done enough to make his bosses happy, but knew well the publicity and notoriety of the train robbery wouldn't sit well. Accidents or mishaps that stalled construction were one thing, but the press *loved* to report railroad robberies. Even worse, the two dead assailants had already been identified. He needed to find a quick way to clean up the mess.

Throwing his smoke on the ground, Wesley raised his voice. "You got two men *killed*, including Dog. Losing a payroll is nothing to the railroad. It won't even pay for a few cars of rails and ties. Who were these other four men and where are they? They've got Dog's body. They can trace it to you and possibly me."

Amos's pale eyes grew cold and he stiffened. "Just some boys we ran into over in Greeley. They wanted to rob the UP payroll train. We thought robbing the Colorado Northern would be easier, and it would aid our cause, so we signed on. I didn't expect such a loot. I don't know where the other boys went. Headed west yesterday."

"I told you this job would take brains, not muscle. What'd you do with the money?"

"We jis split it up four ways." Amos swallowed hard, his Adam's apple moving up and down. "What do you want, a share?"

Wesley shook his head in disbelief. He exhaled a long breath. Why would someone who had just pulled in over seven thousand dollars in a heist still hang around northern Colorado? "No, I don't want a share, damn it. I've got more sense than to get two men killed over thirty thousand dollars. Been two days, you better get a move on, get out of Colorado."

Wesley gritted his teeth, fuming. It might be easier to pull his pistol and end this problem, but Amos might be his equal, at least on the draw. "Not to mention, I'm sure people have seen Dog with you a few times. You're done here. I'll consider us settled. You'll need every penny of that seven thousand dollars. I'd try to go West, over the mountains. Less Indians that way and not likely anybody there will know anything about this train holdup. I'd go today. Those rail bosses aren't very tolerant of robbery. They're likely raising a posse now."

Amos stepped forward, slightly bumping his chest against Wesley's. He flashed his big, sick smile. "Wish I could say it's been a pleasure. Maybe I'll catch up with you somewhere else."

Wesley stepped back a few inches. Lighting quick, he raised his left hand and grabbed Amos's collar as he pulled his pistol with the other hand. He gently put the barrel of the pistol under Amos's chin. "Get your ass out of here, *today*. I'll see if I can buy you a day, but if you're seen in these parts after that, I may be called on to bring you in. I won't be so merciful then." Wesley slowly lowered the gun and shoved Amos to the door.

Stumbling, and then gathering his feet, Amos turned back to Wesley, his hands dangling at his sides. He grinned again, exposing his big teeth, and reached down for his saddle. "Like I said, I may catch up with you again some-time. I'm looking forward to it."

At nine the next morning, Wesley sat in the conference room of the Southwest Pacific's Denver office. Silas Jones wore a black satin vest and string tie. Beside him sat his two minions, Boss Smith and his young aide.

Silas lifted up a copy of the local newspaper. "Did you have anything to do with this? The press loves this shit. Next thing you know the public will be pulling for the Colorado Northern, and God forbid what would happen to us if word got out we were behind this train robbery."

"N . . . o," Wesley stuttered. "Though one of the men killed has worked for me. He was operating on his own. I've done some checking around. It was a gang that rode in from Missouri. Dog Johnson fell in with them. Not much

I could do, the type of men required for this work are free spirits by nature."

"Can he be traced to the railroad?" Silas snapped.

"No chance," Wesley answered. "I never told him or anybody anything. I've never mentioned the railroad to anyone outside this room. Word is, the survivors have all gone west, out of the state. I've only got two men working for me now. One is a guard on the railroad, the other a wagon master."

Silas crinkled his cheeks. "You've done the Colorado Northern some harm, made their construction difficult, but we haven't slowed them down much. I hear they may have three-quarters of the rail built by winter." Silas leaned back in his chair and lit a cigar. He puffed on the stogie hard as his face grew red. He turned back to Wesley and raised his voice. "I *hired* you to stop this rail. You haven't done a very good job. I'm wondering what to do next. Firing you sounds like my only option, but for now," he paused and raised the newspaper, "all we need to do is lay low until everything settles down."

Silas stepped out from his desk, pacing quietly around the room.

Wesley agonized at Silas's mood. For weeks he had feared a meeting like this. He'd spent hours thinking over options to slow the rail work, debating dozens of ideas. He had the brains and skills to do this. He cleared his throat. "I have a suggestion, if I might."

Silas again looked at Boss before speaking in a surly tone. "Why not, nobody else seems to know what to do."

Wesley stood and grabbed a small bag he had brought with him. Out of it, he pulled a map and unfolded it on the table. "Here's the Colorado Northern's proposed line."

All three men looked on with interest.

"Where'd you get this?" Boss said.

"One of my spies got it. It's genuine."

Silas leaned over the table, sliding the map in front of him. "Very interesting."

"They're building here now." Wesley slid a finger across the map. "Across the open plain. You can't hardly stop them without an army of men, but by winter they'll be here, having to build up this steep narrow canyon. It's the toughest portion of their line. I went up there and scouted it myself for two days. Five men in that canyon with a little powder and lead could bring that rail to a standstill. There's cover everywhere. I could hide an army within a rock's throw of the rail and never be seen. I'm no rail engineer, but I'm guessing at least five big bridges will have to be built. There'll also be a lot of blasting and rock moving, and there's only one way in. Weather will be terrible in there. It'll be snowing, neck deep, in two months. I'm saying we lay low for a few months, let everything simmer down, then go to work on them this winter in this canyon. When I get through with them in there, you'll be able to come in and buy the entire operation for pennies on the dollar." He jammed his finger into the map. "This is where we stop them."

Silas sat back down and continued to inspect the map.

"Why don't you just go make a deal with them," Silas's aide said. "Build our line to theirs and connect the two and make some type of agreement to operate the lines together in some type of joint venture. Maybe wait until you've made the construction expensive for them, and they're looking for some help."

"I make no deals," Silas said with a flat, unemotional voice. "I'm a man of industry. I want to leave my mark on the history pages, and I want the satisfaction of seeing Benedict Matson fail. He'd never deal with me anyway.

He'd go bust first. I want that rail stopped, and I don't care if I have to send an army of men into that canyon."

Wesley watched the three faces, all still studying the map. They liked his idea. He knew the talk of a deal would go nowhere. The powerful men who built the rails and tamed the land had headstrong egos. He'd never seen even two men of this nature operate in harmony. It wasn't in their makeup.

Silas turned back to Boss. "When in the hell will Parson Simpson and his posse be back here?"

"Hopefully in a month," Boss said. "Apparently the other job they're on is proving a little dirtier than they initially thought. I'll get a telegraph off to him today."

"Okay," Silas groaned, "let's just sit tight for another month or two. Get ready. I want to get Parson in that canyon too. We will go after the Colorado Northern with everything this fall."

Wesley scoffed, "You don't need Parson Simpson for this job. I've *got* it under control."

Silas said, "We always have a backup plan. Parson and his boys are professionals. They've got a lot more experience in this type of work than you do. We don't give a shit who we pay. You want the rest of that gold instead of Parson, I suggest you get in that canyon and do a little more than you did this summer."

Wesley puffed up. He didn't like this. He still felt supremely confident in his ability to stall the rail, especially when the terrain and weather suited him. Had the crux of this conversation been to remind him that he was expendable? He wasn't expendable, not in northern Colorado. He pointed to the map and spoke in his most solemn voice. "When the rail gets there, progress is over. I, and I alone can raise the men needed for this job, and I'll stop the rail there. Or die trying."

24

The midmorning sun filtered into the room. Marshall sat up in bed at the City Hotel in Fort Collins rolling a smoke as he studied some drawings. Five days earlier, the local surgeon had operated on his arm and left him here to rest and recoup. Fortunately, the slug had only sliced the upper bicep, but it had left a trace of lead in the wound that had to be removed before closing the laceration with stitches.

Bridget, in a plaid dress, sat with her sleeves rolled up plying her needle as she mended one of Marshall's shirts. She had come to Fort Collins with Marshall and had since stayed in the hotel to look after his well-being.

A light knock on the door got Marshall's attention, and Ambrose entered.

"The good news is," Marshall said, "the doctor says I'm going to live."

Ambrose gazed at his daughter. "How's he doing?"

"He's pondering his railroad," Bridget answered, "That's all he ever does."

"I'm terrible!" Marshall groaned, sitting up and putting

aside his papers. "If I don't get out of this room soon, I'm going to go crazy."

"Doctor says two more days and then your stitches come out," Bridget said, "and then you can go back to headquarters. Light duty only."

"I need to get in the canyon *now*." Marshall struck a match and lit his tobacco. "Another week of idleness and we'll be behind schedule. There's a lot of rock that needs moving in there."

Bridget walked over to a table covered with some clean bandages. "Before you men start talking about work, I need to change Mr. Brewster's bandages." She grabbed a pair of scissors off the table and cut the cloth wrapped around Marshall's arm. She then picked up a pair of tweezers, dipped a cotton ball in a bowl of water, and began to clean the wound.

"Ouch." Marshall grunted and looked at Ambrose. "There's a lot of you in her. I saw it in her eyes when she gunned down that bandit."

"Be still," Bridget said. "When I'm done, you can have some of that apple pie I had made for you. And yes, I felt no sympathy for the two miscreants we shot down. My own contribution to cleaning this place up."

Marshall looked past Bridget, stealing a glance at Ambrose. His boss's eyes were focused on Bridget as she judiciously cleaned the wound. Ambrose's facial muscles irritably clenched tight, the veins on his forehead pulsing.

Marshall picked up his plans to avoid Ambrose's piercing eyes. "Did those big iron culverts come in?"

Ambrose said, "Somebody outbid us for them. We built some temporary wood culverts over those ditches. We'll replace them later."

Marshall dropped his pencil and wadded up a piece of paper.

"Don't fret over it so much," Ambrose snapped. "It's a necessary evil to speed rail construction. We'll replace them when the rail is operating and has a revenue stream. You know the general policy, get it down, get it operating, fix it up later."

Marshall leaned back in bed. "What'd you find out about those outlaws?"

"Not much. One of the heathens had a letter in his pocket from Kansas City, and one has been seen around here a few times. Maybe we were just randomly robbed."

"I doubt it," Marshall answered, giving his arm to Bridget so she could wrap it with a new bandage. "They knew too much. Where the money was. The train's schedule. What to put on the track to get under the engine's cow-catcher and derail it, and they stopped the train in a location almost exactly between two guard posts. The assault took place right at dark when the rail guards would be taking dinner. The Southwest, if they're behind this, may have some men on our payroll."

Marshall continued, "When you've been cooped up in this room for a week, you have time to think it all over. Especially since I was there and saw it."

"We can survive the loss of a payroll." Ambrose blew out a long breath. "But not too many. We need to get to the bottom of this."

"What about our people?" Marshall asked. "How'd they come out?"

"One of the guards got scraped up pretty good," Ambrose answered. "A few more got shook up. The local sheriff actually seems cooperative. Seems nobody likes a thief, even around here."

"Any good news?" Marshall put his arm back in the makeshift sling.

"Yeah," Ambrose answered as he looked out the window. "Your nitroglycerin man will be here in about ten days. He's landed in New York. He wired to say he and all his materials are on the way."

"Good," Marshall said, picking up one of his maps. "That may get us back on schedule, and I should be back on my feet by then."

Ambrose turned to Emory. "Anywhere to get a drink around here?"

"Saloon's just down the street, less than a block, across the street."

Bridget finally put down the tweezers after reapplying the bandage.

Ambrose stood and snorted. "Bridget, I need you back at headquarters by dinner tonight."

"But Father," Bridget said, still fumbling around with the bandages on the table. "Who will look after Mr. Brewster, make sure he's fixed up?"

"Paperwork is backing up," Ambrose grumbled. "I'll send somebody else down here tonight to help out until he gets back on his feet in a few days. You can ride back with us this afternoon."

The dusty, one-room saloon had four customers when Ambrose strode through its swinging doors. In the mid-afternoon calm, his spurs jingled as he stepped across the wood floor. At the bar, he tipped his hat to two men sitting at a table near the door.

"Two whiskeys," Emory said, resting his elbows on the bar as he dropped a gold coin onto the polished slab of wood. "This must be Wesley Loomis's hangout. That's him at that first table, the one nearest the door. Saw him here the only other time I've been in this establishment lately."

Boldly and unabashed, Ambrose turned to look. Unlike the other desperate characters present, Loomis stood out in a clean, pressed white shirt under a light brown, cotton coat. He looked strong and able. Ambrose knew the breed, a man easy with a gun, who lived by the gun.

"Here you go, gentlemen," the frail-looking old bartender said, setting the two glasses of whiskey on the bar.

Ambrose picked up the whiskey, downed it, and promptly stepped forward. As he paced deliberately to Wesley's table, he felt like a machine, his instincts taking over. His boot heels clanging loudly against the floor, he stopped at Wesley's table, looking down at the man who read a newspaper. A bottle of whiskey sat on the table, occupied by a second unkempt man, likely a drifter of some sort.

"Well, Mr. Loomis, I've been wanting to meet you."

"And who might you be?" Wesley mumbled, not looking up from his paper.

"I run the Colorado Northern Railroad. I know what you're up to, and I mean to put you out of business around here."

Wesley continued to read. "We were over here minding our own business, and we'd like to keep it that way."

"I *am* your goddamn business," Ambrose said.

The other man at the table slowly stood, staring at Ambrose with roving, wild eyes. "You heard the man. We don't give a shit who you are."

"Sit back down, Joe. I'll handle this," Wesley said in a calm voice. He gazed over at Ambrose's face, before turning in his chair. As he did he slid his coat back with his right hand to expose the pistol on his hip. "Like Joe said, we don't care who you are. The decent people in this county don't tolerate bad manners."

Ambrose's pulse pounded. His muscles tightened. He honed his senses for any threatening movements. Emory sauntered forward and stood beside him, his free hand hanging over his pistol.

Ambrose said, "You ever pull that pistol out around me again, you better be ready to use it."

Wesley smiled. He turned to the four other people in the bar, all now paying close attention to the conversation. "With your manners, I can see now why nobody will be disappointed when you're run out of this county for good."

"You son of a bitch," Ambrose snapped, his emotions taking over his brain. "I will shove that pistol up your ass."

Feet shuffled. The second man again jumped to his feet.

"Settle down, Joe," Wesley said. "Seems as if the railroad man is having a bad day. Nothing to get worried about."

Ambrose lunged at Wesley, grabbing a handful of his shirt. "Damn you."

Wesley sprang to his feet.

Ambrose felt a shove. He stumbled backward. Wesley's pistol rose. The barrel locked on his chest.

Emory slowly slid forward, between the three men, his back to Ambrose.

Ambrose shuffled back a couple of steps as Emory forcefully pushed him away.

Wesley focused over his barrel at Ambrose, his teeth grinding, his face flushed. A few seconds passed with only the sound of heavy breathing.

"Easy," Emory said softly, "everybody calm down."

An incredible urge to lunge forward or pull his pistol besieged Ambrose. Emory backed up a few more steps. Anger washed over Ambrose as he did a quick about-face and strode deliberately to the door. "I will see you again."

* * *

Ambrose sat in his office going over some paperwork. Only the single flame from a gas lamp lit the room. Outside, the moon bathed the sleeping headquarters with yellow light. For an hour, he had been trying to scratch out several letters, but his surly mood had prevented concentration. By the minute his pulse quickened, his skin growing warm and irritated.

Bridget opened the door to his office, poking her head in. "Father, I'm going to bed."

Ambrose dropped the papers on his desk. "Come in and shut the door."

Bridget stepped into the office, gingerly closing the door.

Ambrose spit out a mouthful of air. "What I'm to say is very difficult for me. . . . But your relationship with Mr. Brewster is completely inappropriate."

Bridget put her hands on her hips, relaxing her posture. "Could you please elaborate?"

"Don't give me *that*." Ambrose's voice grew stern. "I wasn't born yesterday. I have a good mind to knock the shit out of him and send him packing somewhere else."

Bridget stiffened, leaning forward. She raised a finger. "What did you expect? You brought me here with instructions to get him to work for you. He didn't want to stay. Are you vain enough to think that he would stick around here getting shot at by Indians and Silas Jones's henchmen just in hopes that he might get to slip my dress off when we're back in Chicago . . . after he's gone through all the formal proceedings? He's here because of me. And he's staying because of me."

Ambrose groaned and swiped his arm across his desk forcefully. Papers flew everywhere and a wooden stand slammed violently into the wall. He pointed his finger at Bridget. "That *is* enough."

Bridget stepped forward, raising her chin. "You want me to say it. I will. I like Mr. Brewster. He's the first man who has ever made my insides tingle. And I'm comfortable with our relationship, whether you and anybody else likes it or not."

Ambrose stepped out from behind his desk. "You're going home as soon as I can send you."

"There's no making you happy!" Bridget yelled. She spun around, walked out of the office, slamming the door on her exit.

"Damn it!" Ambrose screamed. He reached over and pulled a paper calendar off the wall, wadding it up and throwing it on the floor.

25

Marshall lay on his back, his head poking outside his small, two-man tent. Now early September, the evenings had cooled with an autumn nip. He had set his tent on the isolated open plain, the opening to the West. This position also allowed him to see the Front Range. The huge monoliths of rock, silhouetted against the sky and colliding with the ground, were a brilliant contrast and awe-inspiring backdrop for his little camp, especially in the early morning or late evening when the sun shone on the land from the side.

Though a month had passed since his meeting with the Indians, the visions of the warriors remained frozen in his mind, often filling his thoughts for hours. They were out there somewhere in this wonderful wilderness. Where? He'd never know, like deer or elk that ran off to some unknown place, never to be found.

He had been back at work for two days, his arm not completely healed but absent any significant pain or side effects. In the two weeks since the train robbery, the Colorado Northern had pushed forward, completely unmolested. Whoever had been sabotaging the railroad had taken a respite, and the excellent weather and long days had allowed the men to make their best progress to date, averaging almost five miles of construction a week. Additionally, he had finished almost two-thirds of his detailed survey of the canyon and had begun to plan the winter work in the deep gorge.

"You should see it in another couple of hours," Marshall said to Bridget, lying beside him and also looking up at the sky. "An hour after dark, when the stars start moving across the sky. I've never seen so many stars."

"It looks like we're going to make it to Jeremiah Canyon before winter," Bridget said. "The grading crews are only sixteen miles away. We're going to get three of the four sections for government payment completed before fall."

"I know," Marshall said. "Worries me. Things are going too well. When that happens, look out, something's going to happen."

"How about the work in the Canyon?"

"It's going well. The altitude makes physical labor more difficult, and I'm surprised how it dehydrates you. I'll have to account for that with the men." He turned his head to the side. "You need to get dressed and get back to headquarters before your father starts worrying where you are. What would happen if somebody snuck up on us?"

Bridget rolled over on her side. The wind played in her thick hair, now curlier and bleached blonder from flowing unchecked under the sun for the last few months. Her lips seemed fuller and a deeper red set against her now bronzed skin. Unclad, her curves and lines displayed themselves marvelously.

"He knows about us. He's already given me an earful. And he's planning to send me home. I actually came out here with that survey crew to tell you. I didn't plan on this intimate rendezvous, but when you take me with your strong hands I cannot resist turning you into a whimpering boy."

Marshall laughed. "When is he sending you home?"

"He wants to send me now, but still needs me. I'm guessing in a week or two, probably when the line gets graded to here." Bridget's eyes got big, alive, and confident. She rubbed Marshall's chest. "I don't care what Father says or wants. I don't want to go. I want to stay until the railroad is complete. Go see him. Tell him I'm staying."

"Are you sure that's a good idea? He hates this illicit affair. I already feel awkward around him. And are you sure you want to spend the winter here?"

"I don't care about that anymore. It doesn't matter." Bridget brushed back her hair, tucking it behind her ears. "You can't ask a woman to go back to being a girl. I know he's ruthless and mean as a snake. He brought me here. I know him. The only way to handle this is straightforward. You've got a stake in the rail also. You're the key to the railroad. It can't be built without you. Put your foot down, and tell him I'm staying. Show some of the fortitude and determination you've used to build the rail and coax me into your tent. He won't like it, but he'll have to accept it."

"You mean spit in his face." Marshall almost couldn't bear the thought of not seeing Bridget, but was this too much?

"Father is a bear. Though not motivated by wealth or prestige, he craves the battle, winning, transforming things into his vision. He needs it, the colonel without any more battles to fight. He is a steel lever, and when applied by higher powers, he wins, often by means as unscrupulous as his bosses' and at the sacrifice of his own moral standards. I promise you, if I was somebody else's daughter, he wouldn't give a damn."

Marshall gave Bridget a kiss on the lips and then stood.

He ran his hands through his hair. "Let me think about it for a few days. I've already got enough enemies without putting your father on the other side of the fence. I want to marry you. Will you consent to that?"

"I'm not consenting before I go home, if that's what you're asking."

26

In the gray light of dusk, Yellow Horse walked off to his tepee. The two Cheyenne camps had come together for the late-summer sun dance. This was the second ceremony of the year, the other held earlier in the summer before the buffalo-hunting season. He loved the sight of all the tepees silhouetted against the setting sun. The grand events paid tribute to the buffalo. Tomorrow, all the villages would commence packing up and then head onto the plains for one last big hunt before the season of cold winds fell over the land.

The summer hunts had been good, but not great, and Yellow Horse thought one more big meat harvest would comfortably get the tribe through the winter. The last big hunt would sustain them in case of a long, hard season of snows. As the shadows grew long, the drums began to beat. A medicine man walked through the camp lighting the huge piles of wood that the women had stacked all day. The sounds of the rhythmic drums and the pulsing light of the fires gave Yellow Horse goose bumps.

As the drums echoed through the camp, the young braves gathered around the fires. Over the next few hours, the ritual would stir them to a fever pitch, whooping, singing, and chanting. The energy trapped inside the hunters from the dance would propel them to extreme acts of bravery and daring in the coming days. Yellow Horse remembered his first sun dance as a young brave. For days afterward he stormed recklessly into the herds, first confirming to himself, and then to his tribe, that he would be a great hunter for many seasons of green grass.

A soft hand grabbed his wrist. Bird Woman stood beside him looking over at the festivities with a big smile. Short and thin, and with long, smooth hair and big cheery eyes, his wife was well thought of by most of the Cheyenne. The daughter of one of the tribe's medicine men, she was known for her animated sense of humor, aptitude for joking, and her hard work tending the lodges and kids.

"Have you everything ready?" Yellow Horse said. "We will start moving the camp tomorrow."

"Quit worrying," Bird Woman said, playfully pulling on Yellow Horse's arm. "The hunt will be good."

Laughing came from the ground below. He felt something wrap around his leg. He bent over and picked up his daughter, holding her high and swinging her around in circles. Like her mother, she had a streak of mischief, constantly laughing and playing. Her behavior had garnered her the name Always Smiles.

"Always Smiles," Bird Woman said. "Go get your blanket, and put on your big moccasins."

"I am good," Always Smiles said, laughing, as Yellow Horse lowered her.

"Go on," Yellow Horse said. "Do as your mother says."

As their daughter disappeared into the tepee, Bird Woman put her arm around her husband. She looked up at him with a devilish grin. "Maybe when the deer's horns get big and the nights grow long and cold, the Great Spirit will give us another, maybe a young hunter."

"Let us hope so," Yellow Horse said and stirred his wife's hair with the palm of his hand.

Four young braves rode into camp with four spare ponies. With the glare of the fires, he inspected the ponies well, not recognizing any of them. He turned to his wife. "I will be right back. Make sure Always Smiles wears that little robe I made for her. I think it will be cold before the sun comes up."

Yellow Horse paced toward the young braves now dismounting in camp. He inventoried the ponies again. The valuable beasts did not belong to any of the villages camped here for the sun dance. Tribal protocol frowned on any raiding before or during the hunts, the Cheyenne not needing to be disturbed by anyone, whites or other Indians, who might pursue the hunters during the critical work. Yellow Horse approached one of the braves from Sun Walker's village named Big Nose. He liked the young man, probably only in his first or second season of hunting.

"Where did you get these ponies?" Yellow Horse asked, grabbing Big Nose by the arm.

Big Nose looked to the horses, then back at Yellow Horse. "We found them, near the grassy stream by the big jagged rock where Short Legs hurt his foot. They were just grazing."

Yellow Horse studied the horses. He grabbed one by the jaw and turned it broadside, illuminating its ribs with the light of the fires. He felt the area just behind the front shoulder, easily feeling the worn, rough spot from the white men's saddles. "These ponies probably belong to the men building the iron road. You know that Gray Man and Sun Walker have said not to bother the iron road, and you are not to be stealing and raiding before a hunt."

Yellow Horse wasn't particularly disturbed by the stealing of the ponies. He had stolen hundreds in his life. What irked him was that the young braves had disobeyed strict orders from the chiefs, something he hated, and worse, he had been at the council when Gray Man had given the white men his word that the Cheyenne would not hinder the road construction. These transgressions greatly exceeded the crime itself.

"We didn't steal them," Big Nose said. "Nobody was around. We just led them here."

"I will talk to Gray Man," Yellow Horse said. "We will ride over and return these ponies to the iron road tomorrow, before we leave on our hunt."

With the sun rising at his back, Yellow Horse stared down from the small hill at the two hundred or so white men moving and working on the iron road. Around him, the land rolled gently, broken only by a small, serpentine stream that had sliced up the grass. Above the work crew, a gray haze of dust hovered over the land that the white men carved up with their iron tools. Though only mid-morning, the day had warmed. Despite a lengthy inspection of the area and to his disappointment, he did not see any of the railroad chiefs from the parley they had held with the whites during the last moon.

Yellow Horse handed his spyglass to Medicine Bear. "I only see four on horseback." He pointed. "The one riding, with the white hat and gray shirt. He looks to be the leader. We'll take the ponies to him."

"They all have guns," Medicine Bear replied.

"We're armed too. Everybody is armed," Yellow Horse answered, turning to look behind him at six braves, all on horseback, and the four ponies they planned to return. He reached down and grabbed a white cloth, the white man's symbol for peace, and then pointed to the braves. "We are going to ride up. Bring the ponies up beside us so we can all ride up abreast, and they will see we are returning their horses. No war chants or screams."

The braves brought the ponies up beside Crow Eater and Medicine Bear. The nine Indians and thirteen horses stood side by side on the little hill facing the white men. Yellow Horse slid onto his horse, gently put his heels to his steed's ribs, and loped forward as he raised the white cloth. Beside him, the other men and horses moved in unison. Yellow Horse waved the white cloth and looked for one of the white chiefs he had met, the tall man with black whiskers or the young, white-haired chief.

The white men noticed them. They quit working and hurriedly bunched up, forming a line. Yellow Horse raised the white cloth high, waving it side to side as he continued to ride forward. Men yelled. Then a gunshot. To Yellow Horse's right, one of the braves fell from his horse, a bloody hole in his chest. More shots rang out. Medicine Bear's horse fell to the ground in a kicking mass.

All was confusion. Yellow Horse almost didn't believe his eyes, and rage settled over him. He heard the drum of hooves, the high squeal of Indians as five of the young braves raced forward. The braves unleashed a rapid succession of arrows at the line of men. Yellow Horse lashed his pony without mercy and raced forward, yelling as he rode, "Don't make war on the whites. Let's get out of here, back to camp."

Again whipping his horse, Yellow Horse wheeled around and galloped for the cover of a ridge. To his left, Crow Eater had sprinted forward to get Medicine Bear.

Now burdened with the extra rider, Crow Eater fled at a full gallop away from the white men.

Topping the ridge, Yellow Horse dismounted. He fell to his stomach and looked over the hill. The white men still fired away at the young braves, four of whom had taken flight for the cover of outcroppings near the stream. Yellow Horse did a quick count. Two of his party of young braves were missing.

Through his spyglass, Yellow Horse quickly studied the white men, all still clustered along the iron road. One man lay on his back, an arrow protruding from his gut. Another man hobbled along, staring down at an arrow in his thigh.

Crow Eater and Medicine Bear had ridden out of sight. Off to his left, the four Cheyenne braves now also made haste in the direction of the Cheyenne village, a half-hour ride away, splashing across the stream at a full sprint. Yellow Horse's head thumped. What had *happened*?

27

Ambrose sat on a bench at the Colorado Northern's head-quarters. From the porch, he looked over the plains. In the late day, the nip of early autumn filled the air. Where once the fluid, curving grass, long views, and infinite horizons had soothed his mind and body, now it had all become bland. His own eyes had acclimated to the space, became alert, watchful—plains eyes that noticed things in the faraway expanse. Out in the distance, maybe a half-mile, he saw three antelope, where months earlier he would have only seen the wide panorama. He crossed his legs and continued to reread a letter he had written his wife that morning.

My Love:
The weather here has turned delightful, the days growing cooler and shorter. We have made much progress in recent weeks, but I am constantly tormented that the railroad's enemies will reappear. More than anything, I fear these troubles may cause the men to grow weary and frightened

*and abandon the work. Nothing haunts me more
than the fear of failure.*

*I showed Bridget the newspaper article you sent
me about her shooting the railroad bandit. I should
have never conveyed that incident to you, as she
now thinks she's both a society celebrity and
seasoned gunslinger!!*

*I will be sending her home to you soon. I fear
her relationship with Marshall has already trans-
gressed into something not fit for a young lady.
I constantly blame myself for bringing her here.
I fear a confrontation when I send her home.
Please use your considerable powers on her in an
attempt to make her understand how much we love
and care for her.*

*We've had another fight with the Indians, and I
fear more troubles lay ahead. I still cannot get the
visions of our council with the Indians out of my
head. What a strange and frightful event. Images
of the meeting stay burned into my brain, and will
likely remain there forever. Will write again soon.*

Your loving husband.

Ambrose folded the letter and placed it in an envelope.
Inside, Marshall and Emory waited on him.

He stood and walked inside, slowly closing the door and
eyeing both men. "Marshall, I want to make sure we get
the line graded to the mouth of the canyon before the first
freeze. We can lay some track in the early winter, so make
sure we get the dirt moved now. We've got too many men
moving supplies into the canyon. I'm afraid we may not
finish grading. The extra wagons and teamsters you've
rented are costing us a small fortune."

Marshall blinked, exhaling a long breath. "We've only got two weeks of track laying left to the base of the mountains. We're behind schedule in the canyon now. Do you want speed or what you can afford?"

Ambrose sat at his desk and motioned for Emory and Marshall to take seats. The work's progress and cost really didn't have him concerned. It was only small talk. The Indian raid that morning really troubled him. "Let's talk about the Indians."

"We held them off fine," Emory said. "Killed two of their bucks. We lost a man and had another wounded, but he'll be fine in a few weeks. I've told the men to keep their firearms close and at the ready. I think this has taught them a lesson about staying armed and alert."

"Didn't we have a truce with the Indians?" Ambrose blew out a long breath of air.

"I thought so," Emory said. "The men said the Indians just came charging in. Then the fight broke out. Maybe this was another band? Maybe Gray Man changed his mind?"

Ambrose picked up a newspaper, showing its headline. "Looks like the Cheyenne are back on the war path. Tall Bull and Roman Nose had three raids last week. The army can't even catch them. I hope this isn't the start of another war."

"There's Indians here," Emory said. "Nothing we can do about that. We just have to deal with them. Hell, we licked the Rebs."

Ambrose said, "I've been out on the line all day. I think we're all right. The men are looking at this as more of a random event instead of an organized attack, but a few more of these raids and we may have some trouble. Nothing scares them like this, and we might have another month of working weather." Ambrose fumbled through some papers before picking up a telegram. "I sent a telegraph to General Augur, commander of the Department of the Platte, asking for some guidance. He's arranged a meeting for us with a Major Tanner at Fort Russell next week. This Major Tanner knows the Cheyenne well. He may give us some insight or help. The meeting will be next Tuesday. I want to head this Indian problem off before it gets any worse."

Leaning back in his chair, Ambrose propped his feet up on his desk. "Let's put flankers out around the grading crews, and redouble the guards. We've only got another month of good working weather. I'm bringing Bridget to Fort Russell with us. I'm going to send her home from there. It's not far from the UP railhead. I've already told her. She's got about a week's worth of paperwork to finish beforehand. Maybe we can get some help from the army. Let's hope we don't have an Indian war beforehand."

Thirty minutes before dusk, Yellow Horse loped into the large Cheyenne hunting camp, set along a little stream. Through the day, the tribe had moved onto the plains in pursuit of the buffalo and now congregated in several temporary camps before continuing the chase. Most of Yellow Horse's braves and women had combined with Sun Walker's people in the shadow of a rock buttress where the plain rose up and tilted away to the mountains.

The camp was in chaos. Around the long, exaggerated shadows, the women screamed and cried in despair. The eerie sounds rocked Yellow Horse as he watched two young squaws grieving at the news that their young husbands had been killed. One gnashed at her arm with a knife. Overhead, the sky had turned a deep, dark red.

The village criers walked through the camp singing the

war chants. A group of young braves donned their colorful war shirts and crow-feather bonnets. Their horses had been painted, their lances decorated. His good friend Crow Eater stood among the dozen braves. Yellow Horse wheeled his horse around and rode in the direction of the war party.

His own heart burned with hate as the images of the morning episode filled his head. He felt a gratifying sensation as he imagined himself ripping off the scalp of the perpetrators with a quick jerk.

He eased his horse up beside Crow Eater. "What are you doing?"

Crow Eater continued painting his face.

Sun Walker picked up his lance, sharpening it on a stone. "We're going to take some revenge on the whites who killed Big Back and Ghost Bull. They were murdered without provocation."

Yellow Horse rolled his eyes. "Has this been discussed with the chiefs? Does Gray Man know about this?"

"We will avenge this," Sun Walker said. "It is the Cheyenne way."

Yellow Horse sucked in a long breath. Part of him wanted to join in with the war party, but the leader in him reasoned that any retaliation should be thought over and discussed first.

Crow Eater said nothing as he inventoried his arrows. Madness filled his eyes.

An eagle flew over. Yellow Horse's stomach filled with knots at the sign of war.

"Are you coming with us?" Crow Eater finally said.

Yellow Horse sat silently. He turned and searched for his family, his mind filled with confusion. He wheeled his horse around and rode off. "Not unless it is agreed upon by everyone."

28

Ambrose looked at what was left of the work train, only an engine and two flatcars, now burnt and pierced with fifty or so arrows. The scarred ruins of the cars' chassis sat on the tracks under what remained of the train's metal components. The charred remnants of the modern wonder still smoldered, and a few small flames licked over the ashes of the two carloads of wooden ties that had hours earlier chugged along toward the end-of-track.

His eyes aching from the early afternoon sun bouncing off the bright yellow grass in all directions, Ambrose looked over to the tracks where the bodies of three men lay stretched out, stripped of clothing, their limbs severed, their chests filled with arrows. His stomach turned and his lunch pushed up against his throat. The bodies were covered with dark, dried blood. The men lay still, emotionless, like they had only laid down for a nap.

Other than the loss of the engine and flatcars, the Indian raid had done little, materially, to forestall the rail's construction. But psychologically, the effects would have a mammoth impact. Several weeks of early fall remained, and most of the men were already making other plans for the winter. An Indian raid, and the possibility of more attacks, would likely hasten the men's departure for other forms of employment.

"This ain't good," Emory said.

"No, it's not," Ambrose replied. "Especially since the newspaperman from Denver is supposed to be out in a few days. I was hoping the coverage of our progress might aid our cause, help us win over the state authorities and recruit more labor. I'm sure they'll get wind of this, and it will likely be the big story."

"Looks like a party of about fifteen," Emory said with a dull stare, pointing to some tracks on the ground. "They took off due east. This could be retaliation for the killing of the two bucks yesterday. We've got so much track laid now, it's hard to guard it all."

"Why do they maim the bodies so badly?" Ambrose inquired.

"It's a religious thing. I think I heard it has to do with the afterlife . . . their enemies won't have any arms or legs if they meet them there." Emory turned away from the bodies. "I always keep one bullet in reserve, in case they ever get me."

"Maybe this is an isolated incident."

Emory sighed. "I would think most of the Indians are out trying to harvest buffalo before winter sets in."

Ambrose turned his horse back toward headquarters. "Let's get back to the office. I'm tired of losing good men to this."

"It's too late," Patty said.

A cool, stiff wind hustled over the barren brown grass around the end-of-track. In the twilight, a strange, fantastic orange moon sat above the mountains. Marshall studied the group of workers, probably fifty, who had gathered outside the dining car with their bags.

"How many men want to draw wages?" Marshall asked.

"About two hundred," Patty said. "I'm sorry. It's late in the year. There's only a month or so of working weather left, and the men know the payroll will be trimmed significantly then anyway. The Indian attacks spook them much more than the accidents or robberies."

Marshall's forehead grew hot. The railroad teetered on chaos. He held a telegram they had just received. Benedict Matson was en route and planned to be at the railroad's headquarters the next morning. He also had yet to bring up the touchy subject of Bridget with Ambrose.

"This is unacceptable." Marshall said. "The men made an agreement with the railroad, and now they are breaking it."

"I've already tried." Patty scratched his red head, his pale eyes lifeless and his mouth open.

"We've come too far," Ambrose said, butting in. "You lead these men. It's your job to convince them to stay. Make them overcome their fear. That is what leaders do. If you can't do that, you should go too."

"Do you *mean* that?" Patty said.

"Forget it," Ambrose snapped. "I'll address the men. Patty, you're a good man, but you need to take better charge of this outfit. This railroad will only be built by our grit and determination. Matson will be here tomorrow. I will give a seven-day bonus for everybody that stays another month if that's what it takes. But these men will be working tomorrow. Post additional guards as you and the foremen deem necessary."

29

The next morning Marshall stood on the Colorado Northern's loading dock at its headquarters as Benedict Matson stepped off the train from Cheyenne.

Benedict wore a long black coat over a blue suit. As he instructed the rail's steward to get his bags, Benedict stomped some mud off his fine black leather shoes.

Ambrose whispered to Marshall, "He loves to pop in like this, with little notice. I sure am glad we convinced most of the men to go back to work. That would have likely been too much for Matson."

"How many drew wages?"

Ambrose cupped his mouth. "Only about thirty. We'll discuss it later, but I had to make some concessions." He then stepped forward to greet Benedict. "Welcome to the great American desert. How was your trip?"

"Terrible." Benedict placed a top hat on his short, gray hair. "I hate being anywhere uncivilized, you know that."

Marshall motioned to his office. "Let us go inside."

Benedict stepped into the office, taking a brief notice of several maps and schedules hanging on the wall, his face growing red and unpleasant. "Why have we laid only four miles of track in the last ten days?"

Ambrose pointed out the window to five men digging three fresh graves in the railroad's cemetery. "It's the Indians. Nothing else scares the men and slows work like this. What about the federal troops I've been asking for?"

Benedict brushed some dirt off his hands. "I've told you, there are no troops coming." He paused, putting his hands together and then raising his voice in anger. "Is the world to believe the expansion of the great American nation is on hold because of some troubles with a few hundred savages armed with bows and arrows? I'm glad the founding fathers weren't so easily deterred."

A dozen uneasy seconds passed.

Marshall said, "The thought of being scalped, especially here where it is a real possibility, incites fear in the men that surpasses anything produced by a rebel yell."

"What is your plan?" Benedict said, stomping a foot.

Ambrose scratched his beard. "The Indian attacks have only become a problem in the last few weeks. The good news is Silas Jones's hired gunmen have strangely disappeared."

"Well, you *better* come up with a plan to deal with this," Benedict snapped. "If killing the Indians is what's required, you better get to it, and I can assure you Silas Jones is not done with us."

Marshall stepped forward. "It's not all Indians. We've had a few bad days of weather also, but we have a meeting scheduled with the army next week to get some ideas on how to deal with the Indians."

"Gentlemen," Benedict said in a flat voice, pointing a finger at Marshall, "let me cut through the bullshit. I own you two, and I'm tired of these delays and problems. We've laid enough railroad now that I can sell the Colorado Northern and recoup my losses, but you two will get nothing. And neither one of you can stand a public failure like this. If you don't get this railroad built it will mean the end of your careers. You *will* solve these problems and finish this railroad, or I *will* break you. And I will find someone else to build this railroad. Is that clear?"

A rainbow of colors, the green of the aspens, the gray of the tall rugged cliffs, the yellow of the fall fauna, all heightened by the big, bright sun, made for a magnificent setting in Jeremiah Canyon the next morning. Bluebirds, chickadees, and grouse moved and chirped between the abundant timbers. Marshall and Bridget had spent most of the morning giving Benedict a tour of the rail's most imposing natural obstacle.

Every half hour, they had peered out over a panoramic vista, looked down an all-encompassing gorge with trepidation, or stared up at towering sandstone cliffs. The canyon held high mountain lakes, dramatic dips and peaks, wonderful meadows, an entire alpine world not even imagined from a distance. They had seen mule deer, elk, beavers, and even bear tracks, big ones.

"At places," Marshall said, turning in the saddle to Benedict, "the canyon spans almost a mile wide and sometimes it necks down so tight we'll have to blast away the mountain to squeeze the rail beside the stream. There's plenty of spruce, fur, pine, and aspen that we can use for bridge timbers and ties." He glanced toward Bridget in hopes she might employ her charms to alter Benedict's taciturn mood.

"Mr. Matson," Bridget said, "just think of the houses and buildings dotting the plains, built with the railroad's timber. It's right here beside our road. You will be a force in both the rail and timber industries."

In the canyon below, three loaded wagons, pulled by six horses each, trudged up the steep, winding road.

"What good we will do for this wretched area," Bridget continued. She removed her hat, cocked her head, and let her hair fall down to her shoulders to adjust a hairpin. "This is truly an American enterprise. The American people putting their footprint on the continent, the ultimate in making the land productive. The best of America—industry, government, technology, engineering, and free men all working together."

Benedict lifted his eyebrows. "The railroad had its birth in Europe. What we have is the land to give away to make the great railroads happen."

"Yes," Bridget smiled, "but it's *us* who have perfected the technology. Our engineers have developed the new forty-ton engines, stronger rails, more efficient connectors and brakes. In the last twenty years, we've built half the new miles in the world. Other countries can only dream about this."

Benedict produced a small smile. "When did you become such an expert on railroads?"

Bridget tucked her hair back in her hat, glancing smartly at Marshall. "Father and Mr. Brewster have educated me on railroads . . . and many other aspects of business and worldly matters. You didn't know the railroad was getting such a valuable windfall with Father's salary. But anyone can see that harnessing the power of steam equates to national power. Building railroads bathes the country and the men that build them in glory, working machines for the betterment of all. Do not worry. We will get this railroad built despite all of Mr. Silas's efforts to see us fail."

"Ms. Graham," Benedict said, "maybe we should send you to talk with the Cheyenne."

"I don't think they'd be so swayed," Marshall said with a laugh. "They'd likely channel Ms. Graham's energy into skinning buffalo and making feisty babies we'd end up having to fight."

Benedict grabbed his saddle horn. "The last thing we need is another idealist on the payroll, even if indirectly. How far up to Jeremiah?"

Thirty minutes later, Marshall led the way into Jeremiah. Stacked on the wall of a small mountain draw, the hasty community seemed to have popped up out of the ground like a patch of summer flowers. Every structure in town appeared new, the fresh paint and bright planks shining and untainted by weather. Twenty-five wood cabins, a general store, a small café, a bank, a sawmill, and schoolhouse had been completed. Around the city center, dozens of large tents and at least twenty more partially completed wood structures populated the steep slopes.

Two dozen people mingled on the two muddy streets. Six mines, towering edifices in the background, commanded over the town with their tall wood shafts, large warehouses, and heaps of discarded earth cascading from their bases. The surrounding hills had been stripped of timber. Aside from the construction of the community, mining required wood on a larger scale than rail building. Inside the mines, a honeycomb-wood structure, sometimes many stories high and constructed of miles of timbers, supported the underground shaft through the unstable earth as the mine followed the vein of bullion through the mountain.

Troves of material lay open to the elements. Near the

mines, a row of wagons sat lined up and loaded with the priceless ore. A smelter sat on the other end of town. Between the mines and the smelter, more than fifty men worked to construct a short, narrow-gauge rail that would relieve men and beasts of the labor required to move the piles of earth the quarter-mile.

Marshall pointed to three large, disassembled steam pumps. "Those are required for draining the mines. They were disassembled elsewhere and brought here by twenty wagons each, only to be reassembled. Nowhere will steam serve the common good more than enterprises like this that require the transport of large quantities of heavy material."

Benedict leaned forward in his saddle as he inspected the town. "Nothing attracts men and money more than the new silver claims and their possible rewards. The Comstock Lode in Nevada has turned dozens of ordinary men into millionaires. It netted the federal treasury the huge sum of forty-five million dollars during the Civil War, keeping the country solvent and all but paying for the war. It's the reason Nevada got statehood despite the fact the territory didn't have the required population."

"These Front Range claims fill the local papers," Marshall said. "There's never an end to the speculation of the hidden riches in the untamed mountains." He reined his horse off the road and up a steep incline toward one of the mines. "The gentleman we need to talk to is up here, Wolfe Kramer. Represents the eastern interest in three of these mines. I hope we can find him. I sent a telegraph yesterday that we'd be coming."

"How many people are here?" Benedict asked.

Activity at the mine was brisk. Dozens of workers operated the steam engines providing power for the water pumps and hoists reaching into the unseen mine below. Sweaty, dust-covered men and animals pushed and pulled carts loaded with silver-studded rock. Outside, armed men guarded everything.

Marshall stepped down from his horse. "Already four hundred. Nothing here a year ago. I suspect there will be more than a thousand within a year. This is a man-against-earth battle, harsher than rail building. I've heard the temperatures in the mines approach a hundred and forty degrees."

Inside the mine, Marshall led the three into an open office, knocking on a wall as they entered.

Wolfe, sitting at a desk, put down a newspaper and stood. Short and fit, and dressed in ironed brown slacks and a starched white button-up, the mining boss had only a trace of hair above his clean-shaven face. He wore a joyful smile befitting his clean-cut appearance.

"Hello, Marshall," Wolfe said.

"You remember Ms. Graham, and this is the president of the Colorado Northern, Benedict Matson."

Bridget extended a hand. "It is my pleasure. Father sends his apologies, but had to go to Cheyenne for some pressing business."

Wolfe then shook Benedict's hand. "Yes, I got a telegraph from the New York office that you'd be by."

Marshall unfurled a map and laid it on Wolfe's desk. "Here is this map of Jeremiah you gave me." He paused and pointed to a few places. The map delineated the current town and planned future expansions, complete with roads and plots of land for sale. "Looks like the rail will come in here. We'd like to have this plot for our train station."

Wolfe reached into a pocket and grabbed his round spectacles. Placing them on, he spent a few seconds studying the map. "I'd rather have it farther up here, closer to the mines."

"Almost impossible," Marshall said. "Looks to be a

six-percent grade from town to here. It'll take all we can do to get the track here, on the edge of town."

Wolfe removed his glasses and wiped his eyes. "Okay, there then. We'll give you that lot. I'll have the papers drafted and sent to you."

Benedict cleared his throat. "I'd like to discuss the other business I spoke with your home office about. I want some help with the Indians. I explained all this to your boss. We've laid more than sixty miles of track. We should be here next summer, but I want Colonel Bates to help us. It's in your interest, and I know the governor has ordered him to give you a hand on several occasions."

Wolfe fumbled through some papers until he found a telegraph. He scanned it. "Yes, I got the telegraph. My office has asked me to lend you a hand in this matter. I'll be candid. I'm assuming, probably correctly, that other interests in the railroad business control the governor. But Colonel Bates mostly answers to himself. I guess what I'm trying to say is that the colonel has his own political aspirations. Killing Indians is popular. There's little I can do directly, but you should pay him a visit. If you present your problems to him in such a way that serves his cause, the governor's whims may then become secondary to him."

Benedict put a well-manicured hand to his chin, then smiled. "Scheming, kickbacks, and inducements are my specialty. I know how to deal with men that can be bought, whether the price is money or less-expensive things." His dark gaze turned to Marshal. "You will follow through with this, promptly." Benedict returned his glance to Wolfe. "A railroad in this canyon is the end we all want. . . . Can you arrange a meeting?"

"I will have a telegraph sent to him today." Wolfe cleared his throat. "I warn you though. He is ungovernable, and his methods are extreme."

30

The end-of-track bustled with life the next morning as Marshall discussed the construction with a reporter from Denver's largest newspaper. To appease the men, Ambrose had ordered that work on isolated sections of the rail be stopped. All work would be done in the vicinity of the end-of-track, and everything would be guarded with a dozen well-armed men.

For weeks now, Marshall had been in a relentless race to finish the line to the base of Jeremiah Canyon before the weather turned bad. This would significantly aid work in the canyon, allowing men and materials to be moved there efficiently.

Despite the undertone of problems, to the foreign eye, the work site where the rail met the ties looked normal. A telegraph man stood tethered atop a new pole. Around the gray dust hanging over the land, the work went on with little talk. Picks and shovels hammered away below parched tongues, and an endless line of wheelbarrows moved the piles of dirt and rock. A supply train arrived, blowing its air whistle.

"The American never stops dreaming or building,"

Marshall said, putting a hand on his hip and pointing. "We should be to the mountains in two weeks. We will finish next summer. We've only got about thirty miles of line left to build."

The reporter, short and fat, with a shiny bald head, put his pencil to his mouth. "Rumor has it, Benedict Matson is here. Any chance I could interview him?"

"He left this morning on the train to Cheyenne and then on to Chicago."

"I hear you're having trouble with the Indians."

"We've had all sorts of trouble. Building a railroad in an untamed land makes it inevitable. There's supply problems, weather problems, those that don't want the rail built. These are typical and why this is such a grand enterprise. We've only got eleven miles of track left to build to get to the mountains, and we plan to finish that before winter sets in." Marshall paused, wondering about the rail's other enemies that the reporter had failed to mention.

He had told Bridget to be handy. He wanted her to converse with the reporter, her gregarious manners and good looks likely to aid the rail's cause. She sat horseback a hundred yards ahead of the end-of-track, and he nodded as the two made eye contact. "The railroad will aid significantly in the building of Colorado and its economy. Goods and services will travel quickly and efficiently across the northern portion of the state and to the silver mines."

"And what about the Southwest Pacific Railroad?" the reporter inquired. "Do you plan to connect the line with Denver in the future? The word is, the Southwest also has a grant to build a line through this area, and Silas Jones might be delighted if you failed. Would you comment on that?"

Marshall grinned as Bridget arrived on horseback. "Our biggest problem now is the weather. These late September days are showing their ugly side. Twice in the last two weeks, we've been hit with storms, dropping the temperature into the thirties, and hammering the land with gale-force winds and chilling, horizontal rain. . . . Mr. Young, this is Bridget Graham, the daughter of the Colorado Northern's vice president. And to answer your question, no, I don't care to comment on the Southwest Pacific Railroad or Mr. Jones. As you can see, we've got our hands full with our own railroad. Ms. Graham will show you around. We've arranged for you to take a ride on the sixty miles of track we've completed. Ms. Graham will be your escort for the day. I warn you, she can be rather sassy at times."

The reporter turned to Bridget and then put his pen and pad into his pocket. "Yes, I would like to ride the rail, and if it is okay, I'd like to interview some of the workers and some of the men that have been involved in your scrapes with the Indians. No offense. You're in the business of building rails. We're in the business of selling papers, and nothing sells more papers than Indian stories. Public's completely fascinated with and terrified by them."

Bridget reached down and extended a hand to Mr. Young, brushing back her bangs and straightening her dress. "Mr. Young, I have a fine horse for you to ride until the next train arrives and also a nice lunch I made myself. You can talk to anyone you want. By the end of the day, you'll be sure of one thing—we're going to have this rail finished and running by midsummer, next year."

31

Fall had arrived in the mountains, the foliage turning into wonderful shades of yellow, red, and brown, the leaves starting to brown. Here, there was no wide arch of the sky, the canyon walls closing in around everything, the gray rocks blazing with the sunshine. The climate varied dramatically: warm in the day, but with cool, clean autumn winds in the mornings and evenings.

Marshall had spent the last three days in Jeremiah Canyon in an attempt to get the actual construction there started before he departed for Fort Russell. Despite Ambrose's efforts, an additional hundred men had drawn wages in recent days, but Marshall had managed to convince forty of the men to work in the canyon where little threat existed from the natives.

Weeks earlier, he'd moved ample materials here to start construction. Now, he needed to organize the blasting gangs and grading crews on different sites. The blasting required considerably less labor, but it would be time consuming. Fortunately, much of it could be done in inclement weather.

The grading crews consumed most of the labor. Teams

of men and animals lashed away at the soil with picks and shovels, all removed by hand and transported by carts pulled by donkeys or oxen. When the earth consisted of hard dirt, it was plowed first, and when the line collided with rock faces, ridges, or outcroppings, black powder and nitroglycerin blasted the path clear.

Marshall had spent the morning with two young engineers adding and subtracting the cut and fill. These calculations, constantly made, helped ensure that the final grade was set to minimize the quantity of earth moved and the distance it had to be transported. On the plains, the line never rose or fell more than a hundred feet per mile, and grading required little preparation. But in the mountains, the calculations could save thousands of man-hours.

He stepped out of the tent to address Jacob, the Colorado Northern's explosives expert. In his early forties, the quirky Swede spoke heavily accented English, but seemed sturdy, good spirited, and capable.

Marshall pointed. "The grade up to Jeremiah has several major obstacles. On the lower portion, this is our only major hurdle. This pinch point in the canyon will require a small bridge and a six-hundred-foot ledge carved from that exposed rock face. Higher up, three small tunnels and three more bridges will be required, the last of these a four-hundred-foot span across from a ridge down onto a gentle rise that leads to Jeremiah. I don't have it all worked out yet. Much of the work and solutions will have to be invented on the spot. Our success will likely be determined by our disregard for standard solutions."

Jacob pointed to the rock face overhead, a vertical slab of smooth brown granite rising almost a hundred feet. "Yes, quite a challenge, but we'll get along. I inspected it good this morning. I will hang ten baskets down from that buttress overhead. In the baskets, two-man teams can drill the blasting holes for the nitroglycerin sticks. The blasting strength is eight times greater than black powder. Three times a day, we will set off the charges. It will be slow, but it will be good. The rock will fall away. Not much work for the men. No handcarts needed. Once one foot of ledge is cut into the face for fifty feet on each end, the nitroglycerin can be mixed and poured into the holes. Then it is much stronger, but we will need room for mixing it properly. The nitroglycerin is too unstable to be moved or handled in its combustible state." Jacob raised his hands. "Boom. We be very careful."

"When can you get started?"

"Two days," Jacob said as three men began unloading a box. "Will you excuse me?"

As Jacob walked off, Marshall inspected a square rock shelf at the end of the cut. Here, he intended to bridge the canyon with a small trestle, placing the rail on the other side of the canyon where the terrain stood more favorable. The reach up to Jeremiah Canyon required two such crossings. He studied the baffling collection of rocks. What he saw was more intimidating than encouraging. Building a rail here was a Herculean task. Upstream of the natural abutment, the tiny mountain stream fell over a small waterfall. Below the falls, adjacent to the large wall of rock that had to be spanned, the stream took on many forms. In places, it ran clear, sparkling, and docile, and other times transitioned into a torrid, disorderly, foamy, spinning block of water, caged by its banks and displaying its vast energy.

"Looks peaceful up here. Any painted warriors lurking over the next ridge?"

Startled, Marshall spun.

Bridget had ridden up behind him and now grinned from under her big-brimmed hat. "I didn't spook you, did I?" Bridget laughed.

Marshall exhaled as he reined up beside Ambrose, who was discussing something with Patty. He waited patiently until Patty stepped on the train as it departed. Marshall dismounted. "You got a minute?"

"No," Ambrose said, kneeling to inspect a cross tie.

"Well, make some time." Marshall cleared his throat. "It's about Bridget."

Ambrose froze and then gave Marshall a cold stare. "There's nothing to talk about. She's going home. You should feel fortunate I'm not going to whoop your ass."

Marshall felt the blood pour into his cheeks. The wind gusted, kicking up a blanket of dust. He removed his hat and ran a hand over his head. "I aim to marry her. I've discussed it with her. And she's staying."

"The *hell* she is." Ambrose poked out his chest, his face growing beet red. "What's she going to be, your camp girl?"

"My fiancée. That's the way it's going to be and that's final. What are you going to do, tie her up and put her in a railcar bound for Chicago?"

"You son of a bitch." Ambrose grinded his teeth and his face grew tight. "You're not as important as you think you are. Do not fuck with me. I will break your ass. And I'm going to have a word with my daughter this evening. We will see about all this."

"She's in Cheyenne. I sent her there to take care of a few chores. She went on the last train today. You can see her tomorrow before we go to Fort Russell." Marshall put a foot in his stirrup. "You need to come to grips with this. Nothing you can do about it, whether you like it or not."

Ambrose threw his hat on the ground and kicked up some dirt before stomping off down the railroad.

32

"Emory," Marshall said, wiping his mouth and placing his napkin on his plate, "that was an excellent breakfast." Around him, patrons seated at the restaurant's twenty tables chatted over the commotion of the waiters rushing between the tables and the clanging of tableware.

"Fine stuff." Emory reached into a handbag and pulled out a newspaper, placing it on the table. The front page carried several big stories about the current Indian situation.

Emory's voice turned hoarse. "The Indian problems have gotten worse. Paper says seventy or eighty white folks killed this summer. Lots of raids on farms and settlements. Probably why everybody around here is so sullen. Downright depressing. The fighting is fierce just east of here. Cheyenne have been on a rampage. Cavalry finally killed Roman Nose the other day over on the Arikaree River, but the warriors are raiding something every day. Three cavalry regiments are in an almost daily fight with the Cheyenne. It's got all of Colorado and Wyoming terrified. There's a back-page story in there about the Colorado Northern, and a gory, sensational version of our own scrapes with the

Indians, almost like a dime novel. Fort Russell is just a half-hour ride by horse."

Marshall put several dollars on the table and stood. "Where's Ambrose?"

"Going to meet us at the hotel in an hour. He's been in an exceptionally bad mood lately for some reason."

Marshall followed Emory outside. The streets of Cheyenne were utter chaos. People yelled, shouted, or engaged in conversation or bickering on an endless range of subjects. Hundreds of horses and oxen filled the dusty streets. Goods of every kind moved through the town on wagons, and the huge Union Pacific staging area across the street held four steam engines, dozens of railcars, and heaps of rail-building supplies.

"Can't believe how much Cheyenne has grown," Marshall said. "The Union Pacific only founded it just over a year ago."

"Already has four thousand people." Emory pointed to a row of twenty or so wood structures on the town's main street. "Buildings popping up every day." He chuckled. "We finally have gambling houses and saloons. And anything else you might want in the tent city outside of town."

Marshall inspected an impressive new rail bridge spanning a deep gorge, a quarter-mile long and a hundred and fifty feet high, its shiny new wood piers seemingly defeating the impressive natural obstacle. In the other direction, the town's cemetery sat atop a small hill with more than forty tombstones, a foreboding symbol considering the town's youth. A loud steam engine blew its whistle as a westbound train roared by, loaded with rail-construction equipment

Emory nodded to an unsightly scene. Three dead settlers, men, were propped up in their open wooden caskets beside the street. All three had been scalped and mutilated.

Several arrows protruded from the bodies, the display apparently intending to portray the nature of the local savages. The long shadows of the early sun accentuated the gloominess of the cadavers.

The gruesome scene had its desired effect, rekindling the nightmarish visions that had filled Marshall's psyche since his arrival on the plains. Every time he read one of the press's horrid stories or heard about something like this, chill bumps raced up his arms and his skin tingled. What could possibly be more terrifying than a similar demise? Like most, the terror constantly held him hostage.

At noon, Marshall rode into Fort Russell with Ambrose and Emory. Around the long lines of symmetrical, wood buildings, the soldiers walked with a deliberate pace. Instead of pressed blue uniforms, colorful guidons, bright yellow chevrons, polished boots, and perfect lines of toy soldiers, the flat, treeless parade fields were filled with dirty uniforms, sweat-laden overworked horses, and parched, worn, and tired faces. The fort had none of the trappings of its peacetime appearance, but more a working, businesslike façade with the mood and practicality of an army at war. Marshall had seen both sides of the army during the war. Here, these men were engaged in the dirty business of war, and they had given up many of the formal pretenses of army protocol.

The five-acre fort was a city unto itself with more than a dozen buildings surrounding a large parade ground—barracks, quartermaster, commissary stores, offices, stables, blacksmith shops, a chapel, and even a sawmill. A stout, steady wind blew over the plot, kicking up a continuous dust cloud as tumbleweeds rolled over the grounds.

"Can I help you, sir," a sergeant said, riding up to the three and reining up.

"Yes, Sergeant," Ambrose replied. "We have a noon meeting scheduled with Major Kelly. Can you tell us where to find him?"

The sergeant pointed to two small offices beside the fort's large administrative building. "There, that office on the left. There should be an orderly there that can help you."

The three tied their mounts to a hitching post and walked inside the office. There, they found a private sitting at a desk, the only fixture over the wood floor and inside the thin planks, whistling and squeaking under the barrage of the strong breeze.

Ambrose spoke with a stern voice. "We're here for a meeting with Major Tanner Kelly."

The private pointed to an office behind him. "Please step in his office. I'll go tell him you're here. Your name?"

"Ambrose Graham." Ambrose took off his hat and walked for the door.

Marshall and Emory followed him into the office where Ambrose took a seat in one of two chairs opposite a desk covered with papers. Marshall moved to one of the walls that held a large map and motioned for Emory to take the other seat.

Several minutes passed before boots pounded on the wood floor. A yellow-haired officer with a long, flowing mustache entered the room.

Ambrose stood and extended a hand. "Let me make a formal introduction, Ambrose Graham. This is Emory Chapman and Marshall Brewster. We're with the Colorado Northern Railroad."

"Yes," the officer said. "I received a memo from General Augur that you would be here today. What can I help you with?"

Marshall eyed the bright gold-leaf insignia on the major's shoulders. The red scarf around his neck stood out against his regimental blues. The orderly set some papers on his desk and the major returned his salute.

"I'm sure you're aware," Ambrose said, "we're trying to build a railroad south from Cheyenne, and we're having some Indian troubles. I was told you are in good graces with some of the local tribes and might give us some assistance."

Major Kelly grimaced, his alert eyes darting uneasily above his immense jaw. He sat down and propped his boots upon his desk to unbuckle his spurs and take off his leather chaps. "I know most of the local Indians very well. Some say I'm a friend of theirs. That's mostly because I try to treat them fairly, and I've been somewhat outspoken about the way they've been treated at times. On several occasions, and to the detriment of my career, I've even testified against some army commanders who have committed atrocities against the Indians. Due to this, my career has been a ride of ups and downs, pending the sentiments in Washington. Many things are blamed on the Indians, and in general, I'd say that most people are overzealous in their fear of them."

The Major's words, spoken in perfect Queen's English, ran in complete contrast to the rough setting.

"We came here hoping you might help us out," Ambrose said.

"Please sit." The major flashed deep brown eyes at Ambrose and waited for the two men to sit. "I'm sure General Augur has told you that we don't have any spare troops to give you. We've got our hands full. But, if I'm correct in my assumption, you're trying to build a railroad through Cheyenne and Arapahoe country, and you're having to fight Indians to get it built."

"That's correct," Ambrose said. "We met with some of

the local chiefs and thought we had an agreement worked out, but have since had several fights with the Indians. We've lost several men and had a train attacked and burned."

The major rubbed his sun-parched face with the palm of his hands. "I can tell you what I know about the local Indians. It's hard to blame them. They're magnificent, proud creatures, in a war for survival. They've already been broken down into small, scattered bands. Their problem is that we're coming to take their land, and they don't like it. What some of them don't understand is that white men will settle the West, that's inevitable, and they will have to submit to that fact, eventually."

The major paused and scratched the back of his head. "There's maybe two hundred thousand Indians on the plains. There's millions of Americans coming. There's nothing anybody can do to stop it, not the president, not the army, not anybody. It's the advance of civilization. These Indians can't fight this. They don't have the numbers, the technology. There's no other way. If they fight it, they'll be annihilated. They have two choices—change or disappear. Those are not the government's policies, they're just the reality, and no one or no government can change that. They don't realize that every time they fight, the public cries for more dead Indians. They can't win. They must surrender to the power of circumstances."

The major turned his eyes up. "Let me see how to say this. The problem is that we haven't done a good job explaining this to them. We've tricked and betrayed them instead. Every time we run into them and want their land, we simply tell them to go off somewhere else and everything will be fine, but in time we show up at this other place wanting the same things. Now, there's almost nowhere for them to go. The word 'own,' especially as it relates to land, is not even in the Cheyenne vocabulary. Helping the Indians civilize themselves is the only way to save them. That should be our policy, but instead we find ourselves fighting them."

"You sound like an Indian sympathizer." Ambrose laughed.

"No, not totally," the major replied. "I fight them every day. Their demands are unreasonable. They want an area the size of Wyoming set aside as permanent buffalo-hunting grounds. And they like to claim this land is sacred to them. It's not. They've only come West in the last couple of hundred years. Their entire way of life, their roaming, hunting, and horse culture, only began after the Europeans introduced horses here. They've not been directed to live here by some great spirit. The Lakota defeated the Cheyenne and forced them here, and they in turn ruth-lessly defeated the Kiowa to take this land, running the Kiowa farther south. They may deny it, but they are a war-rior culture. They've lived by the rule that the powerful always rule the less powerful, and now they don't like it be-cause a greater power has arrived to subdue them."

"So much for the theory behind all this," the major said. "Let's talk about your problem. I'm guessing you've got a few bad Indians attacking your railroad. Most of the Indians are good, but there are some bad bunches. I hate to say it, but the best solution is to kill the bad ones. That's about all that works. Killing the ones that don't consent helps convince the rest of the inevitable. The problem is— determining which are the bad ones. That's difficult, and you probably can't just kill the bad ones."

Ambrose grunted and sat up straighter. "You haven't told us much. We don't want to fight the Indians. We just want to build our railroad. Isn't there something we can do to appease them?"

The major focused on Ambrose and smiled. "You think these settlers around here want to fight the Indians? They just want to farm or whatever. They don't have any choice. The Indians are like us. They're mostly good Indians, but the few bad ones make it difficult for everybody. Worse, a few bad Indians is interpreted as all Indians are bad. You can try to meet with the local chiefs again. It may do some good, but the ones you parlay with may not be the ones giving you problems."

Ambrose leaned forward. "Sounds like we'll end up having to fight them."

"No, I'm not saying that, but warriors roaming free and hunting buffalo and railroads cannot coexist. You should pursue peaceful options if you can, but you want your rail built. Killing the rebellious Indians might be your only option. Some of these Indians won't listen to their chiefs. They've all been given the chance to go south of the Arkansas River and live in peace. If they're up here, they've refused that opportunity. I wish I could tell you more, but every situation is different. You can always just continue on your current course."

Ambrose exhaled a big breath. "I was hoping we might find a solution, but at least you've given us some guidance."

The major leaned back in his chair. "I can tell you this, if you do have to fight them, do it in the winter. They're easier to fight then, when their travel is limited and their rations are meager. And if you do fight them, don't ever chase them. If you do, you're likely riding into a trap."

Ambrose groaned again and stood, extending a hand to the major. "Thanks for your advice." He laughed. "We may have the only job in the West harder than yours."

The major returned Ambrose's handshake.

"We won't keep you any longer," Ambrose said. "We better get going."

The major stepped out from behind his desk. "I will gladly come down and meet with the Indians if you think it might help, but give me a few days' notice."

"Thank you," Ambrose said.

Marshall started for the door. He stepped out onto the office's wood porch and put his hat back on. The major's knowledge of the local Indians surpassed anything he expected and added a level of complexity to an issue he had previously seen as black and white.

But little had come out of the meeting. He tightened his chin string. The railroad would have to solve the problems with the Indians like all its other problems. They'd have to solve it themselves, and that would likely be dirty. But just how dirty and problematic?

33

Bridget's long, handmade white dress shone in the morning light that poured through the office window. "It seems like a lot of trouble to ride over to Boulder just to go to church." She smiled and pulled a white bonnet over her head.

Ambrose felt his ire easing a little. For a week, he had been stewing. A part of him knew there was nothing he could do about her and Marshall, but the circumstances of it all constantly gnawed at his gut. He loathed it, but had to tolerate it. "We were invited this morning. There will be a lot of local politicians and important people there. It will aid our cause to get in their good graces."

"I sent Mother a letter explaining everything to her. She'll understand. Hopefully, she can come out this winter and see us. I know you don't like it, but you will have me around to help you with all your paperwork."

"If you say so," Ambrose said, grabbing his dress coat. He pulled his watch from his pocket and checked the time. "She'll come this winter and we'll go see her in Cheyenne. Where are Marshall and Emory? We're going to be late if they don't come on. We're supposed to be there by ten thirty."

"It's only an hour's ride. We will make it."

A brief knock came on the door. It opened, and Marshall stood dressed in a black suit.

"Glad you made it," Ambrose grumbled.

Bridget smiled. "I was just explaining to Father that the world is not coming to an end, and the benefits of me staying on with the railroad."

Marshall tipped his hat to Bridget. "I'm sure after your encouraging words, he *now* concurs."

"Let's go," Ambrose said.

"Emory has the horses outside," Marshall answered.

Thirty minutes later, the group found themselves on the open plain, using the mountains to the west as their guide. The little village of Boulder sat literally at the base of the Rockies. Topping a small hill, Ambrose saw five horses, only a quarter-mile ahead.

Emory pulled up. "Looky there."

"What you think?" Ambrose said, reaching in his saddlebags for his binoculars. Before he had a chance to raise the glasses, a bullet zinged overhead. Some dust kicked up about ten paces away. Indian whoops and squeals drifted over the land.

Ambrose's pulse raced. He whipped his horse toward the mountains, a half-mile away, spurring him with all his energy. The horse tore up the turf as he spun and raced off. "Let's go! Find some cover!"

The other three horses bolted in his direction. To his left, the five Indians raced toward the mountains, angling in the direction of his horse's path. His vision jarred. Hearing only the hooves pounding the earth, he calculated the distance of both parties. They were much closer to the edge of the mountains than the Indians and would beat the hostiles there by an easy minute.

The huge mountains got no closer. But just ahead a ridge fell off the high slopes into a small draw. He jerked his horse slightly to the right, toward the slice in the prairie. "That ditch. Let's get in there and get ready."

A dozen seconds later, Ambrose made a running dismount. He reached to his saddle and grabbed his rifle. Around him, Bridget, Emory, and Marshall also jumped to the ground, then led their horses into the ditch in a clumsy dash for cover. In the gully, they flung themselves to the ground.

Ambrose peeked over the bank. The Indians charged forward. The bright paint on the flying steeds and the tall feathers stood out against the tan backdrop. The Indians waved their lances. "Hold your fire until they're close. We get a couple of them, they may run off." He then crouched and ran to Bridget, falling to his stomach beside her and peeking over the ditch's bank. The Indians raced off to their left and swung by them at a distance of a hundred paces.

Up close, the terrible painted faces and bright war bonnets filled Ambrose's vision. The Indians hung low, using their horses as shields, and fired a reckless barrage into the gully, their riding skills displaying a beauty and majesty, even now.

Ambrose, Emory, and Marshall returned the fire, not drawing any blood.

"Only two of them have repeaters!" Marshall yelled. "The other two have muskets. It will take them some time to reload."

Two of the braves thundered by again with another broadside pass, blasting away.

Beside Ambrose, Emory's pistol bucked against his hand.

He heard the thumping of hooves, the red devils' loud taunts. He wiped his face with a bandanna; the awful scene was strangely dreamlike, but starkly real.

The Indians disappeared. The three men reloaded. A few silent, tense seconds passed. Ambrose's eyes stung from sweat.

"What do you think?" Marshall said.

"Don't know," Emory said. "I don't like it."

Ambrose tried to choke down his fear. "I see why we haven't had to deal with the Southwest. The Indians are doing their bidding for them. . . . You think we can hold out?"

"Probably," Emory said, "but one of their favorite tricks is burning you out. There's too much grass and brush around us."

A chill raced up Ambrose's spine as he inspected the thick, dry vegetation. "Up this hill behind us, behind those large boulders." He nodded. "You think we can make it there?"

"Yes," Emory replied, "let's cut the horses loose. They'll likely go after them. They may not come back, but if they do, it will give us time to get some better cover."

"Get all the water and ammo you can carry!" Marshall yelled, jumping to his feet. He grabbed his and Bridget's horses, removed their canteens and two boxes of cartridges from his saddlebags.

Ambrose and Emory hustled to do the same. The swish of arrows filled the air. Ambrose dove for cover, but the four arrows landed harmlessly in the ditch. He removed his hat and slapped his horse with a loud shout.

Marshall slapped the other three horses on the rear, sending them bolting onto the open plain.

Ambrose took a knee, cupping his ear with his hand.

Thirty seconds passed. Then the Indians' screams grew more distant. He sprang to his feet, grabbed his canteen and saddlebag, and lunged out of the ditch, pointing up the hill. "Up there, hurry. Into that little crevice, the one by those three big rocks on the left."

His lungs heaving, he dashed up the hill and dove into the rocky hole. He raised his rifle and crawled up the sides of the four-foot-deep hole. The other three entered and squatted for cover. "We may not get burnt out here, but we don't have any horses either."

Marshall crawled up beside Ambrose and looked down to the plains, thirty feet below. "In all my days on the UP, I never had any Indians get after us like this."

Ambrose squinted, raising a hand to shield the sun. In all directions, he saw nothing, only the rolling, monotonous blanket of golden grass, patched with sparse brush. He turned to Emory. "You think we can hold out? You think they'll be back?"

"I don't know," Emory said, reaching down to get Ambrose's binoculars. "Aim for the horses if they come by again. They're easier to hit." Emory raised the glasses, studying something in the direction they had come.

Terrible thoughts filled Ambrose's mind. "You see something?"

"Think so," Emory said, holding the glasses still with both hands. "Looks like white men, coming our way."

"Maybe someone coming to our rescue," Bridget said.

"Fire a few shots in the air," Emory said.

Ambrose raised his rifle, fired it once, then worked the lever and fired two more shots.

"It is," Emory said calmly. "Think it's some of our boys. They must have heard all the shooting. Might be our lucky day."

Numb, Ambrose stood, exposing himself. The five horses grew closer by the second, the wide-brimmed hats of the riders now visible. Intense anxiety filtered out of his body. A stiff breeze cooled his perspiring forehead. The land sat quiet, but he still heard the echoes of the gun battle pounding through his head. He sat back down on the rock, his face sweaty and soiled.

34

Marshall stepped up on the wood porch of the little two-room house at the Colorado Northern's headquarters where he stayed. He stomped his feet a few times trying to get the snow off his wet boots.

A strong, early-morning gust blew off his hat, only tethered to his neck by a string. Snow covered all the compound's rooftops, and the line of smokestacks billowed dark gray smoke over the steam drifting up from the buildings. He opened the door and stepped inside to escape the howling, bone-chilling wind. The cozy air warmed his insides as he took off his coat, hanging it on a nail.

Bridget sat by the fire, wrapped in a blanket. "There's some boiled eggs on the table."

Marshall grabbed one and walked to the fireplace where Bridget read a newspaper by the light of a sputtering candle. "What are you doing here?"

"Just came to see you."

"Your father doesn't have you working today?"

"Actually, he let the men off. He thinks this is going to be the first major storm of the year. Everybody's getting ready for it, and I'm bored to death."

Marshall glanced at the paper. "Anything going on in the world?"

"They think General Grant got elected president. That's probably good for the railroad business, huh?"

Marshall warmed his hands in front of the fire. "I'm glad we finally got that last twenty-five-mile section complete—it looks like in the nick of time, too. It was the best three weeks of track laying of the entire year. Don't think I could have put up with your father had we not finished it. How many men is Ambrose going to keep through the winter?"

Bridget folded her arms around her knees, still under the blanket. "A hundred and fifty, I think. How's the work coming?"

"The blasting in the canyon has made good progress. With the next patch of sunshine, I plan to lay the track the first four miles into the canyon, past the first major cut. This will shorten our supply run to the first bridge site. I'm starting to think my expectations for the winter may have been too optimistic. We got almost a foot of snow in the canyon last week. The men aren't doing anything now but shoveling snow and probably won't be for another week."

Bridget handed Marshall the paper. "There's a big article about how the Central Pacific is catching up with the UP."

"The Central Pacific doesn't have to fight Indians." Marshall set down the paper and rubbed Bridget's upper arms before poking the fire with a long stick. "The crews have had three minor brushes with the Cheyenne in the last two weeks, one that included an exchange of gunfire."

Marshall sat on the bench beside Bridget. "But the terrible images of that day with you in your white dress still haunt me. Keeps me constantly tossing, sweating, and wincing instead of sleeping. I like my scalp and future wife both where they are."

Bridget scooted over to Marshall and put her hands on his shoulders. "What are you doing the rest of the day?"

"Your father wants me to go to Boulder with him to meet with Colonel Bates of the state militia. I think we're leaving around noon." Marshall put his hand over one of Bridget's, covering it. "I fear he plans to spend the winter hunting Indians instead of building a railroad."

Marshall reached into his coat pocket and pulled out a small box. He opened it, exposing the silver ring. "This came in today. Put it on. The sight of it might ease some of Ambrose's grief."

Bridget leaned over Marshall, her smooth hair falling against his unshaven face. She smelled of smoke and fire, but the rough fragrance did not hide her fresh, feminine scent. He stood up. "I'll bring in some wood. We probably won't be back until tomorrow."

Bridget stood. "I've got you a surprise. A big new coat I made from a buffalo hide. It will keep you warm while Father has you out chasing Indians this winter."

As darkness fell, the temperature dropping into the teens, Marshall followed Ambrose into Boulder. Overhead, under the sweep of gray sky, the apexes of two large peaks loomed, their long shadows draping the town's buildings and three muddy, frozen roads in a blue-gray haze.

Ambrose tightened the collar of his coat around his neck, and blew out a long tendril of white fog. He rubbed his bearded face. "You ought to grow one of these beards. It helps beat the cold down. I believe it's that house there, the one with the big red chimney."

"Maybe he's got a fire going." Marshall spurred his

mount. He trotted forward and then slowly stepped down from the saddle.

Ambrose grabbed a leather case and walked to the door of the residence. He knocked twice, and a man sporting an eye patch opened the door.

"Colonel Bates?" Ambrose said in an agreeable tone.

"Ambrose Graham, I presume," the colonel said, stepping sideways to allow passage inside. "Come in out of the cold. I have some dinner being prepared, roast and potatoes."

As Marshall stepped inside, the thick aroma of onions and fried grease filled the air.

Ambrose presented a hand. "This is Marshall Graham. I believe you two have met."

Several items hung on the wall, including two newspaper clippings, a black-and-white photo of the colonel in uniform with some dignitaries, and several letters of commendation from the governor.

"You fight in the war?" Marshall asked.

"Only in Colorado," the colonel said with a booming laugh and motioned to the table already set for dinner. "Helped keep the Indians and bushwhackers down. I had a brevet federal commission then."

Probably in his late forties, the colonel was a towering man, two or three inches over six feet, with broad shoulders and a big chest. His large, round face, covered with a graying beard, gave no hint of humor. His only eye frequently shifted.

"I hear you're also a preacher," Ambrose said.

The colonel sat. "Well, the Lord's work and the work of the militia is often one and the same."

"I'll get to the point," Ambrose said, sitting. "As I'm sure you've heard, we're having some trouble with the local Indians. Obviously, we have financial and time constraints on our progress. We need to finish the rail by the end of next summer. My concern is that our problems will only get worse. As the rail gets longer, it's harder to protect."

The colonel leaned back. "To solve your problem, you have to run the Indians out of your area. Running them off from your railroad does no good. They only retreat to a camp hidden off somewhere. You've got to get them to move their camp out of the area." He folded his hands together firmly. "The Cheyenne and Arapahoe signed the Medicine Lodge Treaty. They are all supposed to be living south of the Arkansas River. The Indians up here kill and steal because they like it, though they say they're fighting for their way of life. It shouldn't take much to send them south, but if you don't show them that you mean business, they'll hang around here killing and looting forever."

"You mean take the fight to them?" Ambrose said, "And you'd be interested in helping us with the militia?"

"Yes, siree." The colonel's eye brightened. "It's our obligation and duty. Make no mistake, they are warriors. All this talk you hear in the eastern newspapers about conciliatory and humane treatment of the Indians is overromantic. We've tried it. We're having worse problems now than we've ever had. They only understand the sword, and they'll take your scalp if you let 'em."

Marshall found no religion in the colonel's voice. He knew little of the local politics, but something about this man seemed misleading. A month earlier, he had checked around. Colonel Bates had a record as an Indian fighter. Over the last few years, he had successfully hunted down several small bands that had attacked local settlers. He had also inquired into his war record but found nothing.

Ambrose said, "If you were to give us some aid, what would it entail?"

"I would probably muster a company of cavalry, sixty to seventy, and take the field in pursuit of the hostiles. Your problems are Gray Man's tribe and some of his bucks. I'd take the fight to them, near one of their villages. A good whipping, and they'd likely go somewhere else. There may not be any fighting at all. Just the presence of an armed, determined column might send them into flight. If they go south to the reservation with the rest of the Cheyenne, the Office of Indian Affairs can keep track of them. You'll know if they're gone or not. A few bucks won't go, but the army or the militia will get them, eventually, just like they did Roman Nose."

Ambrose leaned back and twisted to Marshall. "What do you think? Did you have any success on the UP going after the Indians?"

"I don't know," Marshall answered. "The army gave us a little help. When we or the army did fight them, it helped move them off the railroad, but they often retaliated somewhere else. I'm guessing the latter just based on what I read in the papers."

Ambrose said to the colonel, "And what would you need from us?"

"I already have the authority to fight Indians at my discretion, but I would like to get a letter from you, on company letterhead, stating that you are requesting help subduing the Indians that are impeding your rail's progress." The colonel leaned forward, focusing his eye. "You understand, I *am* using some public resources. I should at least have something to show that I'm operating for the well-being and betterment of the people of Colorado."

"And once you got this letter," Ambrose said, "how long would it take you to commence your operations?"

"We could move out within a week," the colonel said.

"That is, if we're not busy fighting somewhere else, but I would suggest waiting on a good snow. It makes it easier if we do have to fight."

Ambrose stood.

"Whatever we can do," the colonel said. "Dinner?"

"We would love to, but we have some other pressing business this evening. I will be in touch. Thank you again for your time."

Marshall studied the colonel. He had thought they'd have to beg, coax, and maybe even pay to get the colonel's aid, but instead this man seemed ready to act. It was too easy. He felt unsure about this, but Ambrose had made it clear that he was ready to do something. Where was this going? Would it be as simple and clean as the colonel suggested? His stomach churned a tad.

"We'll keep you no longer," Ambrose said, picking up his briefcase. "I'll have to get all this approved with my employer. We'll talk this over and get back with you. Thank you for your time and assistance. I'm sure you understand." He extended a hand to the colonel and then turned for the door.

35

Inside the large tepee, the orange flames of the fire leaped and wiggled, illuminating the tanned-white walls and dark faces around the fire. The smoke moved up in a vertical column and out of the tepee through the hole in the roof. Yellow Horse listened attentively to the eleven men sitting around the fire.

The last month had been the busiest of the year as the tribes prepared for the long, cold winter. The meat from the summer harvest had been dried and stored. The ponies had fattened up. The tepees had all been patched, the new hides tanned and put to use. Through the winter, they would hunker down in place, the women tending to the four new children born during the summer.

Gray Man twisted his head, gazing at Yellow Horse and Sun Walker, then the eight other young braves. He spoke in a calm but serious tone. "We want to be friendly with the whites if it is possible, but it seems as if they want to fight us. The white men working on the iron road are pulling away from the agreement we made. They fire at us anytime we go near the iron road, and it is impossible to hunt without crossing the road."

Sun Walker spoke. "It is hard for us to believe the whites anymore. They have lied to us. White men don't want to share any of the land."

Yellow Horse leaned forward, barking loud, hostile words. "You *shouldn't* have attacked the whites working on the iron road. You have been doing nothing but raiding for many days. It is not what we agreed."

Sun Walker's big eyes flashed at Yellow Horse, smiling. "When did you become such a friend of the whites? I thought the Great Spirit had made you the next great warrior and hunter?"

Yellow Horse leaned back, almost embarrassed. He usually listened at the councils and rarely spoke, but he had been fuming for days. The tribe had become divided, the loyalty of everyone splintered in different directions. The Cheyenne's numbers diminished with every season of green grass, and with this, they needed to stick together to survive, maintain their way of life.

Gray Man continued, "I have thought about this the whole season of long days. We have had a fight with the whites, and many of Roman Nose's warriors are now raiding in this area. I fear the pony soldiers will be starting a winter offensive soon. We should move the camp south with the next clear sky. We can camp and hunt with our brothers already there on the reservation."

The warm air in the tepee shuddered with a few mumbles. Confusion filled the faces of the young men.

Sun Walker leaned forward, speaking with a loud voice. "Our brothers tell us there is no game at the reservation, and the soldiers do not supply the food and ammo they promised. We have done nothing. This war was brought to *us*." Sun Walker put a fist to his chest. "It is better to die proudly, fighting, than to hold the white man's peace flag. We could have killed many more of them if we wanted.

Yellow Wolf, Big Man, and Lean Bear made peace with the whites, and they were slaughtered at Sand Creek."

Gray Man nodded and waved a stick. "This is only until the ponies shed. Medicine Bear's people have already moved farther south."

Sun Walker leaned forward, raising two hands. "Tall Bull has many warriors with him. I would rather go fight with him. I have good medicine now. It will prevent the white man's bullets from hitting me."

"I will go with you," one of the younger braves said.

"You're too young to even have a woman," another young brave said, and the group of warriors all laughed.

Another brave nudged him with a shoulder, wearing a big smile. "I think Dirty Nose is scared of your sister. He thinks if he becomes a great warrior, she will marry him."

All the young braves chuckled again.

Crow Eater grabbed the pipe, taking two long drags. "I want to trust the white eye, but they have tricked us too many times. It's hard for me to trust the whites anymore."

"I would rather fight!" Sun Walker said.

Two more young braves announced their support of Sun Walker.

Gray Man raised a hand, putting his palm out. "Going south is the best thing to preserve the Cheyenne. It is hard to know what to do. Every man must decide for himself. There is a big snow coming, but after it passes, I will go south to Black Kettle's camp."

Tension filled the tent, the faces around him edgy. The issues of the whites often divided his people, inducing long, heated arguments, even fights. Now, they should be hunting, getting ready for the long winter. Sun Walker's first reaction was always anger, usually without thought, but Gray Man pondered things at length before taking action.

Sun Walker would go on the warpath. What would he do? He did not want to go south. He had heard the rumors of the poor conditions, the starving and sick Cheyenne in the south. But he also did not want to fight. Most of the Cheyenne's great warriors had been killed. Fighting the white soldiers meant constant movement with little time for relaxation, always pursued. He had a wife and daughter.

Yellow Horse studied the eleven men. Some would find their way to Tall Bull's camp on the eastern plains. A few would probably stay. He needed to think about it, discuss it with his wife. Why had life gotten so difficult?

36

Wesley warmed his hands over a woodstove in a café just down the street from the Denver office of the Southwest Pacific. He still had fifteen minutes before his meeting with Boss Smith and Silas Jones.

He retrieved his change from the waitress and stepped outside. As the cold air collided with his cheeks, he turned toward the railroad office, where an ugly sight appeared in front of him. Parson Simpson.

Parson had a tall, slender frame, long black locks, and emotionless green eyes. He moved with a confident, fluid step. He was dressed in neat brown slacks and a white cotton shirt, and two polished pistols hung from his waist.

Wesley stiffened up as Parson paused to grab the café's door. "What brings you this way?" A half-dozen people strolled over the wooden sidewalk going about their daily business.

Parson said, "Got a meeting with some of our common acquaintances. I hear they're in urgent need of some men that can get things done."

Parson's meeting was likely after his. He extrapolated a

negative connotation from this. "Is that so?" He stepped closer to Parson. "Let me tell you something, you little polished-up outlaw." He put a finger to Parson's chest. "I don't care if you think your shit don't stink somewhere else, but here in northern Colorado, I'm the man you have to deal with if you want to get things done."

Parson produced a sardonic grin. "Apparently, your opinion of yourself exceeds the public's perception."

"You better remember that." Wesley grunted and stormed off down the sidewalk.

His temper still stirred, five minutes later Wesley strolled into Silas Jones's office. Boss and Silas were looking over a ledger.

"Mr. Loomis," Silas said.

"You wanted to see me?"

"Yep," Boss snapped. "I'll get to the point. We want to know what's going on with the Colorado Northern."

"Not much," Wesley replied, "they've only built a few miles of track in a month and a half. I still have spies on the payroll. They're about to complete their first bridge in the canyon, and I aim to blow it up in a few weeks. A big, tall bastard with certain parts shipped in from Chicago."

Silas lifted his eyebrows. A few seconds of silence passed.

"Why haven't you already blown it up?" Boss asked.

Wesley chuckled. "I could have, but why? Why not wait and let them finish it before I blow it up? The sooner I blow it up, the sooner they'll start rebuilding it. When it's finished, I'll blow it up. It's a simple task that I've already planned out. They can't move supplies up the canyon until they finish it."

Silas waved at Boss. "What's this I hear about Colonel Bates agreeing to fight their Indians?"

"That's what I hear." Boss grunted, popping two of his knuckles.

"Can't the governor do something about this?" Silas slapped the desk. "Haven't we bought him? Isn't he supposed to be in our pocket?"

"Yeah, we've bought him off," Boss answered, "and he's in our pocket. But he's got lofty political aspirations. He wants to be a senator when Colorado joins the Union. Killing Indians is popular. That crazy colonel of his will hunt down Indians for anybody, and the governor's not too apt to get in his way. Makes for good press."

Silas groaned. "I'm tired of paying for things I'm not getting!" He slammed his fists on the table, his knuckles turning white, then narrowed his gaze on Boss.

"Parson's getting his crew together," Boss said. "When I told him how much money we had budgeted for this job, you should have seen his eyes light up. I've already discussed terms with him, and he's agreeable. He's got ten men coming in and hopefully another twenty a few weeks later."

Wesley studied the scheming men. Was this some type of game? "There's no need for that. I have this under control. The Colorado Northern will be bankrupt before they lay another ten miles of track."

"*Wesley*," Boss said, slamming his fists down on the table, "they've only got twenty more miles to lay before they'll be operating a lucrative line . . . and getting their full government payments and grants."

"They'll never finish," Wesley said, his face growing red.

Boss squared his body to Wesley, muscles bulging.

The two men silently eyed each other for a few seconds.

Silas slapped the table with the palm of his hand. "Enough of this bickering. I've got a backup plan, a good one. A man in my position considers all options." He unfolded a map and pushed it across the table. "We've surveyed our line going north. We plan to start laying track from Denver next year. We've also got a side line planned up to Jeremiah in this canyon just south of the one the Colorado Northern is working in. If you'll notice, about halfway up the slope, the only way to get to Jeremiah is to cut over and use their route for the final access. We'll have to move some rock, but it's doable."

Silas slid his finger over the map, before tapping it. "Here at this point, above the deep canyons, we plan to intersect with Matson's line, then follow this gentle ridge up to Jeremiah. The Colorado Northern, even under the best circumstances, won't be working up here until late winter. Our lawyers have already filed this right-of-way plat with the Territorial Land Office, including the northern portion." Silas grinned. "When Parson gets here, I want his men to take and hold this right-of-way, by force if necessary. As far as I'm concerned it's ours, and I want it. Possession is nine-tenths of the law. We'll see if Matson has the stomach to take it from us."

Wesley put a hand to his forehead. The plan had credence, especially if the local courts got involved, all favorable to the Southwest, but he still didn't like the railroad hiring somebody else to do its bidding.

Silas reached into a drawer and pulled out an envelope that he handed to Wesley. "This plan in no way impedes you from doing what you think is necessary. We'll cross this bridge when we get to it. In fact, it should motivate you to do something useful for us before somebody else gets your money. There's a thousand dollars in here, federal scrip. You get the rest when events transpire in accordance with our agreement. If not, Parson Simpson and his boys will get it." Silas's face got stiff. "I want that rail stopped, whatever it takes. I've now paid you six thousand dollars. I don't give a shit how many bridges you blow or how many men we have fighting for us. Benedict Matson must be stopped. I don't care what it costs."

Wesley gritted his teeth and stood. He snatched the envelope off Silas's desk. "I've got work to do. I wouldn't spend too much effort analyzing that map. It's likely useless." He turned and strode out of the office.

A cool, damp wind rushed over the little valley and the Cheyenne camp. The white clouds moved toward the rising sun, blotting out the midafternoon sky. Behind the camp, five women gathered the day's allotment of wood.

Several of the remaining groups of Cheyenne had just finished setting up their hasty winter camp here, chosen carefully in a small valley and adjacent to a stream and tall stand of timber. The valley shielded the camp from the hostile winter winds, and the stream and forest provided reliable water and fuel.

Sun Walker and four young braves had left the camp five days earlier, heading into the plains to find Tall Bear or the other Cheyenne warriors still raiding the white man's settlements and outposts. Over the last several moons, Yellow Horse had heard the stories of the brave warriors' heroic deeds fighting the pony soldiers from Cheyenne or Arapahoe hunters who had passed through their camp.

The season of snows reduced the Cheyenne to nothing more than camp dwellers, rarely leaving their tepees for long stretches as they were forced to hide from the incessant storms and bitter cold. They only emerged from their shelters during the few breaks in the weather to hunt elk or deer.

An attractive young Cheyenne girl, sixteen winters old, walked by Yellow Horse. She paused and passed a greeting with a big, flirtatious smile. Returning the smile, he saw his wife walking in his direction, a frown on her face.

Yellow Horse picked up his lance, pretending to not notice the pretty young squaw. Cheyenne women were notoriously jealous, especially when several were married to the same hunter. Their bickering and fighting mimicked that of the Cheyenne men, sometimes even resulting in fights or wounds.

"I saw that," Bird Woman said, slapping her hands to remove some mud. "She may be beautiful, but she has the evil spirit in her. And I'm sure she can't take care of you like me."

"What are you talking about?"

Bird Woman balled up her fist, pushed it inside Yellow Horse's coat, and gently tapped against his ribs. "You know what I'm talking about . . . I got a big basket of berries. Always Smiles loves them. She will eat so many tonight, her stomach will get big, and she will fall asleep early. Good for you and me. We can be alone together."

"I would like that, but we have another council tonight. It may be late when I get done."

Bird Woman removed her hand from Yellow Horse's jacket. She placed it on her chin. "When is Gray Man leaving?"

"After this next snow. It is a long ride to the place the whites call Oklahoma. It takes more than half a moon on fresh ponies, and the trip may be dangerous. Big Face says the snows there come much less often."

Bird Woman rolled her eyes and grabbed Yellow Horse's hand. "And what about us? Are we going with him? I think this is a nice place for the winter."

Yellow Horse scratched his cheek. "It is a long trip, but you have the spirit it takes. I think we will go. I think it is much safer for us, and Always Smiles will have more friends there." He paused and smiled. "You may like it. The whites provide rations so you won't have to spend your days skinning buffalo . . . we will talk tonight after the council."

37

From the rear porch of the Pullman car, Marshall sipped hot coffee. The morning was cold, the temperature in the low teens but rising with the meager sunshine hidden behind the white clouds. An easterly wind howled over the plains signaling an oncoming storm that would, in a day or two, blanket the land with fresh snow and send the temperatures below zero. For two weeks the weather had been moderate, and the work crews had laid most of the rail up to the first cut and bridge in the canyon. The progress had been slow but steady, but now the Colorado Northern had again ceased all work in preparation for the oncoming tempest.

Outside, sixty horse-soldiers, mounted, stood in a line. The volunteers, clad in blue coats and matching Stetson hats, sat patiently, smoking and quietly conversing. Two six-pound cannons were hitched to horse teams. He blew on his coffee. These were mostly volunteers, not the professional soldiers he had served with during the war. He wondered about their makeup. He had served with volunteers before. Typically, they tended to be less disciplined and skilled than the career ranks.

Since their meeting with the colonel two weeks earlier,

Marshall had figured Ambrose would ask for the militia's help. Ambrose was a man of action, someone who succeeded or failed by his own hand and someone who never failed without exploring every option. If the Indians planned to harass the railroad, they would, in the end, have to defeat Ambrose himself. A week earlier, Ambrose had telegraphed Colonel Bates asking for help.

He and Ambrose would accompany the column into the field. What lay ahead? The excursion would face the brutal weather. Would there be a deadly fight with the Indians? He walked back into the car where Ambrose sat at a desk talking with Colonel Bates. Ambrose handed the colonel the letter that he had requested.

The colonel briefly read the letter, then blew on the ink, folded it, and put it in his pocket.

"Mr. Brewster and I will accompany you," Ambrose said. "What are your plans?"

"My Pawnee scouts know where the hostiles are camped. It's a day's ride. Maybe we can get to the camp before the weather sets in. If not, we'll have to bivouac, ride out the storm, and then continue until we find them."

The back door in the office opened, and Bridget walked in holding a leather satchel.

"I believe you've met my daughter," Ambrose said.

"Good morning, Colonel Bates," Bridget said, handing Marshall a satchel. "I made you men some biscuits for your trip."

Colonel Bates pulled on his gloves and turned his single eye to Bridget. "I declare, Ms. Graham, I believe you are the best-looking woman I've seen in these parts."

Bridget hugged Marshall, kissing him lightly on the cheek before turning to her father. "You two do be careful out there."

"No need to worry," Colonel Bates said in a loud,

confident voice. He patted his chest boastfully. "We aim to do right. The militia has been trained to fight Indians. We have an exemplary record. I'm hoping we're home in a few days and you folks can get back to building your railroad."

Marshall picked up a stick from the fire, using its orange tip to read his watch. Thirty minutes before sunrise, the morning was cold and calm. To the east, the first pink streak of daylight stretched across the horizon. His hands and feet felt the nip, but inside the huge buffalo coat, his core felt cozy. Around him, the soldiers packed up their hasty camp.

The day before, the column had ridden for six hours through the rolling foothills at the base of the Front Range. The column of horses had weaved its way through the patchwork of low, moderately sloped hills and open grassy meadows filled with gullies and tiny streams. The colors were a checkerboard of browns and yellows, the broken terrain unlike anything in the rail's path. The sky hung big overhead, but many times the terrain restricted visibility to a few hundred paces.

The ride had been uneasy and tense. He constantly wondered if they might stumble onto the menacing Indians, the Cheyenne silently sailing into the column. They had made camp around three, and the colonel had given orders for every man to get some rest. The column would likely move out early the next morning.

Marshall rolled up his blanket and tied it to his horse as Ambrose walked up.

"What's up?" Marshall said. "Looks like the camp is packing up to move out."

"The Pawnee scouts have found the Cheyenne village," Ambrose said, reaching over to grab his bedroll. "It's about two hours away." He nodded to some men gathered around a fire. "The colonel is having a meeting with his officers now. We're leaving as soon as we can. He plans to ride there in force. Says a solid show of force, especially a professional one, might forestall conflict and convince the Cheyenne to go south. Says it's better to arrive at daylight. That way the tribe may not know we're coming."

Marshall's heart leaped to his throat. During his years in the army, he had grown accustomed to the long stretches between engagements and activities. The tension usually mounted for days and weeks. The suddenness of this surprised him. He walked over to the fire where four men were gathered around the colonel as he felt a few tiny balls of sleet fall on his hat, gently pattering against the stiff felt.

The glow of the campfire illuminated the white fog pouring from the colonel's mouth as he passed out instructions, his voice more forceful than eloquent and his face filled with determined intent. His men, all armed with Spencer repeating rifles, busily put grain into their horse's feed bags while others packed their gear. To the west, a row of torches moved in the distance, a column of cavalry already moving out.

Marshall stepped forward beside the four officers and out of the darkness. The colonel flashed his good eye at him as he continued. Around the fire and near the officers, Marshall thought he whiffed the strong scent of whiskey. "Lieutenant Thomas," the colonel said with parting words, "you will be the rear guard. That's it. We depart in fifteen minutes. Keep your eyes and ears peeled."

As the men did a quick about-face, Colonel Bates turned to Marshall. "I've already told Ambrose, but you and him are only observers. You do nothing but observe unless your life's in danger." The colonel waggled a finger. "Is that clear?"

Marshall nodded.

"Get mounted," Colonel Bates said in a stern voice. "My advance party is already on the way."

Marshall spent the next two hours in a miserable daze, riding through the darkness and early sunrise, winding through a large complex of deep, washed-out draws and low hills. The sleet fell, covering the men and animals with a glassy finish. The weather reduced visibility, and riding near the back of the column, he generally only saw the rear of the two or three horses in front of him.

Finally, they topped a small ridge. The sleet had stopped, and the sky had cleared a little. Six horses stood alone on the next ridge, a few hundred paces ahead. In the valley between the two hills, the officers formed their men into a long line. The men's sober, serious mood told Marshall danger lurked nearby.

"They're forming up," Ambrose said, pulling up beside Marshall. He pointed up on the hill ahead to an area off to the side. "Let's ride up there, out of the way, where we can see something." Ambrose spurred his horse and rode forward.

Marshall followed. Seen from the hilltop, the Indian village, about twenty tepees, sat along a creek beside a stand of big timber. Dawn had broken hard and cold, and the glare from the clouds lit the tops of several hills in the distance. In the village, among the long shadows from the hills, the fires glowed in the lodges. Did any of the Cheyenne or Arapahoe he had met at the council live here? Marshall's blood pumped faster. Anxiety, trepidation, and anticipation besieged him.

Six cavalrymen exposed themselves on the hill. One

was Colonel Bates. Another spit out a plug of chew, wheeled his horse around, and slowly led the five horses down the hill toward the village.

The scene stood deathly quiet. Behind the hill, the other sixty or so horses, standing in a line with their heads facing the hilltop, inched forward, stopping just before the hill's apex to remain concealed.

The air escaped Marshall's lungs. Men and beasts sat poised, all the energy of the cavalry company focused on the placid village. Two figures, men bundled in buffalo robes, walked cautiously from the village toward the approaching soldiers. One raised a hand. The seconds passed slowly, time stretching. Behind the ridge, the line of horses moved up the hill a few more steps, exposing their upper bodies. What were they doing and why?

Two quick shots sounded, only muffled pops from somewhere. Then, all was confusion. The long line of horses stepped forward to the top of the hill. Down below, more shots rang out. Dogs barked. Women screamed. Men, women, and kids emerged from the lodges. A bugle filled the air.

"For Colorado, boys!" Colonel Bates screamed, his voice cracking as he rode forward, arms held high and wide.

The soldiers' screams and the thud of the hooves woke the morning as the powerful steeds plunged down toward the village.

Astonished, Marshall watched, not sure of what was occurring. Ambrose pulled his pistol from his hip and trotted forward in the wake of the soldiers to a location closer to the village.

Marshall followed, also securing his Colt. From the new vantage point atop a small knoll and only a hundred paces from the village, he watched the carnage unfold. Instead of a battle, it was a life-and-death struggle. The soldiers rampaged through the village, shooting anything that moved. Four men and two women fell to the ground, their chests covered with blood. The officers barked orders. The troops recklessly fired away.

Marshall slowly rode forward into the mayhem as the men, women, and children of the village scattered, scurrying everywhere. Voices screamed. Guns erupted. Horses raced in all directions.

"I got something for you!" a soldier yelled, chasing a mother and daughter.

A grunt sounded. A cavalryman, an arrow in his forehead, fell from his horse. Two more soldiers fired indiscriminately into several of the lodges. Two Indians tried to surrender, as four more ran for the creek.

A pregnant young squaw ran by Marshall for the cover of the stream. He spurred his horse toward her, internally rooting for her safety, but she dove into the brush on the creek's bank before he arrived.

His temper rising, not believing his eyes and ears, he swung back around and checked his mount. In the village, an elderly woman screamed and clawed at one of the soldiers.

"Kill all their horses!" a sergeant yelled as a barrage of gunfire filled the air from a line of soldiers firing at the large herd of horses hemmed up behind the village.

"Burn everything!" another soldier yelled, lighting a torch. He held it high and then lit three more torches.

A tepee beside Marshall erupted into flames, the heat pulsing on his bare cheeks.

Marshall let out a blast of air, his vision almost going blurry. Two dozen bodies lay stretched on the ground, mostly Indians, but also a few blue uniforms. The attack had lasted only a few minutes. The dreadful firing had ceased, but the village smoldered in death and disorder.

Marshall rode forward, looking down at two of the dead Indians. He instantly recognized one of the faces. It had been fixed in his mind for months, the young brave named Yellow Horse whom he had met at the council, his face frozen stiff with terror, his hand still clutching a young woman, probably his wife, lying motionless and bloodstained on the cold turf.

A young girl ran circles around the bodies, her youthful screams like an arrow in his heart. He jumped off his horse, attempting to cradle the child, but she broke free of his embrace and ran away.

Despair filled Marshall's gut. The sky flickered twice, eerily, and then thunder rumbled in the distance.

"Let's get some souvenirs!" a soldier yelled.

Marshall fell to his knees as he watched a pair of soldiers joyfully chop several ears and scalps. Who were the uncivilized beasts?

"Captain Johnson!" Colonel Bates yelled loudly, trotting into the center of the village. "Put some order into your men or I will. Get your men in line, back up on the hill, and form up, now. That's an order." He wheeled his horse around to Marshall. "Let's go, Mr. Brewster. We're done. There might be other hostiles in the area."

"This was just murder!" Marshall yelled, twisting around and looking for Ambrose. Not finding him, he turned back to the colonel. "Nothing more or less. Look at the women and children you killed."

"These women and children fight," the colonel said calmly. "I'm no different than you, I do my master's bidding, whatever it is. Let's go, now."

* * *

On his back, under a blanket, Marshall stared endlessly at the small tent's canvas roof, lit by a gas lantern and thumping and clattering against the cold gust outside.

He closed his eyes, trying to fall asleep, to free his mind that still raced in disbelief. Had the day been just a nightmare?

A frigid jet of air rushed into the tent. Marshall, his body numb and almost drained of life, turned to see Ambrose crawling inside.

Ambrose sat and bent over to remove his boots. "Colonel says his pickets have seen nothing. He doesn't think the Cheyenne are pursuing. Says we'll likely be back at the railhead tomorrow before sunset if we strike out early."

Marshall rolled over on his back. "I still can't believe what I saw today. During the war, I saw plenty of death. I think more than a thousand killed at Antietam. But I've never seen women and children killed in cold blood like that."

"Well," Ambrose said in a somber voice, "nothing we can do about it. It's not the railroad's business or our place to worry over the doings of those tasked with the country's dirty work."

Marshall closed his eyes. Ambrose's ambivalent tone shocked and angered him.

Ambrose leaned over and blew out the lantern, then stretched out on the blanket. "Hundreds of thousands of innocent men died in the war, basically just in a squabble over what could be done on the land. Sometimes, people have to die for progress. That's just the way it is. We can't change that. Those Indians didn't have much of a future with or without our railroad. Maybe we've ridded ourselves of one of our problems. This was likely inevitable, with or without us."

"I know you don't believe that. This is not a win-at-all-cost war. Maybe you're a different man than I thought you were."

"All I know is I'm paid to solve the railroad's problems. You're just an engineer, so don't go getting all worked up about this. You just build the railroad, let me worry about all this."

38

Marshall rubbed both his temples with a hand as he stood in the center of the railroad. Under the clear, cloudless sky, five hundred feet of newly constructed track in the canyon hung over the new grade, mangled and under a ten-foot wedge of snow and ice. Was there ever an end to his problems?

"When did the slide happen?" Marshall asked Patty.

"Sometime early this morning," Patty answered.

"We solve one problem and another pops up?" Marshall exhaled. In the three weeks since the terrible attack on the Cheyenne village, he had retreated from the railroad's daily business, spending all his time in the canyon constructing the bridge. The work had been his only solace from the haunting images of the slaughter, providing him with a needed escape.

He had avoided Ambrose since the incident, only seeing him twice when forced to go to the railroad's headquarters on urgent business. Further adding a wedge between the two, adding to his daily tension, his relationship with Bridget had frayed. To Marshall's discontent, she had sided with Ambrose after the attack on the Cheyenne village, and twice in recent weeks, they had raised angry voices at each other.

"Patty," Marshall said, "let's get everybody from the bridge crew down here. Start clearing this snow and relay this track."

Patty nodded down the track.

Marshall turned.

Ambrose rode up, raising a hand.

"I'm stopping all work," Marshall said, "until we get this track rebuilt. And we're not going to run any more trains up here at night until after the spring snowmelt. It's too dangerous."

"You think it's too dangerous," Ambrose said, "Maybe I don't. We don't have but ten hours of daylight this time of year."

"*I'm* the chief engineer. And *I* think it's prudent to ensure the work goes on at a steady pace."

Patty said, "Will you two gentlemen excuse me? I need to get the men started down this way." He stepped off quickly.

Marshall's temper rose. He'd been furious for a week. He walked to Ambrose. "I saw the receipt for that ad you placed in those eastern papers for an experienced rail engineer."

"The Colorado Northern needs as many capable engineers as we can get."

Marshall pointed a finger at Ambrose. "You can't fire me. It's in my contract."

"That's something the lawyers will have to decide if it's deemed necessary. Especially if you're not undertaking your duties in good faith and in accordance with the railroad's best interest."

Marshall stomped off. "I've got work to do."

* * *

Marshall oozed with pride and satisfaction. The wonderful bridge, a one-hundred-foot truss spanning the Jeremiah River, rested on a pair of vertical granite buttresses, two walls, falling away more than seventy feet to the rolling river below. The day was cold and overcast, and the modern engineering wonder stood out in the natural cathedral, a testament to man's dominating nature. The structure allowed the railroad to cross the canyon onto more favorable ground for its march forward.

He studied the bright, new wood girders and beams of the trestle. He admired his design as he visualized the train crossing, the beams bending and flexing. The tremendous weight would be distributed along the diagonal beams, balancing the tension and compression, as it transferred the load to the bridge's abutments just as he had calculated. Trepidation stirred in his gut, tempering his bliss. Would the bridge be adequate?

He walked back down the railroad toward the small entourage that had turned out for the bridge's opening. Ambrose and Bridget stood among the onlookers, two dozen bridge builders and two large snowmen erected for the event. Beside the onlookers, on the newly constructed railroad, sat the two twenty-ton steam locomotives.

"This is your New Year's present," Marshall said as Ambrose approached.

Bridget, bundled in a fur coat, smiled.

Ambrose produced a rare smile. "You're two weeks late."

"It's taken all our energy," Marshall said. "Now, track can be graded and laid eight miles into the canyon, all the way up to the next three tunnels and three bridges through those tight granite outcroppings. We tested it yesterday with one engine, but both engines will test it to forty tons."

"Let's hope so," Ambrose answered.

Marshall grabbed the ladder on the rear engine and climbed aboard, motioning to the engineer. "Might as well get on with it."

The engineer twisted a few valves. As the pressure in the boiler increased, the engine crept forward onto the ledge carved out of the mountain. Soon, the ground fell away over the steep ledge, only a foot wider than the track.

Marshall's stomach turned queasy. Walking the ledge had been so frightening that the horses that brought the bridge's material to the site had to be blindfolded and led over the exposed area. The wheels clattered as the engine eked through a curve. The lead engine crept onto the bridge, stopping just past the midpoint, loudly releasing steam. The shiny timbers creaked. Marshall motioned for the engineer to go forward. Holding his breath, he tensed up. The timbers squeaked as the engines slowly rolled on.

Watching to make sure both engines rolled onto the truss, Marshall gestured for the engineer to stop the locomotive, and he stepped down onto the bridge. Grabbing the beams, he walked forward to the space between the engines. Under his feet, he felt the vibrations and shaking from the huge steam boilers. He pulled a piece of paper from his pocket and made a few measurements, checking the trestle's deformation. He compared the measurements to his calculations, inspected a few couplings, and then climbed up on the engine, waving both locomotives back off the bridge.

On solid ground, he stepped off the engine onto the track. Ambrose, Bridget, and the bridge-building crew had all walked up the ledge to watch the crossing.

"Everything looks fine," Marshall said, smiling. "Deformation is almost exactly what I calculated. The bridge can probably hold sixty tons."

Bridget clapped. "Hurrah for the Colorado Northern."

"Just three more to go," Ambrose said, walking back down the track to the covered passenger car he had ridden up to the bridge site. "Barometer is falling sharply. Likely be nasty tonight. Let's get everything battened down this afternoon to ride out the storm."

Marshall followed him. "I figure we can lay the track up to the tunnels and bridges in thirty-five working days. If the weather holds, might be there by mid-February. I'm hoping to have the bridges and tunnels up there completed by the end of March, depending on how long it takes to get the track there, April at the latest. There's only about ten miles of rail to build once we get through Miners' Gap."

Ambrose climbed up on the passenger car, pausing to wait on Marshall and Bridget. "We're already running three trains a day on our existing line to the Pacific Railroad. UP is letting us run those trains on into Cheyenne. The three trains are almost full with freight and passengers. The line may show an operating profit next year even without finishing it to Jeremiah, and the traffic will likely triple once this line's complete. I think we're in good shape." Ambrose paused, scanning the hills. "If our enemies will leave us be."

39

Marshall threw two logs on the fire and walked to the window of his office at the rail's headquarters. His cheek rubbed on the cold glass. The wind whistled, jangling the cabin's door. Dark clouds enveloped the late afternoon sky, almost turning day to night. He returned to the bench beside his desk.

Patty knocked on the door, poking his head inside.

"Come in and close the door," Marshall said.

Patty stomped his feet and stepped inside, nodding to Bridget, who was boiling some water in the kitchen.

"I'm making some fresh coffee if you want some," Bridget said.

"No thanks," Patty said. "We've got everything battened down. This looks like it's going to be a big storm."

"It may break by midmorning tomorrow, or we may be cooped up for days," Marshall said. "Before we can get back to work."

Patty handed Marshall some mail and several newspapers. "These came today. I thought you might be interested in this. Looks like all the Cheyenne that went south of the Arkansas River didn't fare any better. General Custer slaughtered a big group of them down on the Washita River. Got Black Kettle and all his band. Sounds like something similar to what you's went through, though much bigger. He just rode into their camp and started firing away." Patty shrugged. "Depends on which of these stories you read. The eastern papers are calling it a massacre."

"Thanks, Patty. Come get me as soon as it looks like the storm is about to break."

As Patty stepped outside and closed the door, Marshall picked up the weeks-old Denver paper, reading the large headline, *Custer Defeats Cheyenne*. He read through the names of the Indians killed. Only a few were listed, and none that he recognized. What about the rest of the Indians they had met at the council. Were they alive? Had they been killed either by Colonel Bates or at the Washita? Would he ever know?

The story resembled the Colorado papers' recounting of Colonel Bates's attack on Gray Man's village. The narrative painted a picture of brave, outnumbered soldiers risking their lives in heroic deeds against ruthless savages in the cause of the country and civility.

Bridget sat down beside him. "I've hardly seen you in more than a week."

"I know." Marshall put down the newspaper and raised an arm, rotating his right shoulder. "My whole body aches. I'm bruised and battered from climbing around on that bridge all week."

Bridget inspected a large scrape on Marshall's forearm. "Has it been that bad? Are you and Father talking at all?"

"We bump into each other occasionally. Either Ambrose or Benedict, or both, denied my request that the railroad make a formal statement condemning Colonel Bates's attack."

"Have you considered that Father was right? The attack

on the Cheyenne was inevitable. It had to be done to build the railroad. Big fish eat little fish. That is the way of the world. You can't change that."

"Whose side are you on? Mine or his?" Marshall snapped, getting up. "Sometimes I think you are no different than him."

Bridget stood. "And what's wrong with that?"

Marshall grabbed both of Bridget's arms firmly. "You're my fiancée. You're supposed to be in my camp, not his."

Bridget jerked her right arm free, raised it, and forcefully slapped Marshall. "You ungrateful son of a bitch. Father made you. And you wouldn't be here about to be a self-made man if I hadn't pushed you here. Here, if you want something, you have to take it."

Marshall put both hands on Bridget's shoulders, pushing her back into the wall. He expelled two long breaths trying to calm down. "I'm sorry. I think we're both just tired. Tired of everything."

Bridget's face lost its color. She pulled herself free and strode for the door. "I really thought you were the man for me, but I don't know anymore."

The wind whipped through the canyon. The steep, rocky slopes compressed, funneled, and strengthened the bitterly cold air. At times it blew constant, but periodically gusted so strong it made standing a cumbersome chore. The moist, damp air cut to the bone, pushing the snowflakes almost horizontal.

From the narrow ledge, the flurries and forming patches of snow lightened the dark night, but impeded vision to only twenty paces.

"Goddamn, it's cold."

"Shhhhh," Wesley said, stepping behind a large boulder and squatting. He felt the frigid rock. His eyes, now acclimated to the night, followed a few of the small cracks in the granite. "Get over here, Joe."

"Can't nobody hear shit in this storm," Joe mumbled, kneeling beside Wesley. "Only a fool would be out in this weather."

Wesley hunkered lower behind the rocks and felt the constant pressure of the wind ease off his body. He took a knee and turned to look down the canyon. A hundred paces ahead sat the Colorado Northern's new truss bridge, spanning the gorge below. He stared toward the bridge, straining his eyes. There was only the storm, now lashing the canyon with its full might.

For weeks, Wesley had been monitoring the rail- and bridge-building operation, crawling to the apex of a nearby peak on two occasions to reconnoiter the bridge through his spyglass. The bridge had very limited access, and no piers, only resting on two man-made escarpments on each side of the canyon. Destroying it required getting on it via one of its two ends, and since guards patrolled the bridge day and night, his plans had required some thought. Despite Boss constantly urging him to do something, he had patiently waited for the weather to worsen, providing him with his best opportunity.

He turned back to Joe. "Bridge is straight ahead, just down this ledge." He paused and pointed. "The work camp is there, on the other side of the valley, on the other side of that big ledge we spied yesterday. Can't even see the tents' lanterns in this storm. What time is it?"

"About three. I reckon."

Wesley tightened the collar on his long buffalo coat, raking some ice off its sleeves. "This is perfect. Probably below zero, and this wind is enough to even deter Injuns. There's usually a guard, armed, on this side of the bridge. He may not even be there in this weather. If he is, I bet his ass is bundled up and not paying attention. We'll try to sneak by him. If he stirs, just shoot him. In this storm, nobody will even hear the gunshot. But if we do have to shoot him, just try to wound him, not kill him."

Wesley reached over his shoulder and removed a pack from his back. He then pulled a similar pack off Joe's back, setting the two twenty-pound bags of black powder beside each other on the ground. "These fuses are about two minutes. We will have to light them here, in this wind-break, and then haul ass down this ledge. We'll set them in the middle of the bridge and then hightail it back to here. We'll hide behind this from the blast." He lifted off his hat and tapped the back of his head against the outcropping and looked down at the ledge, stirring a few rocks with his boots. "Be careful. It's slippery. You fall off this cut, ain't no saving you. It's more than a hundred feet down there. The wolves will have you for dinner . . . after the storm."

Exhaling a long breath, Wesley stared into the eerie night, the white snow scooting over the jagged rocks. A feeling of emancipation fell over his soul as he grasped his plans coming to fruition. He had the gumption and brains for this. Few men could pull it off, and he was one of the gifted. He mumbled to himself, "Be damned if Boss Smith will sass or second-guess me again."

"What's that?" Joe said.

"Get down low." Wesley grabbed one of the packs and bent over. "And give me some fire. I'll go first with this pack and you right behind me. Now remember, don't get spooked. Just set this on the middle of the bridge. If some-thing's not right, I'll turn around. In that case, just pull out the fuse. And you better not mess around getting back here. This shit turns stone to powder." Wesley lifted one of the packs and then pointed to the little cord. "Now remember, very important, if something goes wrong, don't drop the powder bag or throw it over the ledge. If the powder blows, and we don't destroy the bridge, they'll be onto this trick, and we'll have to come up with a new plan. Got it? It just takes some thinking and wit."

Wesley reached into his coat and retrieved his revolver, placing it in his right coat pocket as the match lit. His heartbeat pattered wildly as Joe quickly lit both fuses.

"Hurry," Wesley said, turning and stepping out into the storm. He took up a quick step down the shelf as he made sure the rock face to his left never got out of sight. Seconds rushed by. He stepped forward, pausing every ten or fifteen strides to regain his bearing and scan the rock wall and burning fuse. His stomach churned. In fifty paces his feet found the rails that now extended a hundred paces past the bridge. The bright tan beams of the truss appeared out of the night. He rushed forward a few more steps. Paused. Searched for a guard. Nothing. At the edge of the bridge, he again stopped. No guard.

He stepped onto the bridge. Veins pulsing, he tiptoed another twenty paces. Don't look down. He squatted and gently placed the pack on one of the large beams. The fuse burned freely, half expired. He stood and grabbed his pistol. Gripping the handle firmly, he walked back. He searched for movement. Nothing out of place. Nearing the end of the bridge, the glowing red sparkles of Joe's pack appeared from the tempest.

Wesley pointed to his rear, nodding. He darted off the bridge another ten paces and crouched. Time slowed, his senses alert. Joe egressed the bridge.

A voice broke the calm, bellowing into the night, "Halt!"

Joe raced forward, past Wesley.

Wesley hurried back down the ledge. His vision garbled, his boots stumbled over the unsteady jagged rocks. His right hand felt his way. He located the stone face that they had sheltered behind earlier. His body tightened. He dove for cover.

Landing on his side, Wesley collided into Joe. He ducked his head and balled up. The seconds passed.

A bright flash illuminated the canyon like a bolt of lightning. The night exploded with an earsplitting boom. The ground shook as the roar lingered, echoing through the canyon. A few pieces of aggregate rained down.

"Let's go!" Joe screamed, disappearing.

Wesley slowly stood, cupping his ear with his gloved hand. He smiled as he heard the delayed crashing and tumbling as something cascaded down into the river below.

40

Ambrose's temples throbbed as he looked over the splintered remains of the bridge, only a stretch of mangled track on its eastern abutment. The snow had stopped falling, but a clean white blanket covered the work site and a raw, bone-chilling wind still swirled. Overhead, gray clouds hid the midday sun.

Ambrose took three deep breaths trying to calm his dizzying mind.

"What time did it blow?" Marshall asked.

"I think about three." Patty said, removing his hands from his pockets and pointing. "The guards said they came in from the other side."

"Anybody hurt?" Marshall asked.

"No," Patty said, crossing himself.

"What now?" Ambrose growled.

Marshall crossed his arms. "It will take at least a month to get a new truss shipped in, if we're lucky. Patty, I think this storm is breaking. Let's get some men down in the gorge. Possibly we can salvage some of the bridge and build some sort of temporary span with a center support. Might be able to build something that will last until the spring rains start. Luckily, there's an engine on the other side, so we only need to build something that will hold a flatcar and a few supplies so we can continue to grade and lay track. We'll try anyway. I'm not making any promises on when or if this can be done."

Ambrose turned an unfriendly eye to Emory. "We've failed miserably." He looked at Patty. "How about the men?"

"I think we're fine," Patty said. "For now, at least. The men ain't got anywheres to go this time of year, but you should probably talk to them. We'll need to increase security again."

Ambrose cocked his head to the towering cliffs, the vast wilderness in the distance. Who or what hid there? Where had he gone wrong? Could the Colorado Northern survive much more of this? What would he tell Matson? He gritted his teeth. "I can see now, we've made some fatal mistakes. We've only been on the defensive till now. That's one of the oldest mistakes in any conflict. We've got to go on the offensive, find and destroy whoever is behind this. I will take over that task. Marshall, I'm leaving the rail building up to you for now. If you got shot, it would be an inconvenience for the railroad. In the short term."

From the apex of a ridge, Wesley's spyglass scanned the bridge site. Snow and ice walled in the entire rail and work camp. From his vantage point, the bottom of the canyon below the railroad lay hidden behind the granite walls, but no wood or rail remained at the rail's intersection with the gorge.

He moved the glass to a man pacing up and down the track on the opposite bank. Focusing the lens, he recognized the hideous face, the surly, arrogant boss of the Colorado Northern he'd had the brush with in Fort Collins a few months earlier. As he took in Ambrose's exasperated expression and wide frown, Wesley's smile grew.

"We done good, Joe."

"I never imagined a storm like that," Joe said

"A hell without heat for those railroad boys."

"The bridge is gone." Joe shuffled backward. "Why are we still here? They may be out looking for us."

"Ain't nobody looking for us." Gratification permeated Wesley's soul. "They're still trying to get their heads out of their asses. That sorry-ass railroad boss don't look that imposing now. Looks like a whipped pup. Bet he won't sass me again."

"You reckon they'll give up and go home now?"

"Can't rightly say. I hear it took six weeks to get that big section here from Chicago and another month working here. I'd say it'll be a few months at best before they're doing anything, that's not counting the weather. Me and you's going to Cheyenne for a few days, have a good time. If they do get back to work, I'll make sure they'll regret it."

41

The engine howled, billowing thick white smoke as it crept forward pushing three flatcars. The two cars closest to the engine were empty, but the front car carried forty new rails, only a fraction of its capacity.

For ten days, Marshall had spent all his mental energy and the work crews' full effort in an attempt to breach the rail gap left open by the destroyed Jeremiah River Bridge. He had salvaged some of the wood timbers and steel pins from the canyon floor and constructed the flimsy, hasty structure that now spanned the gorge, supported by a single wood-framed pier resting on a high ledge above the canyon. To give the bridge added strength, he had lashed eight half-inch steel cables to the center of the span, and anchored them to the canyon wall fifty feet above the bridge.

Marshall studied the rows of numbers scratched on a piece of paper, trying to recheck a few things, but in reality he had little confidence in his calculations. There were too many unknowns.

"You ready?" Patty said, arriving at Marshall's field table.

Marshall exhaled. "I don't have any idea what the

bridge's capacity is. I do think I have correctly determined how much deflection the span will tolerate before it reaches a breaking point. The improvised structure will certainly not support an engine, or even a loaded flatcar, but it might support a partially loaded flatcar."

"Sir." Patty rubbed his red beard. "You been figuring for two days. Only one way to really test it. It looks sturdy to me."

"Okay," Marshall said, "my best guess is it can only take one flatcar, partially loaded. Have the engine push that first car out on the bridge. Have the brakeman be careful. Stop if something doesn't look right. If it works, we'll be able to ferry small portions of supplies by pushing one car across. The engine on the other side will then have to hook up and pull the car down the line. It will be slow, but a hell of lot faster than lugging everything up the canyon road by wagon."

Patty removed his hat and waved it to the engineer.

Marshall held his breath as the lead car edged forward.

The partially loaded car eased onto the bridge. He looked to a brakeman riding between the two empty flatcars. If Marshall gave a signal, the brakeman was to pull a pin and free the two lead cars from the engine and one remaining flatcar. If the bridge failed, this would result in only the loss of the two lead flatcars, and not the valuable engine.

Marshall's muscles tightened. He put his right eye to the transit, focusing on some marks painted on the bridge's pier. Having already calculated the allowable deflection, he studied the pier's movement. He'd done his calculations meticulously, checking them three times. But that was just theory. This was real.

The lead car moved forward. Almost all its weight now bore down on the bridge. Marshall raised a hand. The train stopped. He squinted his right eye, putting a hand over the end of the transit.

"Looks good!" he yelled. "Only four inches of deformation. We're still three inches from the elastic limit. Move her forward." He raised his left arm and motioned the engine onward.

A dozen more seconds passed. The lead car landed safely on the opposite abutment. Another brakeman ran forward and released the car. The engine then quickly backed down the track a few hundred feet.

The tense scene erupted with applause, and Marshall turned and bowed to the dozens of workers standing along both sides of the makeshift bridge.

Relaxing for the first time in weeks, Marshall sat down at the table and took in the day. It was clear and bright, but a far cry from the mountain paradise of wildflowers and cool, sweet air of the summer. The land had become a hard, almost lifeless, ice-covered world.

Two weeks had passed since the terrible storm and hellish, dreamlike night when the bridge had been destroyed. Since then, he and his men had been pushed to their limit. For the first time he wondered if this entire effort might be folly. Would all his hard work be for naught? Or worse?

The bridge's destruction had stirred his temper to something close to Ambrose's disposition. They *had* to finish the railroad. Matson had recently reminded him of the consequences of failure. He had no choice. He was backed into a corner. And there was Bridget. Was he about to lose her, too? He had to succeed, no matter what that required.

"I'll be goddamned if they blow this," Ambrose grunted, riding a tall sorrel up beside Marshall. "I will have fifteen men here, twenty-four hours a day." He pointed to a hasty shack under construction on the far side of the gorge. "I knew your sorry ass would come in handy sometime, else I never would have tolerated that bullshit with my daughter."

Marshall put a flat hand over his eyes and took notice of Ambrose's sunburned face, and sharp, focused eyes. The land and hours of exposure had hardened Ambrose. He now resembled a soldier more than a rail boss, a stark contrast to his appearance nine months earlier. But he had mastered the role before in the war.

Marshall cleared his throat. "I guess it's just our luck our enemies are dumb-asses, blowing up the bridge while we had an engine on the far side. Might take a lot of switching and scheduling, but we'll be able to move men and materials ahead by steam."

Ambrose scratched his beard. "If they had brains, they wouldn't be outlaws and bushwhackers. Probably ex-Rebs. We cleaned up a lot of the blood in the war, but maybe we should've done more. . . . Those forty snow shovels you ordered a month ago finally came in. Might help us get out from under the weather next time."

"This is not our last battle with old man winter. My feet are still cold."

A racket came from the canyon. Four hundred feet below, beside the frozen river, two teamsters waved as they trudged up the rough mountain trail at a fitfully slow pace.

Ambrose dismounted. "This is a tough land. What we once thought were requirements are only troublesome luxuries here that require more work than benefit. Men and materials are pouring into this canyon every day, bound for the mines and promise of a fortune without a master. We need to be in business. . . . Let's go up to Miners' Gap. I want to look over our operations there, make sure we don't have another debacle like we had here."

* * *

From the apex of a ten-foot rock chimney, Marshall looked over Miners' Gap, a geologic anomaly ten more miles into the canyon that the rail had to surmount. Here, the rail moved away from the river and through three jagged pieces of bedrock that poked up almost vertically from the mountains.

"How's this going to work?" Ambrose asked.

Marshall pointed. "We're tunneling through these three wedges of granite, and we're going to construct two bridges to connect the tunnels. Once out of the final tunnel, the road crosses the largest structure on the entire line, a four-hundred-foot bridge across a one-hundred-foot-deep chasm."

From his horse, he inspected the tunneling operation. Though the most time-consuming operation on the line, it was the only enterprise on the railroad not affected by the weather. The work required little material, and the tunnels gave the men cover from the frigid snow. The work also went on twenty-four hours a day, a repetitive chorus of hand drilling followed by the blasts that heaved up the ground, followed by the labor-intensive removal of the debris.

Ambrose's inquiries perplexed Marshall. Overcome by an almost ungovernable rage after the destruction of the Jeremiah Bridge ten miles down the mountain, Ambrose now had forty men guarding the railroad. He had divested himself of the details of building the railroad. He now spent all his hours with his security detail, the job of finding the bandits consuming all his time and attention.

"How's the tunneling coming?" Ambrose asked.

"About a foot a day, that foot costing more than a thousand dollars."

Ambrose nodded to one of the tunnels, only a black hole in the granite face that led to a cavern. "What about this big bridge up on the other side of this rock that gets off of this ledge?"

Marshall pointed. "That will be difficult. It will require men and materials to traverse five miles around the buttress. Why do you care? I thought you had given up daily management of the railroad to deal with security."

"How about the Jeremiah River Bridge? When will we have the new truss? And when will we have rails to here?"

"I've hired twenty more men. Depends on the weather. The new trusses won't be here for six more weeks, then probably another three weeks to install them. We need to have the new bridge in before the snowmelt, which will likely wash out that temporary pier holding up the current bridge."

"And what's our schedule up here?"

Marshall frowned. "What's today?"

"February 8th, I think."

"Well, we got lucky, staging all the timbers, steel, and mortar on this side of the river before the bridge fell. Probably only take us six weeks. The little bridges, maybe another week or so, but the tunnels won't be complete before the end of March. That will be the critical path work, and there's little we can do to speed it up. Possibly, once the big bridge is built we can blast the big tunnel from both ends, but I'll have to check with the nitroglycerin guy to see how that will affect the bridge. I plan to start hauling material for the big bridge's foundations this week. We're about halfway through the tunneling. You've got to walk around a mile and look up almost a hundred feet just to see the backside of it."

"How you going to know where we come out?"

"I've surveyed it four times . . . two times myself and two times with another survey crew, but there's no guarantee. I think about it twenty times a day. Let's just hope you've got a good engineer. Since I know I'm not perfect, I've got two feet of wiggle room in the bridge. We can miss by that much and be all right."

Ambrose shook his head. "That's pretty damn thin. I've watched those little men with odd scopes and steel tapes for years. I know their work is important, but at times like these I'm reminded how expensive their mistakes can be."

Marshall grunted. "We won't find out for ten weeks or so, will we?"

"We've got another six weeks of hard winter, and then another month of marginal weather, but we're on schedule." Ambrose walked up a steep incline.

Marshall followed him up to a point overlooking the work site and vast obstacle the rail had to scale.

"Beautiful, isn't it?" Ambrose said.

"Be prettier with a rail across it," Marshall answered with a heavy breath as he reached the peak. "We will probably start surveying the last stretch in March. Can't hardly send the surveyors out until the weather starts to break in earnest."

Marshall put his hands on his hips and admired the setting, a mile of jagged rock, and a high mesa beyond. The hard landscape, falling away in the distance, took on every shade of black, gray, and brown, all sparkling wonderfully from the sun, now halfway between the horizon and its apex.

Ambrose tossed a rock off the ledge. "The West will not be conquered or even mapped in our lifetime. It's the last great prize, its fortunes and faults still a mystery. A land of opposing promises and ideas. It will take generations to tame it, but we are at the forefront. All others will stand on our backs." He looked up at the clear sky. "If the weather holds, I want to ride over there tomorrow and scout that high flat that leads up to Jeremiah."

"There's nothing we can do there now."

"I want to look the place over, be ready when we get there." Ambrose shook his fist. "This final bridge is where they're likely to strike. I think I've found the spy in our midst."

"Really." Marshall stood on his toes. "Who? Have you run him off?"

Ambrose's face got tight. "I don't want to run him off. I want him to lead me to Loomis. I've thought this over good. No matter what I do, I can't protect this railroad. I'm going to have to hunt Loomis down. I've got a plan I will discuss with you later." Ambrose stepped toward Marshall, tapping on his chest with a forefinger. "We have to defeat our enemies. There's no shirking that task. It's us or them. There's no third option. It doesn't matter what we do if we don't lick the Southwest."

Marshall squared his shoulders to Ambrose. "I'm in for whatever it takes to hunt these outlaws down. Whether you realize it or not, there's a difference between killing bandits and women and children. And let's get another thing straight. I've reread my contract. I can only be terminated for incompetence. After I rebuilt that bridge down there, there's no way you or Benedict Matson will get my stake in this railroad. I'd fight it. And there's plenty of good men on our payroll that would attest to my competence. So, we should put our differences aside and solve this problem."

42

Gray clouds swept over the sky, the midday sun only occasionally showing itself. A light breeze spoke in the fir and aspens, but the day was pleasant, the temperature hovering in the forties.

Wesley reined up beside the small tent, set against a thirty-foot rock wall in a five-acre stand of timber. His help, a young, healthy ruffian named Joe, with long, stringy blond hair and cold blue eyes, milled around the camp, unloading a few supplies.

"Secure those anchor ropes good," Wesley said. "The wind can be fierce up here. We may be here a few weeks. We're not leaving until the Colorado Northern abandons their railroad. When that happens, you can have the rest of that gold I promised you. Come give me a hand."

Wesley handed his reins to Joe, dismounted, and walked to the packhorse he had led to camp. He untied a few knots, releasing one of the two-foot square boxes strapped to the horse's back, and the two men slowly set the box on the ground.

Opening the wood crate, Wesley lifted a piece of the box's precious cargo.

"What the hell is *that*?" Joe said with big, curious eyes.

"Nitroglycerin," Wesley said, examining the crate's contents. Thirty-six long sticks an inch in diameter. "This shit is ten times more powerful than black powder. We've got enough to blow up an entire mountain."

Joe picked up one of the sticks. He removed his faded Confederate kepi and scratched his head. "Where did you get this?"

"Ain't none of your *business*," Wesley snapped. "I'm a man of resources. I've got contacts. This work just requires a little smarts. Now help me get these two boxes in the tent. We need to keep this dry, and then we're going to ride over to that high pass we came in on the day before yesterday. I saw some men over there milling around on the high side of that new big bridge. I want to see who it is."

An hour later, Wesley leaned forward on his pommel as he studied four men in the distance. He lowered his glasses and inspected the high, gentle plateau, covered with sparse brush and boulders.

He had been amazed at how fast the Colorado Northern had gotten back to work after the destruction of the Jeremiah River Bridge. In fact, it had stirred his constitution so much he had now moved into the mountains. He had to stop the rail *now*. This was likely his last chance. Almost begrudgingly, he had come to grips with the fact that either the rail would be stopped, or he wouldn't come out of the mountains.

"What the hell are they doing?" Joe said.

Wesley groaned. "Looks like they're building a little cabin."

"Is the railroad about to start work up here?"

"It's some unwelcome and unneeded guests, trying to get a cut of our stake in this job. Let's ride over and make our acquaintance." Wesley slapped his reins, picking up a quick canter. As he approached the group, the sorry lot overseeing the work turned to face him.

Wesley rode forward slowly, his horse taking one step at a time. "What you boys doing way up here in the high country?"

Parson Simpson stepped forward. "I believe you're familiar with the interest I represent. In fact, I was told to find you and you'd show us around. We'd like to get a look at the rail."

Wesley fired a smoke, inhaling a long drag. He casually looked over Parson's emotionless eyes, rangy, slender body, and big shoulders. Two glossy Navy Colts hung from his waist. He turned to the three other men erecting the little cabin. "What's the construction for?"

"We may be here a few months or more. We're occupying the Southwest Pacific Railroad's legal right-of-way until they get here. Going to keep the Colorado Northern from stealing it. We've got nothing to hide. Boss Smith told me to make a point not to conceal ourselves and go out of our way to let anybody who strays into this area know who we work for."

Wesley took another long drag, then stared at the smoke's orange tip a few seconds before flicking it to the ground with his middle finger. "You're wasting your fucking time. The Colorado Northern will abandon this canyon long before they ever get here."

Parson smiled, thin lips stretching to his ears. "It appears any work you've been doing for your current employer isn't yielding acceptable results. The problem with you, just like most old wore-out lawmen, is you don't put fear in anybody—not any fear that will matter anyway."

Wesley growled and wheeled his horse.

Parson stepped forward, tipping his hat. "Boss Smith also told me you'd show us around. Believe me and Tex will go see that railroad now, while the weather's good."

"I'm a busy man," Wesley said. "It's almost a two-hour ride."

Parson tightened the chin string on his hat. "I don't give a damn how busy you are. I'm giving you instructions from Boss."

The shiny bronze timbers of Colorado Northern's new bridge crisscrossed each other like a web, climbing from the rocky earth up the vertical wall a hundred feet. Through a spyglass, Wesley inspected the dozen men working near the top of the bridge, banging away with mallets and drilling holes. He had made weekly inspections of the progress on the sturdy structure for more than a month.

Demolishing this bridge would be much more difficult than the lower truss. Almost four hundred feet long, the bridge had eight foundation piers supporting the maze of wood. Destroying a single support column, or even two, might not bring the structure tumbling down. He studied the substantial brick foundations. Would the new explosives undermine these? He moved the lens up, where the wood timbers anchored into the stone, pondering the height of the brick foundations. He needed to know this.

"How many men are in that work camp?" Parson said.

Wesley turned to Parson and another man, a short stocky fellow with ammunition belts crossing over his chest. Both lay beside him, looking through their glasses at the Colorado Northern's bridge from the hilltop.

"And how many workers and guards do they have total?"

Wesley moved his glass to the dozen tents off to his left. "Probably forty at this camp, maybe a hundred and twenty-five total. Come spring, they'll have as many as five hundred on the payroll."

"And guards?" Parson didn't look up from his inspection.

"Twenty to thirty," Wesley said.

"What'a you think, Tex?" Parson said.

"Honest to God," Tex said, "that is the best-looking woman I've seen in these parts. I'd like to pick that flower."

Wesley moved the lens over the camp until he found the woman, who was tall and wearing sunglasses. A long coat covered her lower body, but her long blond hair flowed abundantly from under a big-brimmed hat. She walked along with Ambrose Graham, inspecting some of the work.

"She does look like a spicy bitch," Parson said. "Might be a nice prize once we take over the rail work."

Wesley put his glasses on the woman. Certainly not camp help. Was this the woman he had run into in Fort Collins back in the summer? He frowned at Parson and Tex. His employer would likely frown on any indiscretions against a society woman. "You boys need to stick to what you've been hired to do," he grumbled and nodded back in the direction they'd come. "The people you work for ain't too pleased when you get off into other business. Until the railroad gets over there, which is unlikely, I'm in charge of the railroad's interest, and that's the way I aim to keep it."

Parson lowered his glasses. "My instructions are clear. That rail right-of-way behind us belongs to the Southwest Pacific, and I'm to protect it, whatever it takes. If you've got some problems with that, you need to take them up with Boss Smith." He turned to the man beside him. "Tex, let's me and you get back to camp before dark."

Parson and Tex slid backward, shuffling off down the hill and out of sight.

His forehead growing hot, Wesley watched as they disappeared. He spied the sky. "Joe, be ready, me and you's going back to work. Soon."

43

Marshall gazed into the fire and sniffed the pure air. Patches of snow spotted the hills surrounding the work camp. Thirty minutes shy of dusk, the temperature had already fallen into the twenties. Around him, the merry talk and laughter of the camp filled the air.

Patty approached.

Marshall motioned to a chair. "The men have made good progress for the last two weeks."

"Only two days of weather," Patty said. "The track-laying crews are within a mile of Miners' Gap."

Marshall's body ached, and the mud and ice covering his boots kept his feet perpetually cold and wet. But he beamed with pride, excitement, and anticipation. They might finish by midsummer. In a few days, he planned to return to the base of the canyon to take care of some logistical business. He'd get to take a break from the all-consuming demands of work and see Bridget in private for the first time in weeks.

Below, a train approached. The clacking, vibrating, and rattling of an engine battled the grade. Cinders and smoke flew out of the exhaust pipe. The engine's engineer poked his head out to study the smoke and sounds as he turned a few knobs. The violence of the engine reminded him of the immense forces cradled and tamed to push the machine forward and surmount gravity, space, and time. The engines were wonders of the industrial age.

Three brakemen patrolled the cars with a watchful eye, ready to set the cars' brakes or jump off the train in a life-saving leap. The loss of the lone engine across the temporary bridge would slow work to a snail's pace.

"Fifteen thousand dollars," Patty said, "for one of those modern coal steamers, ah."

"And a hundred pounds of fuel a mile, maybe double that in the mountains. Operating the engines on this steep incline is dangerous work, especially the descents."

"I tells ya, chief. Nuttin' much scares the men more than a runaway train on the steeper grades. I've seen it. Out of control, the engines usually meet a violent and destructive end . . . There's nuttin' left but a mangled pile of steel and flesh."

"I wish we had a second engine this side of the Jeremiah River Bridge to use as a helper engine."

"How's the work coming?" Ambrose said. He grabbed a wooden stool and sat down beside Marshall, offering him a piece of cornbread.

Patty nodded to Ambrose. "I'd better check on the men."

Marshall grabbed the cornbread and picked up his notebook. "It's going well. We're still on schedule."

"And our budget?" Ambrose asked.

"Railroad is pretty sound," Marshall said. "With the grants and bonds we should have enough money to finish. Might be close at the end, but once we get across Miners' Gap, we'll be all but done, and it will be easy to borrow money. We don't consume near as much stuff on a daily basis in the mountains . . . why do you give a damn? I thought you quit worrying about the small details. You're supposed to be taking care of the rail's security and burying our enemies."

A few awkward seconds of silence passed as a wolf howled in the distance.

"I love to listen to the wolves," Ambrose said, turning to scan the camp. "I love the silent wilderness, the twinkle of the fires, the white tents glowing. It reminds me of the war."

"This is another form of war, but the world is better off after we win it."

"This land is unscarred, in complete contrast to the East, or the maimed turf of the battlefields." Ambrose's voice got more serious and blunt. "When will the big bridge be complete?"

Marshall scratched his head. "It's all but done now, except for the rails, and we won't install them until the tunnels are complete. Be a waste of time to lug them all the way around there without steam. I need to go back through the structure and shore up a few things, add some compression members, beef up some of the critical-load joints. Take about a week, but that's about it. But there's no hurry. We're waiting on the tunnels, and that's still weeks away."

Ambrose looked up at the bright, clear sky, a few clouds blotting the stars. "There's a storm coming. Probably a big bastard. Stop all work on the bridge. Move all your men back to the track between here and the Jeremiah River Bridge. Touch up some of those trouble areas. Finish running the telegraph lines up to this camp."

"That's not a judicious use of men and materials right now."

"I don't give a shit about that. Do it." The color drained from Ambrose's face. "I'm going to meet with the guards in the morning, move five of the men guarding the big bridge back down on the line where your men will be working. I'm figuring Silas's outlaws will try to hit this new bridge during this next storm. When I tell the guards the work on the bridge is done and we're moving men back down the line, their spy will likely pass this to Loomis. I'll keep an eye on the spy this time. When he sneaks out of camp, I'll follow him. Hopefully I can kill Loomis before he ever springs his trap. I know he's out there. I've seen the reflections of glass on those far ridges several times in the last few weeks, and I've seen the fresh tracks. Somebody is keeping an eye on that bridge from a safe distance."

Ambrose removed his revolver from his hip, inspecting it with the light of the fire. He blew some dust off the chamber. "I'm the hunter now. I may need you. Distribute rifles to some of your best men, ten or so, the ones you trust and the ones that can shoot. Be ready when this storm hits. This will happen fast, and when I signal you, I want your men to move down into that tight canyon just south of the Jeremiah River Bridge. He may try to escape through there, but if I'm above the big bridge, we'll have him trapped in there, like a bear in a cave. There's nowhere to climb out of that canyon. Be nothing to do then but consummate the hunt."

A quarter-moon illuminated the rim of the canyon, and the rugged, steep slopes of the hostile, isolated land. Ambrose's healthy figure was equally impressive and silhouetted against the light of the camp. For sure, it was a blessing to have him at your shoulder during a fight, but what was he up to? For weeks, he and a few men had disappeared into the mountains for hours, if not days. Where was this going?

44

Outside the wind whined, flapping the walls of the little tent and rattling its wooden support poles in an incessant rhythm. By lantern, Ambrose lay on his cot reading over a letter he had scratched out to his wife earlier in the day.

The front flap of the tent opened, sending a gust of frosty air in as Emory strode in, bundled in a large coat.

"We get any news?" Emory said, stepping inside and removing a wool scarf from around his face.

"No, just writing my wife a letter. Reminding her that I love her and trying to encourage her not to come out here until the spring . . . what's up?"

"I think our spy just slipped out of camp. He went down to the trail leading to the river ten minutes ago and headed upstream."

Ambrose set down the letter, swung his boots to the floor, and stood. "No hurry. No need to spook him. He'll be easy enough to follow with this snow."

Emory removed a wool toboggan, running his hands through his shaggy hair. "I've got horses already saddled down by the river."

Ambrose grabbed a large coat and then looked at his

pocket watch that read ten o'clock. "Only five of us. I don't want to spook him, just find out where he's going. Get your three best men . . . how's the weather?"

"Not that bad yet. I don't think the brunt of the storm will hit until early morning. Just a few flurries, maybe twenty degrees, but it will likely dip to zero before daylight."

Outside, the beautiful campfires now all burned low, only the cherry coals glowing and pulsing. Men snored under the tents dusted with snow. The night was especially quiet at the Miners' Gap camp, all the men let off early to prep the work site for the storm. Even the periodic blasts from the tunneling that went on most nights had ceased. The men would need their rest to dig out when the sun returned.

Ambrose lifted the hood on his coat and put on his gloves as he followed Emory down a tight trail of switchbacks to the canyon floor.

Beside the frozen stream, three men stood holding the bridles of the five horses. One struck a match and lit a lantern, reducing the flame until only a small ring of light covered the earth.

Ambrose and Emory approached. One of the guards kneeled to the ground, pointing to a set of boot tracks. The guard pointed upstream. "He went toward the Miners' Gap Bridge. There's no way out of this canyon until he gets past the bridge. He only has two options when the river forks. We'll have to stop and pick up the trail again there."

Only a few flurries fell. Emory said, "He should be easy to track with fresh snow, at least until the brunt of the storm hits."

"Cut that lantern off," Ambrose said, pulling on a saddle horn, and swinging a leg over one of the horses, "and keep the talk to a minimum."

For the next forty-five minutes, Ambrose led the four horses farther into the mountains, following the rocky path on the south bank of the frozen stream. The steep canyon was dark, the bare willow stands on the stream's banks only black voids beside the trail. They stopped at the fork in the river. The tracks crossed the frozen stream and continued up the dry draw in the direction of the new rail bridge.

His eyes now fully acclimated to the night, Ambrose saw the bridge's tall maze of timber—a black monolith against the sky—a quarter-mile before they rode under it. Reining up at the bridge, he raised a hand to stop. He looked and listened, scanning his surroundings. The horses exhaled long streams of smoke. "Looks pretty quiet." He pointed to one end of the bridge. "Emory, take two men and check that side of the bridge. We'll check this end."

Ambrose dismounted, pulling his Henry rifle from the scabbard. He then led one of the men along the bridge, checking the foundations and rows of timbers above. Not seeing anything out of place, he returned to his horse.

Emory knelt, striking a match and illuminating the ground where the boot tracks continued into the mountains.

"He's headed to see somebody," Ambrose said, his stomach turning with anticipation, his hands almost shaking with a combination of satisfaction and rage. "Let's see where's he's headed. Maybe we can end our problems tonight."

"In a half-mile," Emory added, white breath escaping his mouth, "the land opens up, he will be hard to follow then."

Ambrose climbed on his horse, swinging the mare around. "Let's go. Keep your eyes and ears open."

The five rode on another thirty minutes, the terrain

opening up into a large sage flat, the brush as tall as the horses.

Ambrose wheeled his horse around. Over the field of sage, a few ridges were visible in the distance.

Emory pulled abreast of Ambrose, putting his gloved hands in the pockets of his coat. "This is hopeless." The icy mix of flurries fell more abundantly. "It's almost one, and the storm is getting worse. Wind's picking up. Our best plan is to get in this brush, take some cover till daylight. Then we can likely pick up the trail. Might catch Loomis sound asleep."

Ambrose raised his gloved hands to his mouth, blowing into them as he scanned the horizon. He strained his eyes. Was that movement on the ridgeline a few hundred paces to the north? He pressed his spurs against his mount's ribs and rode ahead a dozen paces where the sage parted. He stood in the saddle. The black silhouette of four horses moved along the ridgeline. Men sat atop two of the horses, leading the other two, laden with bags. Ambrose's breath got quick.

He pointed to the ridge as Emory and the other three men arrived. "Hell, he's going to try and blow the bridge tonight. I hadn't planned on this." Ambrose paused. Out of sorts, he held a quick council with himself. He studied the four men beside him, then the worsening weather. "This will be perfect. We'll be able to sneak up on him in this weather. Emory, you go back and get on the river, where it forks. We're going to flush him in that direction. When he comes by you, pour a lot of lead in their direction, send him on down the canyon."

Ambrose turned to another of the guards. "You ride back to the camp. Get Marshall and tell him *now*! Tell him to get his men and move down below the Jeremiah River Bridge. Go, with all haste!" Ambrose grabbed the bridle of the guard's horse, turning it back in the direction they had come and then slapped the horse's rear. "Hurry! You too, Emory—get in that river fork. Get back a piece and fire away. If they get there, they won't see anything. Make them think there's a bunch of men in there, and they'll head downstream."

Dismounting, Ambrose led his horse into the bush, kneeling and taking cover from the weather. An ungovernable fury built in him. "Let's just squat here fifteen or so minutes—let them get down there by the bridge. Then we'll sneak up there. If we get a chance to kill them, all the better. If not, just fire away, send then scurrying into the canyon. We need to spread out when we start shooting so they'll flee the other way. This is our chance. Let's not mess it up."

45

The sleet pelted the ground, a steady clatter, as the rocks beneath Marshall's feet turned white. He climbed onto the engine and found the engineer bundled up and asleep in the engineer's cabin. "We need to get this train moving. I need to get to the Jeremiah River Bridge in a hurry."

The six men Marshall had rousted from their cots ran down the slippery railroad to one of the Colorado Northern's engines, tethered to four empty flatcars a few hundred yards downhill from the Miners' Gap camp.

The engineer wiped his eyes as Marshall opened the door to the furnace. He grabbed a shovel in the cabin and began to feed coal into the furnace. The little fire, only a glowing pile of coals, produced a small flame. "Get up. I need this train moving in ten minutes."

The engineer stood, shook his head twice, and grabbed a railing at the cabin's door, leaning outside. "It's awful icy out there."

Marshall continued to shovel. "We'll go slow and easy."

"It's too icy, and it will take at least twenty minutes until the boiler gets hot enough to operate."

Marshall inspected the furnace, the flames getting a little bigger. He studied several of the engine's knobs and levers.

The engineer stepped forward, reading a few gauges.

What were his options? He looked outside at the four flatcars hitched to the engine. He took a big sigh. "We'll just cut that rear car loose, ride it down!" he yelled as he descended the engine, getting his footing and pointing to the six other men. "Everybody, get on."

The engineer poked his head out of the engine. "Be careful, and lean on the brakes. Don't go faster than fifteen miles an hour or you'll likely lose it. If that happens, don't try to stop it, just jump off."

Marshall ran to the rear of the train, pointing at the flatcar's wood planks. "Jump on." He pulled the coupling pin attaching the car to the train, and then ran to the train's rear, climbing on. Standing on the slippery floor, he slowly turned the steel braking wheel protruding up from the rear wheels.

Staring into darkness, he turned the wheel another half-turn. They eked forward a few inches. Another quarter-turn of the wheel and the flatcar crept away from the train. His stomach churned as they gained speed. Marshall tightened the wheel a quarter-turn. The squeal of metal and gnashing of steel filled his ears as they slowed a tad. He removed his gloves to better grip the wheel.

The tracks led into the darkness, the symmetrical twin lines of iron following a steep ledge. Their pace increased. The wind rushed onto his face. The falling ice tapped on the brim of his hat. The ground rolled past. He tried to gauge the speed. Behind him, the flickering lights of the camp faded into nothingness.

Moving along at what he figured to be ten to twelve miles an hour, he tightened the brake a little more. Around him, the night was bizarre, slightly illuminated by the winter mix, the deathly quiet of the land only broken by the car's clattering and squeaking, strange without the roar of the engine. The six men, all clutching their Henry rifles, stretched out on their rears to secure their places, their eyes as big as his, their guts likely churning.

Marshall tried to determine their location by the terrain. The car jerked as it made a curve, jostling his insides. Then it fell down a steeper section of track. His stomach got stiff. He tightened the brake again, exhaling a long breath as the brakes grabbed. The car lurched again, turning and clanging onto a stretch of straight rail.

They rolled over a small hump. Marshall recognized a culvert under the track. From here, the track ran straight for another mile until it made a big bend before crossing the Jeremiah River Bridge. Then it weaved through another tight curve, before straightening again.

The seconds passed tensely. The eerie, recurrent clattering of the wheels was the only sound as the car rolled through the otherworldly ice. Marshall twisted the brake more. Only a car's length ahead, the tracks merged into the night. They jerked right. He worked the wheel again as the bridge rushed into his view. He leaned on the brake with all his might. The car bumped up, over the shaky bridge, and then slammed to the left.

Marshall crouched low, securing his footing. Ahead, the rail straightened. His hands shaking, his fingers so cold he felt almost nothing, he turned and stole a glance at the bridge as it quickly disappeared into the night. He yelled over his shoulder to the men, "Up here, about a half-mile, there's a pile of rails on the right. That's where that trail goes down to the river. Help me find it."

Two or three minutes passed. The neat stack of rails

appeared out of nowhere. Working the brake, he brought the car to a sliding stop. The night turned quiet.

Marshall exhaled two long breaths. Dear God. They made it. He listened for anything amiss, but only heard the ice colliding with the ground. "The trail's just up the track, maybe fifty paces. Be careful, it's steep and probably slippery."

In less than ten minutes, Marshall and the six men found themselves on the banks of the frozen Jeremiah River. His legs weak and cramping, he studied the scene, a narrow gorge encased by steep, jagged walls maybe four hundred yards wide. The night hid the faces of his six men.

"Fan out," he said. "I don't want anybody to get through here. The outlaws will be coming from that way." He pointed upstream. "Ambrose and his men are also coming. Don't shoot anybody until you identify them. See somebody, yell out to them. If it's not one of our men, fire away. Might be thirty minutes or more than an hour before we see anyone."

Marshall found a boulder beside the river and took a seat. He put a wool glove on his left hand and then wrapped a scarf around his neck. He levered the Henry, set it in his lap, and stared into the darkness, his ears trained.

Boring, monotonous, and frightful minutes dragged by. The shadows from the trees swaying in the wind produced a myriad of movement on the canyon floor that constantly kept his attention.

For almost an hour the men waited in the cold, damp air. From the distance came the muffled sound of gunfire. "Be alert, I think I hear something!" he yelled to his men.

"I hear it too!" one yelled back.

A few more shots rang out, louder. Faint voices filtered through the canyon. He honed his senses, the noises growing closer. He crawled behind the boulder, kneeling and resting his elbows on the rock to support the rifle.

In the darkness, Ambrose was likely charging down the riverbank, devoid of caution. The voices and random shots grew louder. This was a primitive hunt, the sounds of the hounds replaced by men—the prey more cognizant of the ordeal.

A yell came from Marshall's left. A few tense seconds passed. A single shot pierced the night. Then two more. Hazy muzzle blasts permeated the trees. Up the riverbank, something moved. He blinked. A large black blob raced forward.

He fired once, purposely above the horse. "Who is that?"

A red flicker came from the horse, the lead ricocheting off the rocks around him. Marshall steadied the rifle, placing the sights on the fuzzy image charging forward. He squeezed the trigger. The lead thudded into flesh. He quickly recocked the Henry and fired again.

The horse, stumbling in his direction, plunged forward onto its front shoulders. A man fell off on the stream's bank, staggering toward the river. Marshall fired again. The silhouette spun sideways, falling to the ground. It lunged for some brush on the river's edge. Marshall crept forward, pumping two more rounds into the brush. More movement, shuffling from the brush.

More random shots rang out from upstream. He crept forward. Something slid on the frozen river. He stepped up on a small rock ledge to spy the ice. The other side of the stream abutted a vertical wall of stone.

"It's us. It's Ambrose!" a voice yelled from upstream, only forty paces away.

"I think I got one of them!" Marshall yelled back. "Come on."

Two horses appeared out of the night.

"Don't shoot," Marshall said, darting forward.

"Where?" Ambrose said.

Marshall pointed. "In the stream. Not sure if he's dead or wounded. He's on foot."

Ambrose dismounted, regripping his rifle and pointing it downstream. He stepped to the river. "You two get downstream a piece. I'll try to flush him that way."

Marshall ran down the stream bank to a small bend in the river. He motioned for the other man, still horseback, to go downstream. He stepped onto the frozen river. His feet slid from under him. He fell, his rifle butt jamming into his ribs painfully. He struggled to his feet, regaining his bearings. Upstream, a lantern flickered.

"You find him?" Marshall yelled.

No response. Marshall walked forward, his rifle against his shoulder. He scanned the stream through his sights. Ambrose appeared, holding the lantern with one hand, his rifle with the other.

Marshall sauntered forward, his footing precarious, stopping beside Ambrose, who raised the lantern. In a crevice beside the stream, a man sat, blood gushing from his right leg.

"Wesley Loomis?" Ambrose said. "You don't look that daunting and daring now. A bushwhacker and common outlaw about to meet his end."

The man's eyes roved with terror, his chin quivering. "Damn you to *hell*," Wesley snapped. "Don't give me any of your self-righteous bullshit. You're no different than me. The same aims, just fate has put us in opposing camps."

Ambrose handed Marshall the lantern and raised his rifle.

"You wouldn't shoot a defenseless man?" Wesley growled.

Ambrose's black beard was covered in ice, his hat plastered with snow above his steady eyes. A chill ran down Marshall's spine as Ambrose lifted his rifle. Marshall studied the frozen earth, his hands shaking. After everything they'd been through for the last nine months, were two strips of steel worth this?

A loud shot jolted the night. Marshall flinched. A second blast.

Ambrose lowered the rifle. "Leave him for the wolves and coyotes."

Around Marshall, the ice hung from the trees. The wind whipped, gusting and funneling through the canyon, chilling man and beast to the bone. The sun rose casting a patchwork of crimson light between the long black shadows as he followed Ambrose into the little cabin he had built two miles below the railroad's work camp.

Marshall rubbed his gloved hands together, blowing into them. Inside, two men sat at a table, their hands bound behind their backs and their feet lashed together. One had two scrapes on his face, the dried blood smeared around his left eye. Both were bundled in damp overcoats. Under their big-brimmed hats, their beards were covered with ice. Their eyes roved, nervously blinking.

"This one's the one that snuck out of camp last night," one of the guards said and pointed, white breath billowing from his mouth as he spoke. "We caught the other an hour before you got Loomis."

Ambrose struck a match, lighting two lanterns. The fluid light danced around the dark room, partially illuminating the two men. Both looked similar, middle-aged, plain bearded faces above their thick clothing.

"Give us a minute in private," Ambrose said to the guard, sitting on the table.

The guard departed, a gust slamming the door loudly against the wall as it was opened.

Ambrose lifted up a rope, one end already partially woven into a noose. He meticulously added another band to the noose's knot.

Both men looked down at their laps.

"I want to know who else Loomis has on our payroll," Ambrose said in calm, icy words.

A few seconds passed, the only sound was the wind hooting and roof rattling.

Ambrose sprang to his feet. He rapidly raised his fist and backhanded one of the men with all his might, almost knocking him out of his chair.

"I asked you a *question*," Ambrose snarled.

Marshall took a deep sigh.

The man wiggled back into his chair. "We don't know nothing. Wesley ain't tell us nothing."

Ambrose picked the rope back up. "I'm aiming to hang you sacks of shit. Dump you into the canyon. You'll be bear shit this spring. It will make me feel better about myself. . . . I'll be doing my own little part to clean up the Colorado blood before civilization arrives. But if you tell me what I want, I'll throw your stinking asses on a railroad car, and you can take your chances with the federal marshal. I've got cause either way."

Marshall studied Ambrose, his mind racing, his insides uneasy. Would Ambrose actually hang these men? Did he have cause? Had he completely fallen into a dark abyss?

Ambrose's cheeks twitched as he stared at the two men. He slid the coarse rope through his hands and stood. "I'll give you two a few minutes to think it over. Wesley Loomis is nothing but a frozen carcass. He ain't hardly worth hanging over. I'll be back in fifteen minutes. I'll do you a favor and make sure I find a good, sturdy tree."

Marshall opened the door, stepping back out into the freezing, eerie morning. The sun was now up enough to illuminate the otherworldly ice-covered landscape.

Ambrose walked out of the cabin, nodding to the guard. "Keep an eye on them, but leave them alone." He strode off to the meadow beside the cabin, turning his head up to inspect the tall trees. "We'll hang them one at a time. The second one will be more agreeable."

Marshall strode to Ambrose. "You can't hang these men."

Ambrose continued to pace off. "I thought you said you were prepared to do what it takes to rid ourselves of these criminals? You can't make up your mind, what you want to do."

"We're not judge and jury. Just send them to the marshal."

"Mr. Brewster, don't you have some things to do? This storm has broken. We may be able to get back to work by tomorrow afternoon."

Marshall stepped in front of Ambrose. He extended a flat hand, putting it on Ambrose's chest.

Ambrose looked down at the hand, his face flushed red. "I'm not going to let you do this."

Ambrose huffed. "You're too busy playing with my daughter and your bridges to get anything done."

"This is bullshit."

Ambrose jerked Marshall's hand down. "If all the dirty work required to build this railroad had been left up to you, the Colorado Northern would have been bankrupt months ago." Ambrose turned and walked back to the cabin. He tossed the rope to the guard. "Throw this over that big spruce. We'll hang them from a horse. Maybe they'll get talkative."

"You're not God!" Marshall yelled, following Ambrose back to the cabin, stopping over the threshold.

Inside, the two men sat silently, heads held high.

"You boys have anything to say?" Ambrose reached into his pocket, pulling out a toothpick. He broke it in half, balling the pieces up in his two fists. He stood in front of the two men. "We'll draw. Short stick hangs first." Ambrose stepped forward with a smirk.

The man Ambrose had slapped cocked his head back, his glassy eyes roving. "I've told you. I don't know nothing. I've never even seen this man before last night. I only worked for Wesley. Our camp was over that saddle-shaped mountain by a little stream. I can take you there."

Ambrose shuffled over in front of the other man, throwing the ends of the toothpick on the floor. He grabbed the man's chin, turning his face up to him. "Well, if that's the case, we'll end the games. We'll hang you first, and then Johnny here might realize I'm serious." He squeezed the man's mouth, distorting his face. "I want to know who else Loomis had working for us."

Marshall's hands shook. Uncertainty besieged him. Was Ambrose right? Did this need to be done? Ambrose's earlier words rang in his mind. He retreated from the cabin. He couldn't watch or be a part of this.

46

A cold midday breeze brushed across Marshall's cheeks as he stepped into his tent at the railroad's Jeremiah Canyon work site. In the four weeks since the death of Wesley Loomis, the railroad had gotten back to work, but progress had been slow, the men battling the weather as much as the canyon.

Marshall fumbled through the mail as Patty sat at a table in the tent, its front flap open to allow the bright sun in.

With a big smile, Patty picked up a paper and began to read. "The *Daily Frontier* has learned that three men are currently being held by the Federal Marshal in Cheyenne for allegedly impeding the construction of the Colorado Northern's railroad to Jeremiah. The marshal would not comment other than to say an investigation is ongoing. If these accusations are found to be true, a bigger question looms: who is behind this? We have learned through sources that the three men were apprehended by the railroad's vice president, one Ambrose Graham, a Union colonel during the war under General Dodge. To date, inquiries by the *Frontier* to the Colorado Northern have not been answered."

Marshall grabbed a letter and stood. "I thought Ambrose was really going to hang those men if they hadn't offered up the third man. It wasn't as pleasant as it sounds." He stepped out of the tent, the sun radiating on his cheeks. "This is the best weather we've had in weeks. Let's get the rest of those ties moved up here today."

Ambrose rode up, relaxing in the saddle.

Marshall handed him a letter from Benedict Matson. "This just came in." He waited patiently as Ambrose read, studying his eyes as they moved down the paper. "Mean anything?"

"Yeah." Ambrose wadded up the letter up and threw it on the ground. "Matson's sending his hatchet man out to check on us. This Mr. Smith is the railroad's lawyer, and Dalton is Matson's problem solver, a real asshole with a bad attitude. . . . Matson may be trying to steal the rail from us, or more likely he's lost confidence. Possibly he'll try to replace us this summer. Doesn't matter, now that I've killed Wesley, we'll be through the tunnels before long. The worst of the weather is now behind us. We'll soon hold all the cards." Ambrose grabbed his pommel, turning his head down at Marshall. "They won't be here for two weeks. And I *expect* you to have some significant progress completed by then."

Emory walked up, putting a hand on Ambrose's shoulder. "Excuse me." He pointed to two horses riding up the canyon road to the work camp. "The local sheriff is here."

"What the hell's he want?" Marshall asked.

"Don't know," Emory said. "But we're in Boulder County now. You can bet the local sheriff is in the Southwest's pocket."

Ambrose wheeled his horse around to face the two men riding toward him.

Marshall raised a hand. "Can we help you?"

One of the men raised a hand, the two horses continuing to walk forward, one step at a time.

The lead man was bundled in a black coat, his gray hair and stubbly face shaded from the sun by a large tan Stetson. His brown, bloodshot eyes scanned the railroad camp as he pulled back on his reins, leaning forward on his saddle horn. "Name's Colburn. I'm the sheriff. This is Deputy Hatch."

"What can we help you with?" Marshall asked, studying the deputy, a younger, thinner version of the sheriff sporting a shiny silver badge on his black coat. Above his tall collar, the deputy's blue eyes took in the campsite.

The sheriff exhaled a long breath. "Just thought I'd come up here and see what all the fuss is about. . . . I read in the paper that several men up this way have been arrested, and another from these parts is missing."

Ambrose clicked his heels, his horse moving closer to the sheriff. He pointed farther up into the canyon. "If you're talking about Wesley Loomis, you might find what's left of his corpse there. I sent three more of his henchmen to the federal marshal in Cheyenne. If you want some details, you'll need to go see the marshal. We signed several affidavits relating to all the events that transpired."

The sheriff reached into his coat and pulled out a cigar. He struck a match and lit it, taking a long drag. "I ain't too keen on people taking the law into their own hands in my county."

"You've got your laws." Ambrose grunted. "And we've got ours. This is a federal right-of-way."

"Don't cross me," the sheriff said. He flashed his gaze at Marshall, clicked his heels, and ambled off.

Thirty silent seconds passed as the sheriff and his deputy rode out of camp.

"What do you make of that?" Emory said.

"Just a bunch of hot air," Ambrose said. "I won't worry too much with him."

"We've got another problem," Emory said. "Maybe killing Wesley hasn't ended all our problems. We found another man snooping around the rail today . . . just the other side of the high bridge. Armed with two pistols on his hip. I thought there might be a fight for a second, but we've got him detained at the north camp. You want to go up there?"

Ambrose popped his knuckles on his right hand, one at a time. "No, send him down to headquarters on the next train, then on to the marshal in Cheyenne. I'm going to do some looking around, see what I find. And see what that sheriff's up to."

The train scooted along, rocking rhythmically to the incessant clattering below. The last few months had been the worst of Marshall's life, surpassing anything he'd experienced during the war—the slaughter of the Cheyenne, then the fight with Wesley, and the unending battle against Mother Nature. It had all been like a dream, a nightmare, almost not real.

Through the window, the late day sun shone wonderfully over the endless brown grass, beaten down by months of wind and wilted from frost and a lack of sunshine. In the rear of the car, three of the railroad's guards watched over the captive, his hands bound behind his back, a brown burlap sack over his face. Despite numerous inquiries, the man had given no hint of his identity or the reason for his presence that morning on the rail's right-of-way.

Marshall had thought they had finally defeated the railroad's enemies. But had they? And then there had been the letter from Benedict Matson earlier in the day. There seemed to be no end to his problems. The more of his heart, soul, and grit he put into the Colorado Northern, the more its completion eluded him.

The train's brakes engaged. Two of the guards lifted the masked-man from his seat.

Marshall stood. "Let's transfer him to one of the box-cars. We'll take him to Cheyenne on the five o'clock train."

The train stopped and the two guards led the man out of the passenger car. Marshall walked to the car's door.

Bridget stood on the loading dock, a shotgun resting in her arms. She pointed to a boxcar. "Put him in there, lock the door, and keep two guards on the car until it leaves."

47

When Marshall walked into the railroad's headquarters the next morning, Bridget stood in an apron in the kitchen flattening dough, her sleeves rolled up and face covered with flour.

"I'm making you a warm meal," she said. "It's so lonely here with everybody in the canyon. What did the marshal in Cheyenne say?"

"Not much. He's going to do some checking around, but said he can't hardly hold or charge a man for just being on our right-of-way."

"When do you think Father will be back at headquarters?"

Marshall reached into his haversack and pulled out some fresh bread. He set it and a bottle of wine he'd purchased in Cheyenne on the dining room table. "He didn't say, but he's settled down a bunch in the last few weeks. He's even started to look back over the company books. I'm sure he's off worrying about his railroad somewhere."

"It's our railroad, too. . . . Maybe our troubles are over. It's been over a month since Father killed Wesley Loomis, and the work is going fine. A little normalcy may be returning. I like you men a lot more when you're working on the road and not worrying about it."

"Well, my shriveled feet are starting to dry out, and my bones are thawing." Marshall walked over and kissed Bridget on the cheek. He had gone out of his way in recent days to reconcile with her. He couldn't bear the thought of her rejecting him. If he had differences with her father, he would keep them to himself. "I got a telegraph yesterday from Chicago notifying me that the new truss for the Jeremiah River Bridge has left the factory via train, and in the next week or two, the tunneling crews will finish their work. Though we've got a small bridge to build, the way to the upper canyon is almost open. The rail will likely be finished by midsummer unless Silas Jones sends some more hired outlaws our way. Which wouldn't surprise me."

Bridget walked a few steps away from Marshall, keeping her back to him. "There's something else I need to discuss with you." She ran her hands through her hair a few times. "I think I may be pregnant. I'm feeling sick in the mornings. And I'm late."

Marshall cocked his head back, looking at the ceiling. A few silent seconds passed.

"Well?" Bridget said.

"I'm sorry," Marshall said. "It's not bad news, just more shit I'll have to confront Ambrose with."

"I will see the doctor in Cheyenne this week."

"Let's make sure before we make a fuss out of it. Please let me know when you find out. If you are pregnant, we may have to get married before the summer."

Bridget nodded to the window.

Marshall turned. In the distance, a horse rode toward the house, the frame on top of it unmistakable. Ambrose. "Wonder what the hell he wants." He stepped back from

Bridget. "We'll finish this later. I'm not going back to Miners' Gap until the first train in the morning."

Shortly, boots rattled on the porch. The door opened and Ambrose entered. "Think we've got a problem," he said, stomping through the front door and tipping his hat to Bridget.

"What's that?" Marshall replied.

"There's a bunch of armed men on the high flat, about a half-mile past the big bridge on the other side of the last tunnel. Don't know what they're doing."

Marshall scratched his head. "I sent the surveyors up on the ridges past that bridge a few days ago to shoot some azimuths and start setting up some control before we get started in earnest, and they said they saw some men down there. Hell, I thought it was probably you or Emory just out scouting the line. What about that sheriff we met yesterday?"

"It's not him. He rode back toward town. . . . Be at Miners' Gap tomorrow on the first train in the morning. I'm going to take a party over tomorrow and check it out. This is worse than fighting the damn Rebs; at least they knew when they were licked."

Marshall squinted at the bright glare of the early afternoon sun reflecting off the tan and black rocks. The light breeze was almost cold, but in contrast, the sun felt warm on his cheeks. From the little ridge, atop his horse, he looked out over the rock-strewn and sage-covered plateau above Miners' Gap. Here, the hills parted and the land opened up, a gentle mesa, maybe a half-mile wide, guarded on the right by a tall, rocky ridge. To his left, the plain fell off into a deep ravine. From here, the flat worked its way up into the mountains almost ten miles until it collided with a set of small, rough ledges at the base of the mining town of Jeremiah.

Ambrose lowered his field glasses and turned to the four guards of the Colorado Northern and Marshall. He asked Emory, "How many did you say there are?"

"We counted about thirty this morning, all pretty well-armed."

"Hell, this can't be good." Ambrose moaned, pulling his Stetson down tight on his head. "We might as well get on with it. Put that white shirt on the end of your rifle, hold it up high, and let's ride up there. Everybody stay calm and cool. Don't do anything threatening. Let's just go slow and easy."

Marshall rode forward abreast of Ambrose and Emory, who carried a flag of truce. For much of the day, he'd tried to fathom what the men were doing so brazenly armed and in the open on the upper mountain. If they were there to fight the railroad so bluntly and boldly, they'd likely only need to summon the army, the U.S. Marshal, or maybe even the sheriff to run them off. Fighting Indians or outlaws was a gray area, but loitering on a federally issued rail right-of-way backed by Congress was another matter. The government had to make good on the deeds, or the entire enterprise of rail building at the government's direction would fall apart. Or at least so Marshall believed.

The group approached the two men they had been spying, fitted with big-brimmed hats and long wool coats. Each was well-armed, a pistol holstered to their hips. One man wielded a shotgun, hanging down to his boots, the other held some type of European breechloader casually at port. One extended a flat hand.

Ambrose reined up, twenty steps short of the men. "Who's in charge here?"

"What do you want?" the man yelled back.

"I'm Ambrose Graham, vice president of the Colorado Northern Railroad, and we've got a rail right-of-way through this area. All I want to do is speak to whoever's in charge."

The two men mumbled to each other softly, and then one walked to a horse, mounted up, and disappeared into the brush. The other cupped his mouth and yelled, "Stay there for now!"

"What you thinking?" Emory whispered to Ambrose.

"Same as you. Not sure what's going on. Let's just sit easy, see what we can find out."

Marshall grabbed his canteen and poured some cool water onto his dry throat. As he lashed the canteen back over his saddle horn, three riders approached, quickly, before bringing their horses to a slow trot.

Ambrose waved as the horses stopped a few yards away.

"Name's Parson Simpson," the man on the lead horse said. "What can I do for you?"

Marshall spent a few seconds inspecting the man. He wore knee-high boots, wool trousers, a long coat with the collar turned up, and a Stetson over his long, straight black hair that hung down to a red bandanna around his neck. His eyes were gray and emotionless. A man of danger.

"We're with the Colorado Northern Railroad," Ambrose said. "We've got a right-of-way to build a railroad across this plateau." He paused. "And we mean to start building here in a few weeks. I'm just wondering why all of these armed men are on our right-of-way."

Parson cut a piece of tobacco off a plug, placed it in his mouth, and chewed it slowly a few times.

The two men beside Parson were both of similar appearance, but not as imposing. Less polished, both wore unshaven faces and untidy, dirty attire. Each looked threatening but not as competent and cool as Parson.

Parson reached into his coat and pulled out some papers. "We've got nothing to hide. We work for the Southwest Pacific, and we're up here readying our own rail right-of-way. Believe it's right here. Here's the paperwork. It's all proper, stamped and sealed by the Colorado Land Office. This is our right-of-way, so long as we build a railroad on it." He rode forward a few steps and extended the papers to Ambrose.

A few seconds passed, the only sound was the rattling of tack. Ambrose said, "I don't give a shit what that paper says. This is federal land, and we've got a federal right-of-way. We mean to build a railroad here, whether you're here or not."

Parson put the papers back in his coat. "Mr. Graham, you must be wrong." He smiled, his grin showing off his big, wide teeth. "This is our right-of-way, and we aim to hold it peaceably. But if you try to force yourself onto our land, we are perfectly within our legal rights to defend it— with arms, if need be. And make no mistake, we intend to do that, and I can assure you we have the necessary grit. There's no sense in a fight."

Marshall sucked in a deep breath. He stared at Parson's now wild eyes, then the veins pulsing on Ambrose's forehead. His own temper rose. They had to solve this problem, whatever it took.

Ambrose sat up in the saddle. "You piece of shit. You will regret you ever met us."

"What's that?" Parson said with a smirk. "You want to forget about this business, me and you can ride off into the bush, discuss this more intimately."

Marshall worried Ambrose might jump off his horse onto Parson.

"We'll slap him around later," Ambrose said as he wheeled his horse back in the direction they'd come and gritted his teeth. He whipped his horse as he lunged forward in the saddle.

48

Marshall sat in the railroad's small office near the Jeremiah River Bridge. He spooned some sugar into a cup of coffee and took a big sip, the rich aroma drifting into his nose and heightening his senses. For four days, the Colorado Northern had been trying to piece together the encounter with Parson Simpson. Nothing about the confrontation had slowed the work, but in a week or two, they would finish the tunneling and be ready to cross the contested high approach to Jeremiah. Ambrose had instructed the guards to stay clear of the area, and the railroad's only contact with Parson's men had been two surveyors run out of the sage flat at gunpoint.

After the encounter with Parson two days hence, Ambrose had again retreated from the job of building the railroad, spending his days scheming and organizing his guards.

By default, Marshall had assumed operational control of everything else. The day before he had hired a lawyer in Denver to do some snooping and research the Southwest's right-of-way title claim. Earlier that day, he had gathered all the information available and transcribed a long telegram to Benedict Matson in Chicago. He had yet to receive a response.

Ambrose sat at a table cleaning his rifle. He slid a cleaning rod down the barrel, then wiped the oil and grime off the tip with a towel.

"Why can't we go see the army again," Emory said, "or send a telegraph to your people in Washington to see if they can help? That's a federal right-of-way."

Marshall stood. "I hear Silas is making a big fuss with the governor and the Federal Land Office. He's saying he just wants the courts to decide. Sounds fairly reasonable, but that might take months, or years. He's just trying to slow us down. If we get delayed, we'll miss our federal deadline. . . . Possibly we could get an extension from Washington. Seems reasonable if we're locked up in court."

Ambrose slapped the desk. "An extension until when? Next winter? And our creditors don't care about that. A lengthy delay will mean Silas gets the rail, not us, and that's why he's concocted this scheme."

A knock on the door interrupted Ambrose. A guard entered and handed Ambrose a box of shells and quickly departed. Ambrose began feeding them into the rifle and nodded to Emory. "What'd you find out about Parson Simpson?"

Emory put his hands on his hips, his face turning white. "Pretty well known east of here. He's hired muscle for some of the big cattle and corporate interests. Heard a rumor he's wanted for murder in Texas under another name, Johnson Parish."

"Just what we need," Ambrose said. "A real Wild Bill Hickok."

Another man knocked on the door, then entered and handed Marshall a telegram. "From Mr. Matson."

Marshall unfolded the letter and read the brief passage.

Ambrose said, "What kind of wisdom did Benedict bestow on us from his comfortable desk in Chicago?"

Marshall refolded the paper. "He says build the railroad."

Ambrose chuckled. "I already knew that."

Marshall scratched his head. The only sound in the room was the shells sliding into Ambrose's rifle. For weeks, he had not been able the get the awful visions of Wesley's bloody demise out of his head. He had thought the killing might be over. He pondered their options, sucking in a large mouthful of air. He couldn't lose now, not after all they'd been through, even if it meant bloodshed. "We've got to defeat them, whatever it takes. I doubt we have enough willing men to run them off in an open fight." He turned to Ambrose. "Whatever you've got in mind, I'm behind it."

Ambrose asked Emory, "What about the other gentleman we discussed?"

"Beetle Wilson," Emory replied, taking a seat. "He's agreeable, so long as you put it in writing he's working for the railroad and that all his actions are at your direction for the defense of our right-of-way. He'll be here tonight."

"Who's Beetle Wilson?" Marshall asked.

Ambrose stood. "I've decided we need our own professional help." He picked up his rifle and fed two more shells into the magazine. "I've had about all this shit I can stand. I know Parson's type, full of piss and vinegar. There's only one way to deal with his type. I'm going to deal with it and end this with the least blood possible, but I *will* end it." Ambrose's face contorted as he turned to Marshall. "How many men do we have that can and will fight?"

"Ten or twelve not including your guards."

"That's enough," Ambrose said. "We'll likely shut work down on the rail in a day or two. And Emory, I want to see this Beetle Wilson first thing in the morning. I want to go up on the ridges around Parson's camp and look around with him tomorrow. We should be back here tomorrow night, and we'll have a meeting here then."

A purple dawn broke across the wide panorama. Among the long shadows, the cold morning to the east transitioned from orange to turquoise. In the mountains, the sunlight only bathed the tall summits.

Marshall panted heavily. They'd been climbing the steep trail for more than an hour. He looked up discouragingly to the rocky path that led over another ridge to a spherical summit.

Ahead, Ambrose led the group at a steady pace. Cresting a small ridge, Ambrose stepped into the cover of some timber and took a seat on a fallen tree.

Marshall followed, sitting beside Ambrose, his lungs heaving and calves burning. Emory and Beetle Wilson followed, both sitting on an inclined block of granite. Beetle was a big, burly man with a chummy round face and curly red hair that fell down to his neck. A smidgen over six feet tall and probably weighing two hundred and twenty pounds, he had said little all morning.

Marshall unbuttoned his wool shirt and grabbed a canteen from his pack, turning it up and pouring the water into his cotton-filled mouth. He nodded to Beetle. "How'd you get a name like Beetle?"

"I'z shot me a beetle one time, when just a lad, at almost a hundred paces," Beetle replied in a coarse Irish accent.

"Summit's only another fifty feet up," Ambrose said, wiping his brow on his sleeve. He pointed to the east. "Sun will come up over our backs. It'll be calm for the next two hours or so before the breeze picks up. When we get up there, everybody get on your bellies. We can crawl forward and peek over the backside of this hill. From there, we'll be looking right down on their camp. It will be two hours before they'll be able to see anything looking into this sun. Let's ease on up there."

They stood, Marshall still perplexed as to Ambrose's plans. The night before, Ambrose had returned to camp after a day of scouting with Beetle, not saying anything to Marshall but instructing him and Emory to be ready to depart at four this morning.

Reaching the rocky summit, the four got prone and shuffled forward to peer over the hill's gentle crest.

Ambrose pointed to a small log cabin. "That appears to be where they congregate."

Marshall scanned the vast sage flat two hundred feet below, the mountain's shadow concealing the nearest half, but retreating by the second. He pulled out his field glasses and gave the area a close inspection, everything exaggerated with the sun at his back. To his left sat the slab of granite the rail tunneled through. Three of Parson's men, only faint images, stood maybe a half-mile away.

Over the sage and rock, off to his right, two more men sat horseback. Beside Marshall, the other three men silently inspected the scene.

"What's the elevation here?" Beetle said, lowering his spyglass.

"Little over seven thousand feet," Ambrose answered.

"Be perfect light in about twenty minutes," Beetle said. "I gauge it to be less than a quarter-mile to that cabin." He turned to Marshall and scooted back from the crest. "Give me a hand with the Prussian Big 50."

Marshall shuffled back a few body lengths.

Beetle removed the long, leather scabbard from his

back. Opening it, he removed a large rifle and a few leather pouches. The Irishman briefly inspected the weapon, checking a few measurements on the optical scope with a micrometer. "Reach in that little leather bag and get me three of those cartridges."

Marshall pulled out the heavy shells, almost three inches long and a half-inch in diameter.

Beetle inspected them, looking over the casings and meticulously studying the bullets. He opened the rifle's breech and carefully fed in one of the cartridges, watching as it slid into the barrel. He put another cartridge in his shirt pocket and handed the third back to Marshall as he turned a small knob on the scope. He handed the rifle to Marshall and pulled a small tripod from the scabbard. "I'm going to crawl back up beside Ambrose. Hand this to me when I get there. Don't bump it on the ground."

Marshall clasped the rifle, noticing its weight, about ten pounds. He waited a few seconds for Beetle to slide forward and work his big body into position beside Ambrose. Easing forward on his knees, he handed Beetle the rifle. Ambrose continued to study the brightening scene through his glasses.

Beetle set up the tripod and rested the barrel on it as Marshall crawled up beside him.

"Two men came out of that cabin," Ambrose whispered, "but neither was Parson."

"Look a here," Emory said and pointed to the left.

Marshall raised his glasses. He saw the upper bodies of two men bobbing through the brush on horseback as they moved toward the cabin.

Ambrose swung his glasses in their direction. "I believe the second rider is Parson. Looks like they're headed for the cabin." He lowered the glasses and turned to Beetle. "He's the one with the red bandanna around his neck. If they get up here and mingle around the cabin, shoot the son of a bitch.

Marshall lowered his glasses. "You going to shoot him?"

"Hell, yeah," Ambrose said.

"Sounds like a good plan," Marshall said, raising his glasses. The two horses neared the cabin. "He's already threatened to shoot us if we try to get on our property. We've got five witnesses to that, and we need to get on our property. The legal system won't miss him."

Beetle put the rifle butt to his shoulder and scope to his eye, adjusting the rifle's trigger.

Marshall swallowed as he picked up his glasses again, resting his elbows on the ground to steady the view. Parson had dismounted and now stood in front of the cabin conversing with two more men, his side profile visible. He turned toward the cabin, his back exposed. A metallic click. Then the earsplitting roar that jolted his glasses from his eyes.

His mind humming, Marshall put the glasses back to his eyes. Parson lay sprawled on the ground, one of his legs slightly moving. Marshall strained his eyes. One of the outlaw's arms lay separated from the body.

"You reckon he's dead," Ambrose said in an even tone.

"Yeah," Beetle said, removing the spent casing from the rifle. "That 50 cal hit him anywhere north of the balls, and he's taken his last breath."

Ambrose shuffled backward. "You all get back to camp. Beetle and I are going to scout around for a bit. I want everybody to meet at the Miners' Gap camp an hour after dark tonight."

49

Ambrose poked the fire with a stick, stirring the coals. He loved to gaze into fires, entranced by the hypnotizing effect of the dancing orange flames. Tiny pricks of starlight stood against the clear sky. Beside the fire, the two shiny rails slithered through the work camp and up the mountain.

He'd spent most of the day hiking or crawling around the hills observing Parson's men. He had also sent out eight of his guards to do the same from a safe distance atop the surrounding peaks. One of the groups had gotten into a brief melee, exchanging gunfire. The scuffle had only kicked up dust, the shooters too far apart to be a real threat.

Ambrose turned to the railroad's headquarters tent where Emory, Marshall, Beetle, and two of the railroad's guards now congregated to await their meeting. Two dozen more of the railroad's guards mingled around the camp, all wearing urgent, apprehensive faces.

Ambrose sucked in a deep breath. He'd spent the day observing, thinking, and scheming. To his disappointment, Parson's death had not deterred the squatters. There had been a few hours of confusion and bickering among the desperados in the wake of Parson's death, but by mid-afternoon, the hodgepodge outfit had regrouped and coalesced under the command of Parson's two lieutenants they had seen under the flag of truce a few days earlier.

The railroad's survival teetered on his actions in the next twenty-four hours. And the men would only go so far. Now was the moment of truth. He not only had to convince the men he had a viable plan, but also had to lead them to its successful implementation.

He tossed the poking stick into the fire and walked into the tent, grabbing a lantern off the wall and setting it on the table where he had laid out some maps he'd drawn earlier that day. He turned a knob on the lantern to brighten the tent and waved everyone to the table.

Ambrose cleared his throat. "I was hoping killing Parson might end this, but I think we've got a little more work to do." He pointed to the large terrain map he'd drawn that day. "It looks like those two slimy bucks we met with Parson the other day are calling the shots. For most of the afternoon, most of them stayed in that house or hiding here, behind these rough stone breastworks they've built just the other side of the tunnels, near the area we met Parson the other day." Ambrose slid a finger across the map. "Today, they built another set of breastworks here, to the east, facing the hilltop Beetle shot Parson from. I guess they figure those are the areas we'd most likely attack from."

Emory pointed to the map. "It looks like somebody over there has some brains. Each set of breastworks makes for a good fallback line for the other, and they cover the only two logical approaches."

Ambrose tapped the map. "Looks to me like most of them hang out around this front set of rocks facing the tunnels. It's the farthest from any hills. Beetle's sure put the fear of God in them."

"You say they've got thirty men?" Marshall said. "I know we've got the high ground, but we might lose twice that many taking those defenses, and I don't think any of them will be dallying around in the open anymore to let Beetle pick them off one at a time."

Ambrose shook his head. "We're not going to attack them. That's not how we solve this. We're going to shoot those other two little greasy pricks that are in charge, then see if anybody else wants to step up and be boss. That, and a good show of force will likely have them out of here with nightfall, and back to whatever other illicit endeavors they were up to before they took Silas Jones's money."

"Sounds easy enough," Emory said, "but we'll probably have to attack these breastworks to kill any of them."

Ambrose scratched his cheek. "I've been thinking on it all day. Those two underlings hung out around these breastworks facing our bridge most of the day." He pointed to the map. "Those breastworks were thought out well, too far from any hills for us to shoot at them, but there is a flaw. To move between the two sets of defenses, they have to skirt this little finger protruding out into the valley. If a bunch of us, say eight or ten, snuck down here in this ravine and came at this breastwork from the rear, they'd likely all move over to these other breastworks. We'd never be able to take them over that open ground, just show enough stomach so they'd get behind these walls. We'd put a few men on these hills to the east. Have them fire down on them so they'd take the bait. We wouldn't hit anybody from up there, but they'd think moving was a good option."

Ambrose put a finger on the map. "Anyway, when they

move, Beetle could likely shoot one or both of Parson's minions. Especially from this ridge when they move between their defenses. He'll have the sun at his back if we do this late in the day."

Ambrose turned to Beetle. "You remember what they look like? One has the crossing chest-ammo belts and the other will be easy enough to spot if you find him before all hell breaks loose."

"I got 'em," Beetle said.

Ambrose said, "We need to make an effort not to shoot anybody else. We don't want a slaughter or a war. Marshall, we need to get any and all of your men that we can and have them stand on this ridge when it's over, around dark. The outlaws' two honchos will be dead, and then they will look up and see fifty or sixty men staring down on them in the twilight. I bet they all haul ass by midnight. Anybody got thoughts or suggestions?"

The room sat silent.

"Marshall," Ambrose said, "your men knock off late morning tomorrow. See if you can get forty or fifty to come over. Don't lie to them. Tell them they're not going to fight. We're just trying to make a show of force to Parson's boys to run them off, that's it. What's critical about this plan, if it succeeds, is we take the right-of-way with all our guards and hold it. Then if Silas comes back at us, he'll have to remove us from our right-of-way. And Marshall, if this does work out, I want grading crews over there working the next day. I don't care if they'll be grading in the wrong place. Once we're working in the area, it will be ours, both by possession and in the eyes of any court."

Ambrose leaned back from the table. Did the plan have a fatal flaw? "Tonight, we'll start assigning a command structure and assault teams. It may not go as planned.

What's important is we get Beetle a good shot at Parson's cronies. Everything else will then likely work out." Ambrose pointed his finger at each of the men. "I don't want to lose any men in this, none. Emory, have some detailed assault teams to me by midnight to go over."

50

A voice startled Marshall. He jerked forward. His palm stayed on his revolver where it had been when he had dozed off sometime earlier. He shook his head to regain full consciousness as he leaned forward from the wall of the small gully, shaded by a few scrub trees. He gauged the sun, a few hours shy of setting, the clear, warm day winding down.

What a long night and morning. And now in the mid-afternoon, he and eight other men sheltered in the deep ravine on the south side of the high plain occupied by the thirty hostile men. They had spent the midday anxiously hiding, waiting for a runner to arrive with the word that Beetle and the remainder of the Colorado Northern's little army of almost fifty men were in place and ready to execute Ambrose's ambush.

An hour earlier, Ambrose had ridden ahead to find an ideal location to exit the gorge and make their assault on the railroad's enemies.

Ambrose led a sweaty roan into the washout, his hat pulled tightly down on his head.

Marshall stepped forward, stiff and weary.

"Everybody," Ambrose said, squatting and pointing, "finish a canteen. About a half-mile up this draw we can get up on this plain. We'll have good cover there until we get within a quarter-mile of those breastworks by the bridge." Ambrose took a big gulp from his canteen. "It looks like there's fifteen to twenty men at the front breastworks. Remember, we don't want to assault them, just get them out of that cover. After we've got them on the move, we'll fall back to the ravine, then back to here. Everybody got it?" Ambrose grabbed his pommel. "Okay, let's go."

Horseback, Marshall weaved up the deep draw, the sun moving from over one shoulder to the other as the horses' shoes clattered on the rock floor. In the gully, he lost all sense of direction among the myriad of colors and shapes. All the men wore tense faces, their smiles long gone.

Ambrose reined up at a small side draw and dismounted. He pushed away the mare, hobbling her, and removed his rifle from a scabbard. "Up this draw, then we've got three or four hundred yards of good cover until we get to a ledge, with four or five feet of cover. We'll rally there. Let's be quick about it."

As Marshall dismounted, his horse blew, his ears high. He grabbed his rifle, the events unfolding with more haste than he'd imagined. He followed two men up the draw where he climbed a four-foot bank, and continued into the thick sage. He zigzagged through the brush, hunched low and darting as he kept an eye on the man he followed.

The terrain rushed by, without details, only a montage of gray and green colors as he sliced through the dry, coarse vegetation. Four more men came into view, each kneeling behind a four-foot escarpment. He rammed his shoulder into the natural obstacle and took a knee. Marshall wiped his sweaty brow as four more men arrived.

Ambrose spun the cylinder of his Smith and Wesson

revolver. He placed it back in his holster and levered his Henry. He pointed over the rock ledge. "About fifty paces ahead the sage gives way a bit. We should be able to see those forward breastworks from there. Let's take cover there, then open up on them. When our boys hear us fire, they'll start to pepper them from above. I'll shoot first, then everybody open up. Be careful. When they break, I'll order everybody to fall back. Fall all the way back to our horses, then back to camp. Everybody ready?"

The eight men silently nodded.

"Okay, on with it."

Marshall's stomach danced. He tried to suppress his emotions as he dug his fingers into the rock to pull himself from behind the cover. One of the men said a quick prayer, crossing himself. Marshall raced ahead behind Ambrose, hearing only the sound of footsteps and heavy breathing.

Ambrose ducked behind a shrub, looking forward and pointing for the men to spread out.

Four hundred paces ahead, into the glow of the setting sun, a dozen men milled around. He put a hand over his eyes to shield the glare. Around the wall, four men stood, the remainder leaning or sitting on the stone abutment smoking and conversing. He propped his forearm against a fir tree. Staring down his sights, he scanned the area. The sage gave way to a few willow and juniper trees. He tried to lock his sights onto one of the men, the image too tiny to draw a steady bead, and the targets too casual and unthreatening to focus his aim.

Two loud shots pierced the air. Then five or six more.

Marshall fired twice. More shots erupted in the distance. Loud voices barked. More alarming, two rounds zinged overhead. He fell to the ground. Unable to see anything, he promptly returned to a knee.

Ambrose darted ahead and jumped into a small washout. "Keep firing and come on!"

Marshall ran forward another twenty steps to the cover of a small aspen. He fired three more shots. Around him, a barrage of gunfire opened up.

"We've got them moving!" Ambrose yelled.

Around the breastworks, the men scattered, the dust being kicked up from the salvo of gunfire. One of the squatters hunched over and plummeted to the ground. Five or six more took off running.

"They're moving to the other breastworks!" Ambrose screamed. "Everybody fall back!"

A few more shots came from Marshall's left. Then, silence. Behind him, three men retreated. He yelled to Ambrose, "Fall back! It looks like we've run them out from behind those rocks."

"Go on," Ambrose said. "I'm going to make sure."

Marshall lingered, his mind dizzy and racing as he nervously spied the setting. He secured his footing, the time passing slowly.

Ambrose studied the scene through his field glasses.

He finally stood and stepped off quickly. "Let's go. Back to that escarpment."

Marshall picked up a trot, falling in behind Ambrose. Out of the corner of his eye, he saw some rapid movement to his left. Two horses raced in his direction, their riders visible above the brush, both men's arms extended. Marshall screamed and dove to the ground as the pistols popped. He raised his rifle and fired at the lead man, who stooped over, out of sight.

The second rider whipped his bridle, swinging his horse in his direction and raised his revolver.

Marshall steadied his barrel, covering the outlaw with his sight, and squeezed the trigger. He never felt the recoil as the man fell backward, over his horse's rear. Racing forward, Marshall heard shuffling to his right. He stepped into a small opening. A rider, still horseback but hanging on the side of his horse, struggled to reseat himself.

Levering his rifle, Marshall pumped two quick rounds into the desperado, one spattering the man's face and the other sending the horse to his front knees with a snort.

Marshall spun. A man lay sprawled on his back, his hands twitching at this side. Marshall stepped forward, raising the rifle. He recognized the face—one of Parson's two henchmen he'd encountered in their brief meeting several days prior.

Heart racing, he pulled the trigger. The slug splattered into the outlaw's chest. He wheeled around and yelled, "Ambrose!"

In the long shadows, the day got deathly quiet. Farther to his right came a groan. He stepped toward the sound. Ambrose lay on his side, his shirt spotted with blood. He pushed himself off the ground, took two steps, stumbled, and fell.

"Lay back down," Marshall said, a lump in his throat. He shuffled forward, taking a knee beside Ambrose and lifting the mangled, gory shirt.

Dark red blood gushed from Ambrose's chest, saturating his shirt and dripping down on his groin. "I'm done for sure."

"No, you're not," Marshall replied, looking around, trying to judge the distance to the horses.

"Even if I could get up, the ride would kill me."

Marshall flopped down, the air escaping his lungs. "Oh, my God."

Ambrose mumbled something, then stared silently at the sky.

Marshall moved to block the sun from Ambrose's face.

Ambrose's eyes turned glassy, his face pale white.

"What does a man say with death closing in?" he said, with a small grin. "This is what happens when you find out you've only got a few minutes to live."

His chin shaking, all the air escaping his lungs, Marshall put a hand on Ambrose's forehead. "The last moments of a lifetime full of excitement."

Ambrose's breath got long. He grabbed Marshall's hand, squeezing it gently. "Be good to Bridget. She deserves it. I'm responsible for what flaws she has." He squeezed Marshall's hand tighter. "You have to finish the railroad. You can't let Silas win, just on principle. It's hard to believe, but he makes Benedict Matson seem like a saint, if that's possible."

"I will." Marshall felt Ambrose's pulse weakening. Even now, this man loomed large against the land.

"I hate I won't see it finished. My wife has all the papers of what we're entitled to." Ambrose leaned his head back against the hard Colorado rocks, and closed his eyes.

Ambrose's chest scarcely rose, the blood from the wound barely flowing. The sky got bigger. Everything turned quiet.

51

From the top of a hill behind the Colorado Northern's headquarters, the Front Range glowed brilliantly with the rising sun. June had thus far been mild, the mornings filled with the glory of spring sunshine and fresh breezes that spruced up mind and body. Under the tall white clouds and perfect blue sky, the landscape had exploded with flowers and green.

Marshall loved the flutter of color with the swaying grass and never tired of the space. He turned to the small cemetery behind the headquarters. He counted sixteen tombstones, the dirt still fresh over its newest occupant, Ambrose Graham. Behind the cemetery, in the distance, sat the men's labor camp. Almost like a portrait, one of the Colorado Northern's engines, its boiler huffing, pulled a train of seven cars over the plains en route to the end-of-track, now only a mile from Jeremiah. The steady *ch . . . ch . . . ch . . .* the only sound for miles. Amazingly they had succeeded.

Since Ambrose's death two months earlier, the work on the rail had gone on unhindered. As Ambrose had predicted, Silas's men had disappeared after the Colorado

Northern had shown its strength, killing four of the squatters, including two of its leaders. After occupying the railroad's right-of-way, they had spent a dozen tense days, with every available man guarding the right-of-way but had seen not a hostile soul.

Adding to the lore of the fracas with the Southwest, one of the two villains Marshall had killed was Blanco Winston, a gunhand of some reputation. One of the local papers had actually done a small story on the event, referencing Marshall as a trained Civil War marksman and experienced crusader against Confederate guerrillas.

In a high mesa on the far side of the hill a small herd of buffalo, maybe fifty, grazed below the metallic sky. The sunshine spilled across the prairie accentuating their brown coats.

Marshall sensed someone riding up behind him. He wheeled around to see his wife sitting horseback.

"What are you doing?" Bridget said.

"Just enjoying the view." Marshall pointed to the railroad's headquarters and the cemetery.

"Love," she said, "you can't bring him or any of the others back."

"You can't blame me. I was there when they shot him and spent almost an entire night getting his body off that mountain." He nodded to the buffalo. "They'll be gone before long, too. The Cheyenne call them *hotowa'e.*"

Bridget put a hand over her eyes. "They *are* beautiful."

"It must be something to see the big herds. I hear they stretch for miles, as far as you can see. A brown blanket over the grass that shakes the ground when they stampede."

"Have you got everything packed? The train back to Cheyenne will depart at noon."

Marshall raised the day's mail and a day-old newspaper. "They've driven the golden spike in Utah. Everybody is talking about the completion of the Pacific Railroad. Says here, the news is filling the front pages around the world." He smiled. "I passed on that for you."

"Don't worry, your day is coming."

Marshall rode over to Bridget and handed her an open letter. "Benedict Matson will be here in two weeks to officially open the rail. He's already scheduled the federal rail inspector. I'm sure he's gone out of his way to inform half the press in Denver and Chicago."

"I swear, I am going to finally buy that new dress to celebrate such a grand occasion. Will we make it?"

"Of course we'll make it." Marshall grabbed Bridget's hand. "Since we've completed the tunneling, I've got every man grading and laying track. I'm guessing we'll be through in a week, so long as nobody else shows up to get in our way." Marshall raised a letter. "I'm wanted now to build a new rail in Utah."

"Don't get too high in the saddle. And I don't know if I'm going to Utah. And just because we're west of Kansas, you're no Brigham Young. I'm all you're going to have."

Marshall plucked another letter from the stash and held it up. "Here, a letter from your mother. Maybe she's coming out for the rail opening."

Bridget grabbed the letter, rubbing her plump stomach. "More likely she's getting ready for us to come home and have the baby in Chicago."

Marshall swung his horse around. "I've got to get some paperwork done before the mail run. What are you doing the rest of the afternoon?"

"I'm going to get some fresh bread from Mr. Stewart and then make some dinner."

Marshall spurred his mount, galloping off to his office. There, he found two men standing inside. He recognized one, the sheriff of Boulder County. The other man was small and thin and wore a nice black suit, top hat, and a pair of wire-rimmed glasses. He brandished a piece of paper.

"Can I help you?" Marshall said, sitting at his desk.

"I'm Mr. Davis," the man in the black suit said, removing his hat. "I'm an attorney for the territorial land office. I've been ordered by the state court in Denver to investigate some official complaints that your right-of-way may be in conflict . . . that you may not hold a clean title to it. I'm sorry, but I've been ordered to go through your records . . . you do understand."

The sheriff leaned on the wall waving a second sheet of paper. "It's all legal and proper."

Marshall dropped his feet to the floor, his boots colliding with the planks. "When is Silas Jones going to realize he's lost? This is not his rail and never will be. I've had some reliable sources tell me that the Southwest has cut its losses and given up their pursuit of the Jeremiah line. They've now focused their resources on potential markets south of Denver."

The sheriff stepped forward. "We're not concerned with your thoughts on Mr. Jones's intentions."

Mr. Davis glanced at the sheriff, then Marshall. "And your name is?"

"Marshall Brewster. The vice president of the Colorado Northern."

"Mr. Brewster," Mr. Davis said calmly. "I don't mean to inconvenience you. I'm sure you're a busy man. I'm just doing my job. And I just need to go through some of your records. I've been ordered here by the courts."

Marshall extended a hand.

Mr. Davis stepped forward and handed him the paper. "It's all in there."

A boot stomped on the floor near the office's doorway. The two men turned to look.

Bridget stood in the threshold, a pistol extended from her right hand. She pointed the weapon at the sheriff. "Do you know what this is?"

The sheriff squared his body to Bridget.

"It's a Colt pocket revolver," Bridget said, lowering the pistol to the sheriff's groin. "Thirty-one caliber. It will make a mess, even if I miss your little pecker. So get your ass out of here before I take away your manhood. We have a federal right-of-way, and if you want to see any of our records you better go get the federal marshal."

Bridget stepped into the office, keeping her sights on the sheriff.

"But Miss," Mr. Davis said, "we've been ordered here by the court."

Bridget quickly lowered the pistol a few inches and fired. The wood floor burst into shards below the sheriff. She raised the pistol, pointing it at the sheriff's chest. "Don't try me. As far as I'm concerned, you're trespassing now."

"We'll be back," Mr. Davis said, stepping for the door. "Let's go, Sheriff."

"You better have a federal warrant," Bridget said. She reached over and grabbed the court order out of Marshall's hand and held it up. "Our lawyers and the federal marshal will take this up with the Denver court tomorrow."

52

Nervous energy filled Marshall as he supervised two men touching up a rail switch at the Colorado Northern's intersection with the Pacific Railroad. The hot rock burned the bottom of his feet as the two laborers drove the last few spikes, their bare backs glistening with sweat.

"That's good," Marshall said, bending over to inspect the track. "You boys are done. Get cleaned up. We'll have plenty to eat and drink at the festivities."

Marshall turned to a temporary grandstand set up beside the track. Red, white, and blue streamers and regalia covered the wood planks. One of the Colorado Northern's engines, freshly painted, straddled the rails on one side of the stage. Beside it, an eight-piece military band worked away, banging out patriotic tunes.

The engine tooted its horn, then blew a few whistles and rang some bells. In front of the stage, more than a hundred onlookers, all dressed in their finest attire, stared up at the stage.

Marshall strode up the steps behind the platform, but as

he reached the center of the attention, the crowd grew quiet.

"Let us pray," a voice said.

Marshall slightly bowed, catching a glimpse of the black suit stepping to the front of the stage. As the preacher began to give thanks, Marshall stole a few more peeks at the setting—what a contrast to the desolate land he'd first glimpsed more than a year earlier. He thought about Ambrose, the horrific images of the Cheyenne village's slaughter, Wesley Loomis's death, and the shooting of Blanco Winston. The holy man's deep, gentle words seemed like a moral double standard in this land.

"Amen," the preacher said.

Bridget, standing near the front of the stage, smiled at Marshall. Under a blue parasol, her long blue dress stretched from her shoulders to her ankles, a red ribbon in her shimmering blond hair matching the trim around her waist and the colorful setting. Every ounce of her appearance radiated charm and sophistication.

Benedict stepped to the podium. He wore a black vest over a white cotton shirt, his sleeves rolled up. The attire produced the façade of a grounded workingman. He held up a stogie, altogether conveying the image of a politician as much as a wealthy aristocrat.

"The Colorado Northern is here to stay!" Benedict said in a loud, confident voice. "We will employ Coloradans, pay taxes, and more importantly, bring a needed service to this vast, fruitful land, aiding in the moving of people and material. Railroads are the key to statehood and a full place in the Union for Colorado and Wyoming. The railroad means prosperity for everybody."

The assembly applauded as more than a dozen reporters scribbled away on their little pads.

One of the reporters raised his hand. "Do you have anything to say about Ambrose Graham, or Silas Jones's cutthroats that murdered him?"

Benedict scanned the audience, raising a flat hand. "Ambrose Graham was a man of big ideas. He left his mark on this land. He was a man that spent all his energy trying to remake the world into an image of himself, not trying to make himself into an image of the world. He was a benefit to the land and to those who had the pleasure of working with him."

Marshall's throat got thick.

Another reporter spoke up. "What do you think about Silas Jones? Some are saying he tried to steal your railroad with underhanded schemes."

Benedict leaned back from the podium, chuckling. "What's this? I thought the Colorado press adored the Southwest and Silas Jones. And if you're wondering, a federal judge ruled this week that we have a clean title to this railroad."

"We adore winners!" the reporter shouted back.

The crowd laughed.

"What about your chief engineer?" a man in the back yelled. "Can we ask him a few questions?"

Benedict stepped to the side, extending a hand to Marshall.

Marshall put two jittery hands on the podium.

"What about all your amazing men?" the reporter said, "The public wants to know more about the engineer and men that carved the road through those rugged, impenetrable mountains. Do you have more magnificence planned with them?"

Marshall cleared his throat. "The men are mostly going away to do more glorious work for the Republic, somewhere else. But first, I suspect they're now probably indulging in that most celebrated habit of railroad men, set on reckless debauchery, gambling, and drinking that will likely fill the local merchants' pockets."

The audience erupted in laughter.

Marshall flashed his gaze at his wife, her doting approval putting some stiffness to his weak knees.

The reporter continued, getting up on his toes, "And what are your thoughts on the federal railroad acts, the huge sums of land and credit provided by the Republic? The eastern papers say the corruption ranges from deep to extreme—they're an insanity of riches."

Marshall grinned. "I think the idea is great, bold, and filled with greed and graft. The country at its worst and best."

A few in the audience snickered.

A short, well-dressed man elbowed his way forward, raising his pad. "How many Indians did you have to kill?"

Marshall's stomach turned queasy. He paused a few seconds.

Another reporter filled the void, butting in with a shout. "And Mrs. Brewster, what are your thoughts on the new railroad?"

Bridget stepped forward. "I love it. It's all a totally American endeavor, winner take all."

The spectators exploded with cheers.

Benedict stepped forward. "One more question, and then we'll get some photographs. The refreshments are courtesy of the Colorado Northern."

"Mr. Brewster," a reporter near the stage said. "They say you're a man of gumption and foresight, the type of man that can conqueror the West, fulfill our manifest destiny. What do you see for the West, Colorado? The army killed Tall Bull and the last of the Cheyenne warriors last week. Now that we're free of that scourge, can Colorado be the next Illinois or Iowa?"

Marshall stuttered, scratching his chin. A few awkward seconds passed.

Benedict took a step toward the podium. "Those states' mineral riches pale in comparison to Colorado's. Now that we can be accessed by eastern markets, Colorado will, in time, be the envy of Illinois."

A quick flash, accompanied by a pop, lit the stage.

"Photographs in front of the train!" someone yelled as most of the crowd stood, hustling for the engine.

Marshall stared at the endless savanna. Would anybody again ever see the Cheyenne or buffalo roaming freely over the plains or feel the incredible peace and isolation in the fields of grass as the wind blew free?

HISTORICAL NOTE

In less than a hundred years after the Louisiana Purchase, the American nation had developed most of the continent. The vision for the West is still debated today. Should we exploit or conserve this landscape, one of the most spectacular and astonishing in the world? The settling of the West is a story of conquest, of utmost valor and cowardice, of brutality and dignity, of delight and dishonor. To this day it still attracts and resists. Despite the riches of this vast expanse, it has been a somewhat guilty treasure, at least in the American psyche. This triumph shaped our national character, demonstrating all our inventive spirit while compromising many of our country's hallowed principles.

In 1879, General Nelson Miles, one of the nation's most decorated Indian fighters, who often expressed his sympathy for the plight of all native peoples, summarized his thoughts on the West and the Indian problem shortly after the subjugation of the last Plains tribes:

> In our treaty relations, most extravagant and yet sacred promises have been given by the highest authorities, and these have been frequently disregarded. The intrusions of the white race and the non-compliance with treaty obligations have been followed by atrocities

that could alone satisfy a savage and revengeful spirit. Facts that have been already referred to make it almost impossible for the two conflicting elements to harmonize. No administration could stop the tidal wave of immigration that swept over the land; no political party could restrain or control the enterprise of our people, and no reasonable man could desire to check the march of civilization. Our progress knew no bounds. The thirst for gold and the restless desire to push beyond the western horizon have carried our people over every obstacle. We have reclaimed the wilderness and made the barren desert glisten with golden harvest.

The iron road led the way in the taming of the West, and hence, the end of the Indians' way of life. The railroad wars of the West did occur between companies vying for the federal government's lucrative land grants and bonds. Many of the details are sketchy, the battlegrounds ahead of civilization. In one incident in Colorado, the Sante Fe Railroad hired such notable gunhands as Bat Masterson and Doc Holliday to raise a small army to protect their right-of-way up the Arkansas River to the silver mines of Leadville. But in the end, the Denver and Rio Grande Railroad's army prevailed, claiming the route for its backers, who operated the line through the Royal Gorge until 1988, when they were bought out by another rival railroad.

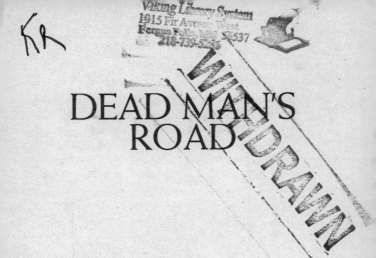

DEAD MAN'S
ROAD